PLAYING WITH FOREVER

THE PLAYERS CLUB SINNERS
BOOK ONE

ERIKA WILDE

Chase Noble always seemed unattainable...until one night with him at the Players Club changed everything.

I've wanted Chase for years, but much to my frustration, he's always considered me off limits. When I walk into the Players Club with one goal in mind, to find a man who will give me what I need, it's the maddeningly dominant, possessive (and I soon discover, *pierced*) Chase who refuses to allow any other man to touch me. He gives me a night I'll never forget, a taste of what is possible, and I want more. With him.

But Chase is a man with a dark past and secrets, and even though we come to an agreement, where I'm the student and he's the teacher, he insists this is all it could ever be. That he's not capable of anything more.

Just as things begin to heat up between us, someone starts leaving me cryptic messages and watching my every move. Chase insists I move in with him so he can protect me, and the moment I do, our undeniable chemistry ignites into something deeper than either of us expected.

Soon, his protection isn't enough. I want all of him —his body, his heart, and his trust. And this time, I'm not letting him go without a fight.

Playing with Forever is a steamy romance with high stakes tension, a possessive alpha hero, and a love worth fighting for.

CHAPTER 1

Andrea

Biting my bottom lip, I glanced at my reflection in the decorative, floor length mirror propped against my bedroom wall, taking in the slinky black dress and strappy heels I'd chosen for my evening of debauchery. Thin spaghetti straps held up the light, silky fabric, while the material caressed my figure in a way that was meant to accentuate my curves. I could have worn a strapless bra, but decided to go without because tonight was all about being daring, taking chances, and embracing those bad girl tendencies I'd suppressed for too long.

I shifted to check out my backside, and the movement caused the dress's fabric to brush across my bare nipples, making them furl into visible stiff points. Instead of being self-conscious, I felt sexy and confident. I was young, and my breasts were still high and firm and perky, so why not enjoy that benefit while it lasted?

This wasn't just an evening out at a club or a casino. I had done that plenty, especially since my breakup with Heath two months ago. No, tonight's adventure was hopefully going to show me everything I'd been missing.

After years of wishing and wondering, I was finally going to The Players Club, thanks to the invitation my older sister, Madison, had given me. Her and her husband, Rick, were members of the exclusive club in San Diego, but I'd moved back to Las Vegas where I'd been born and raised. About a year ago the owners, Mac and Dean, had opened a second club on an estate in Summerlin, just a short drive away. I was beyond ready and excited to see, learn, and experience everything the club had to offer.

With a combination of nerves and excitement dancing in my stomach, I grabbed my small purse and headed into the living room. As soon as I did, my half-sister, Violet, looked up from where she was reading a book on the sofa, her eyes widening in surprise at the dress I'd chosen to wear, because it was more risqué than I'd normally opt for.

Violet was the reason why I'd moved back to Las Vegas two years ago. After Madison and I had submitted our DNA to an ancestry site on a whim, we'd discovered, much to our shock, that we had a half sibling. I'd been the one to tentatively reach out to Violet, only to learn that our deadbeat—and now deceased—father had been having an affair with Violet's mother while our own mother had still been alive, and she'd been a product of that tryst.

Shockingly, despite our vastly different personalities, we'd become fast friends, and wanting to establish a true relationship so I could get to know Violet better, I'd made the decision to return to Vegas. After I'd secured myself a job at an advertising agency, we'd moved into an apartment together at first, and since housing was so affordable in the area, after a year of paying rent, we'd decided to buy a condo together as a mutual investment.

"Okay, what do you think?" I asked her, giving a little twirl so she could see the full effect of the outfit. I'd pulled my dark hair back into a sleek ponytail, and the ends brushed my shoulders when

I turned. I could easily picture a man tugging on that thick rope of hair with his strong hands, and the thought made me shiver in anticipation of that possibility.

Violet grinned. "Damn, you're definitely going to turn heads as soon as you walk in the place."

That was exactly what I wanted to hear, and my self-esteem increased with my sister's compliment.

Violet, too, was already dolled up, wearing a head turning, body hugging red metallic dress with a dip in the front low enough to expose a good amount of cleavage and showed off the pretty floral tattoo on her arm. Her overall look was very much retro vintage glam—a Rockabilly fashion style she loved and embraced. She'd piled her silky blonde hair on top of her head in a stylish updo, giving her a more sophisticated look.

But instead of accompanying me tonight, she was about to leave for work as a poker dealer in one of the high end casinos on the strip. Her spiky black heels were on the floor next to the sofa, looking dangerous, a perfect match for the tough attitude and street smarts she'd developed growing up in a not-so-great neighborhood on the outskirts of Vegas.

"Okay," I said, exhaling a deep, fortifying breath. "I think I'm ready to do this."

Violet dog-eared a page in her book—because she was a heathen who refused to use a bookmark — and stood up, sliding her feet into her heels as she eyed me with sparkling green eyes and a gregarious grin. "All I can say is, eat your heart out, Heath."

"Are you kidding me?" I said with a caustic laugh. "Heath would have a coronary if he knew what I was about to do."

Violet smirked in agreement. "Well, then it's a good thing the prudish bore is a thing of your past."

I had to agree. The truth was, despite our initial attraction, Heath and I had been incompatible in the bedroom. He was a nice, dependable guy, but all during our six months together our sex life had been dull and uninspiring . . . which eventually made it a tedious chore and not something I looked forward to. While I was sure there were plenty of women who'd appreciate the soft, tentative, missionary sex that Heath preferred, it had left me unfulfilled and unable to orgasm.

I could remember all the times I'd lay in bed after sex, Heath asleep and satisfied while I stared up at the ceiling wishing that there had been *more*. Something a little harder, a little rougher—I wished he'd flip me over onto my hands and knees and fuck me from behind while smacking my ass, or pin me down on the bed and drive into me until I was tender and sore from being fucked good and hard. I wanted to be ravished and blissfully ruined by the time we were done, instead of disappointed and frustrated.

I'd tried talking to him about the situation, opting for honesty, open communication, and expressing my desires, instead of harboring them. I'd suggested roleplaying as a start to ease us both into the experience, and even bought some toys for us to try out—leather cuffs, a flogger, a vibrating wand, and even a cock ring for him. I'd honestly been hopeful, that maybe by me initiating things it would give him the freedom to let loose, that he might enjoy exploring fantasies and being primal and dominant with me.

Yeah, that plan had completely backfired. Instead of excitement, he'd been appalled and told me that kind of perverted sex was for sluts and whores. I'd been shocked, hurt, then royally pissed off with his attitude and insinuation that what I desired was abnormal. Seeing my reaction, he'd tried to back-peddle and apologize, but the damage had been done.

I'd packed up my things from his apartment that night, along with my new *perverted* toys, and ended our relationship. Surprisingly, Heath had tried to grovel his way back into my good graces, but I knew I would always want and need more than he would ever be able to give me.

Which was why tonight's invitation to The Players Club from my sister Madison was such a gift—and her way of supporting me after I'd confessed the reasons for my break-up with Heath. That a part of me craved a dominant lover who pushed my boundaries and satisfied those salacious needs I could no longer ignore.

Madison assured me that there was nothing shameful about my inclinations and had decided it was time to let me figure out my kinks at The Players Club, hence the invitation. This was my chance to explore and test my limits in a safe place where I wouldn't be ridiculed for those darker proclivities, or that little slice of pain I'd always secretly wanted to add into the mix of pleasure.

With both of us ready for our evenings ahead, we walked toward the front door, my gaze once again drawn to my sister's very sexy dress. "By the way, I can't believe they're asking you to work in that outfit." Normally she wore black trousers, a white blouse, and a brocade vest with the casino's emblem on it.

Violet shrugged as she dropped her cellphone

into her purse. "It's a private poker game in the casino's penthouse suite with high rollers. They like to look at pretty things while mulling over the cards in their hand. If my boss wants to pay me extra to get sexed up and be some distracting eye candy, I'm happy to do it. Besides, it helps with the tips. So long as they keep their hands to themselves, I'm good."

"I know you're more than capable of breaking fingers if someone gets too friendly, but I worry about you."

She rolled her eyes at my concerned tone. "The last thing you need to worry about is *me*," she said, then gave me a pointed look. "*You're* the one going to The Players Club. And, for the record, I'm envious as hell." She flashed me a grin. "I expect all the sordid details tomorrow."

"Of course," I said, then let the tiniest of nerves take hold. "I just hope I don't stick out like a sore thumb, being a newbie and all."

"Trust me," Violet drawled as we exited our townhouse and she locked the door behind us. "I don't think you're going to have any problem finding someone to take care of you tonight."

The idea of a man whispering in my ear *let me take care of you* made a full bodied shiver course through me. "I'd rather keep my expectations low.

Be pleasantly surprised. Maybe all I do tonight is mingle and meet some potentials."

"Do not waste your night at the Players Club by over thinking things," Violet said, almost chastising me for my thoughts.

I sighed. "I know. You're right. I just don't want to get my hopes up, only to be disappointed," I said, because if I was truly being honest with myself, I was pinning my hopes on finding a dominant, confident, alpha personality who would make all those lust-fueled fantasies of mine a reality. . . and wouldn't consider me *perverted* for those desires.

Violet stopped on the sidewalk where both of our cars were parked at the curb, and glanced at me in that perceptive way of hers. "Look, I know you well enough to know what you're thinking after the shitty things Heath said to you. But the beauty of a place like The Players Club is that most everyone is there for the same reason. Which is to explore and indulge in all their dirty, kinky, depraved predilections in a safe, consensual space where no one is going to judge or ridicule them for their unconventional sexual practices."

I smiled at her, my anxiety ebbing. "You're right. Again."

"I usually am," she replied cheekily. "Just leave

your inhibitions at the door, follow your instincts without overly analyzing the situation, and be honest about what you want. Then, let the good times roll with some hot stud who is capable of giving you the kind of experience you're there for."

After that last little pep talk, Violet waved me off as she got into her car and headed to work. I slid behind the wheel of my vehicle and followed the directions on my phone to a private gated community in Summerlin, completely in awe at what I encountered when I arrived at the address' gated entrance—an enormous three story mansion that spread out over an expansive property, the magnitude of the Mediterranean style structure matching the size of at least five houses put together.

It had been built in a discreet and secluded location up on a hill overlooking the city, and there was no doubt in my mind that I was eyeing a multi-million dollar piece of real-estate. Despite the grandeur and exclusivity of the place, nothing gave away from the outside what went on inside. It just looked like another beautiful mansion among other equally huge, luxurious estates.

I had to scan my invitation at the fancy, high-tech security system at the gate, and once it beeped its approval, the heavy wrought iron panels opened, allowing me entrance. I navigated my way along the wide paved lane that gave way to a circular drive in front of the house where I handed my car over to a valet.

Excitement and nerves buzzed through me as I headed up the polished steps to the courtyard, my heels clicking on the terracotta tiles as I approached the entrance. I couldn't hear anything from the outside—no music, no voices, or screams of pleasure, I thought in amusement. I was sure that the neighbors down below had no idea of all the debauchery that went on inside this building. It made it all feel even sexier, the secretive, hidden nature of it.

When I reached the doors, they opened automatically for me and I stepped inside, with the same doors gently closing behind me, enfolding me into the house like the wings of a butterfly. Like I'd entered a cocoon.

I'd stepped into a foyer with soft lighting, and immediately a young man was at my elbow to check me in. He was extremely good looking, but also looked like he bench pressed elephants in his spare time. I was sure that if anyone tried to put a toe out of line, this guy would make sure they regretted it.

"Member code or invitation?" he asked, clearly

not recognizing me as a regular member, and scanned the latter from my phone when I presented it to him. "You can put any of your personal items that you don't want to worry about in one of those lockers," he said, pointing out a sleek black panel, that upon closer inspection was sectioned off as a discreet wall of lockers. "And no cell phones past this point, please. We can't allow pictures."

"Of course." Madison had told me to expect that, and I secured my purse into one of the cubbies, locking it with a code so there wasn't a key to worry about.

He passed me an iPad, on which was a list of club rules I already knew but as a first timer needed to sign off on in person. There wasn't anything surprising. There was a two drink maximum, and a reminder of the club's safewords and hand signals to security if needed. And no drugs allowed, of course.

I'd filled out all the pre-approval information online, along with a required blood test for health reasons and to rule out any issues, and completed another document with my hard and soft limits. I was told there were screens imbedded in every room of the house that allowed a person to peruse their partner's boundaries before the fun began, which could also prompt any discussion that needed to be had for clarification.

After signing all the forms, the man took back the iPad and opened another door. "Enjoy your evening."

The sound proofing on this building was amazing, because the moment I stepped through that door, it was like I was in a whole other world.

I was now in what must have once been some kind of large grand entrance foyer, back when this was an actual house and hadn't been gutted for renovations. They'd kept the grand staircase, but a large circular bar had been set up around it. Bartenders worked, while behind them people could head up the set of stairs to the right or left, where there seemed to be private rooms.

All along the walls were intimate booths. To my right was a doorway into what looked like a public sex room, filled with beds, in what had once been a dining or sitting room. To the left through another doorway was a room with a lounge and a stage where people performed—burlesque, extreme kinks, sex shows.

There was music, but none of it was so loud it was overwhelming. The lighting was tasteful. The walls, at least in this room, weren't done up in the traditional red but in black with gold accents. It was possibly the classiest room I'd ever been in—and it was a sex club.

Dean and Mac had clearly spared no expense with this second club, and from what Madison had told me, their wives, Jillian and Stephanie—who owned Fantasy Bedrooms and Interior Designs, and where Madison worked for them, as well—were responsible for all the aesthetics and décor, including the various special custom themed playrooms.

Feeling almost giddy at finally being here, I headed straight to the bar to grab a drink, deciding I'd take my time and see who might approach me. Who I could flirt with and who might give me those dominant vibes I was searching for.

The moment I ordered my mojito and glanced back into the lounge area where another show was starting, I saw *him*. The one man who had the ability to make my entire body light up in ways that left me breathless and restless and irritated all at the same time.

Chase Noble…because of course life liked to tempt and tease me with what I wanted, but couldn't have.

He sat with a small group of men and his brother, Austin, who I also knew and recognized. Part of what I found so annoying about Chase was that if I didn't know the guy, I would already be trying to get his attention in a place like this because he embodied all those traits I found irresistible. Muscular body, bad boy tattoos, and alpha tendencies with dark hair and dark eyes. Even wearing a crisp white dress shirt with the sleeves rolled up to showcase the artistic ink on his arms, and nice black slacks, he still had that rugged, brooding, assertive look about him.

I eyed him from across the room, reassuring myself, not for the first time, that Chase was *not* my type—at least not in personality, which was moody and reserved. Okay, maybe it was more that I wasn't *his* type, which meant he couldn't be mine...and I'd be lying if I didn't say that knowledge didn't hurt. Yeah, he'd made it pretty damn clear he didn't want anything to do with me...for the past six years, in fact.

I knew Chase through Madison. His parents, Jillian and Dean, were one of the co-owners of the original Players Club in San Diego, and now this one. By association, Chase was a part of Madison's world because she worked with his mother, and I also knew that Chase was now employed at the Noble and Associates security firm here in Vegas that had opened up a few years ago. We were all intertwined, however tangential.

When I'd first met Chase at a barbeque at my sister and Rick's, I'd felt such a thrill and the kind of infatuation that set butterflies fluttering in my belly. Chase was so gorgeous, and he'd had this enigmatic air about him after having recently been discharged from the Navy. At the time, through my twenty-one-year-old eyes, I could've sworn I'd seen him looking at me with a spark of interest.

I'd clearly been wrong, or maybe my lack of maturity at the time had shown and been part of the problem. I couldn't pinpoint any one thing, but by the end of that barbeque, it had been clear that something had changed and shifted between us. That what might have started as a mutual attraction had somehow, someway, turned one sided.

Since then, he'd been polite but cool and distant every time we met, even as Madison and Rick's other acquaintances greeted me warmly. Chase made it almost feel like I didn't exist for him, and that indifference stung. I couldn't even figure out a way to ask him, or say *look, let's bury whatever hatchet this is and play nice, okay?*

Over the years, I'd come to realize that Chase was infuriating that way because he never did anything that I could truly call out. Just little things that got under my skin and made it clear that he was avoiding me whenever we were in the same vicinity, and keeping me at arm's length...and I had no freaking clue why or what I'd done to cause his dismissive attitude.

Annoyed by this unexpected and unwanted surprise, I lifted my chin in determination, because I wasn't about to let the presence of Chase Noble ruin my evening. I'd come to the Players Club with a singular goal in mind, and that hadn't changed. There were plenty of other attractive men around, and I put on a sultry smile as one approached me.

The night was young, and before it was over, I was determined to find myself that thrilling, dominant partner I craved to play with...even if that man wasn't Chase Noble.

CHAPTER 2

Chase

I knew it would sound insane to anyone outside of our family and friend group, but I was genuinely just at The Players Club to have a drink and hang out. Oh, sure, maybe if the right woman caught my eye I'd have some fun, too. I certainly wasn't opposed to releasing a little tension. But I was there first and foremost to catch up with friends and co-workers in a more relaxed atmosphere, including my brother, Austin. It was always nice to spend casual time with him outside of the hectic pace of the office.

We were sitting in the lounge area, the guys

discussing one of the security cases that had just wrapped up while the next show began onstage—a demonstration on Shibari techniques, which wasn't my thing, but it was always interesting to watch a skilled rigger tie up his partner with intricate knots in pleasurable ways.

That's when I saw Austin, who was sitting to my left, shift his gaze to someone, or something, behind me. The knowing smirk on his lips definitely didn't bode well for me.

"What's that look for?" I asked, taking a sip of my bourbon.

Austin gave me a full-fledged grin. "I just see someone I recognize. You'll never guess who."

"If you say *Mom*, I'm going to strangle you." It was always a possibility, considering my parents owned the joint with my dad's best friend, Mac, and they all frequented the club when they were in Vegas visiting.

My brother grimaced. "Jesus, if mom and dad were here, then I wouldn't be. That's just way too fucking weird. *But*, I guarantee someone far more interesting *is* here tonight. Take a wild guess."

Clearly, he was goading me. We were two years apart, and he'd been doing annoying shit like that since we were kids. I had always been the more serious one, even before I enlisted in the Navy and that stint had changed my mental disposition and temperament, while my brother had opted for college. Despite being close in age, our personalities couldn't be more opposite, and Austin had always enjoyed pushing my buttons to get a reaction out of me. The guy was lucky I loved him.

"Austin, please," I said on an annoyed sigh. "I'm not playing this game."

"I can really make it a game if you want," he quipped, his eyes returning to whoever it was that had caught his interest to begin with. "I spy with my little eye..."

"Oh for fuck's sake," I groaned, and looked at the other guys sitting around our table, hoping for a little support. "Please, someone, make him stop."

"You think we can stop him?" Ford asked me, laughing because he'd seen this sibling rivalry and just how relentless Austin could be. "That drink you're sipping must be a lot stronger than you realize if you think any of us have that kind of influence over your brother."

Jaw clenched, I flipped him off. I'd known Ford and the other guys at our table for a couple years now, since I'd moved to Vegas to help open the new branch here for Noble and Associates security firm. I hadn't expected Austin to tag along with me, of course, but I supposed that was just how it was. Younger brother chasing after big brother. Even after all these years.

"I'm not the one you need to stop," Austin said, more serious now as he nodded over my shoulder. "*He* is, and you'd better do something quick, before it's too late."

I frowned, then followed my brother's gaze because now I was admittedly curious to know what the fuck he was talking about. Shock rippled through me when I saw that none other than Andrea Corbin was here.

Oh, fuck no.

My stomach tightened and heat flooded straight to my dick with a surge of lust. I hated how I couldn't stop my body from responding every time I saw her, and it didn't help that she was wearing a short, body-hugging black dress that showed off her perky breasts, highlighted her curves, and exposed way too much damn skin.

Normally, she wore her hair down in loose waves, but the fact that she'd pulled those strands back into a sleek ponytail made me feel a little primal, especially in a place like this. I could easily imagine wrapping my fist around that silken rope, completely controlling her as I forced her onto her knees and did unspeakable things to that lush mouth of hers while she looked up at me with those bright blue eyes, all while swallowing my cock like a good fucking girl.

What the hell was she doing here? Everyone who knew Andrea described her as a bit demure, hardworking, and practical. Someone who kept their head down and stayed out of trouble. But from the moment I first met her, I'd seen that daring spark in her eyes, and it made me think maybe Andrea was someone who liked dancing with fire. That was a dangerous notion for someone like me who liked to deliver the heat in ways that would undoubtedly singe every single one of her sensibilities.

I'd known six years ago that I wanted her. Visions of stealing all that sweetness and inno-cence and making her sob with pleasure, or whimper from the carefully administered pain I inflicted, made my dick throb. The idea of her begging *please, sir, another,* as I used one of my toys on her, while I corrupted her, was the hottest thing I'd ever imagined in my entire life.

That was exactly why I had to stay away from her. I wasn't a man that people would describe as demonstrative or emotionally engaged, and I preferred it that way. After the shit I'd endured in the military, I'd learned to keep my feelings locked down tight, for my own sanity. Sex, physical release, was easy, but I was smart enough to know that I wasn't cut out for any kind of a committed relationship, or even marriage...and girls like Andrea eventually wanted those things.

And ultimately, Andrea was the sister of someone I knew and respected. There was no way I would ever start something with her, only to inevitably disappoint her and potentially cause tension and friction in our extended friend group. Which was why I'd spent the past six years trying to keep my distance from her, even at the expense of making her dislike me. It was safer that way.

Andrea's light laughter yanked me out of my dark thoughts, forcing my attention back to her and the man who was flirting with her. My jaw clenched before I could stop it. I knew that my brother could see my response, but I couldn't hide my reaction. Someone as guileless as Andrea had no business being in a club like this. She probably had zero idea how to handle what went on in this place...what depraved men like *me* did in the play-rooms that were equipped with implements that delivered equal pain and pleasure.

Someone had to do the right thing and tell her to cut her losses before she got in way over her head.

"You look like you're having a stroke," Austin said, his tone amused.

My dick of a brother was enjoying this—my annoyance and the tension this situation was causing me. He was one of the few people who knew why I'd deliberately maintained an aloof attitude with Andrea, because the last thing I'd ever want to do was lead her on, or make her believe I was a forever kind of guy, despite how much I wanted her.

I glared at Austin, finished off my drink, then stood up. I didn't know or recognize the guy Andrea was with, but that didn't matter to me and what I was about to do. As I strode over to the two of them, I told myself I was protecting her. Trying to keep her safe and from making a mistake she'd regret later. Logically, I knew what she did here was none of my business. Illogically, I was about to insert myself into a situation that would undoubtedly piss her off.

It was a chance I was willing to take, because the thought of her fucking anyone in the club tonight was raising my blood pressure to alarming levels.

The man said something to Andrea, flashing her a charming grin as he dared to run the back of his knuckles down the side of her neck. As I neared, I caught the last of his words to her. "...I'm thinking one of the themed playrooms upstairs could be fun. What do you say?"

I spoke before Andrea could. "I say, unless you'd like to walk out of here with a few broken fingers, I'd suggest you don't touch her again," I replied, startling them both with my sudden appearance. "She's with me."

The man immediately dropped his hand back to his side, and they both glanced at me. Him, a bit warily, which I was used to considering the intimidation factor of my size. I was taller than him by a few inches, broad shouldered, and solid muscle compared to his much slighter build.

The man put his hands up in that classic sign of surrender. "My apologies," he said quickly, and I nearly rolled my eyes at his timid reaction. "I had no idea."

Andrea's lips pursed, her eyes flashing with annoyance at me before she shifted her gaze back to the other man. "I'm not with him," she insisted.

The man looked thoroughly confused, apprehensive, and unsure how to proceed.

"What can I say, she likes being a brat," I said with a shrug and crossed my arms over my chest. "It's a little game we like to play, and we both know where that bratty behavior of yours leads, don't we, sweetheart?"

She narrowed her gaze at me, infuriated at my interference. "Go to hell, Chase," she snapped.

That fiery attitude of hers made my dick hard. I was almost disappointed that this wasn't real, that I wasn't going to whisk her away to a private room to dole out the kind of punishment that would make her bare ass red, while she cried out an apology for being so mouthy.

"Look, I'm not into couple drama roleplaying, so I'm out," the guy said, clearly not the confrontational type, because he walked away from Andrea without a backwards glance.

She stared after him, looking frustrated that he hadn't fought harder for her, but then she straightened, squaring her shoulders as she glared at me. "What the fuck was that, Chase?" she demanded angrily.

I ignored her question. "I didn't know you were a top," I said instead, purposefully provoking her, when I should have been leading her toward the exit.

Her jaw dropped open, then closed again. "I'm...I'm *not* a top," she sputtered, clearly flustered —which I had to admit I found adorable.

I was impressed that she understood the

meaning of being a top, but her denial only pushed me to goad her a bit more, because I was enjoying this encounter far more than was wise. "Well, he's clearly as submissive as a puppy, so where would that put you in that dynamic, had you gone off to one of the playrooms with him? I'm guessing with him on his hands and knees, and you holding the crop."

Her fingers visibly tightened around the drink she was holding, which judging by the mottled mint leaves inside the glass, looked to be a mojito. "I'm *not* a domme," she said, but I already knew that.

This woman in front of me was dying to be submissive, to have a man take her in hand and bend her to his will. *To claim her*, as that dipshit who'd just walked away from her hadn't had the balls to do. I'd been living this lifestyle for six years, since the age of twenty-five, and all the signs were there. That defiant, daring attitude was like cat nip to a dominant man like me, who enjoyed having the upper hand and saw that rebellion as a challenge.

She finished the last of her drink, then turned around and headed to the bar, dismissing me. I followed, because obviously I was a glutton for punishment when it came to her.

"How did you get in here?" I asked.

She set her empty glass on the counter and rolled her eyes at me, something I wouldn't have tolerated under different circumstances, or if we'd been in a playroom alone together. "I broke in through the underground tunnel," she deadpanned, and when I gave her a disbelieving look, she continued with her snark. "Oh, wait, you didn't know there was a secret passageway that doesn't require an invitation?"

I braced an arm on the bar counter, the corner of my mouth twitching with the urge to grin, of all things. It actually took real effort to keep my tone and expression neutral. "Oh, I'm aware. I just prefer to walk through the main doors like a civilized person."

Aggravation rolled off of her in waves. "Do you think you're funny?"

"A little bit," I admitted.

She looked completely exasperated with me. I'd created this tense situation between us purposefully, for the sole reason to make sure I didn't cross any lines with her. Our encounters over the years had been brief, my attitude always cool and distant. Whenever we'd been in the same room together, I'd walked away, avoided her, and I should have done so now but the thought of

28

another man swooping in and doing *anything* with her was unacceptable.

I had to get her the fuck out of here before I lost my mind and did something incredibly stupid...like drag her off to one of the rooms to finally give in to the urge to slake my lust with her, *in her*, until she was completely and utterly mine.

While I was mentally contemplating all the ways I wanted to wreck her, she stepped closer and stabbed me in the chest with her finger, her eyes flashing a combination of fury and frustration. "What gives you the right to interfere with my evening here, anyway?" she demanded to know.

"That was me, saving you from making a big mistake," I replied. "So, you're welcome."

Andrea's brows shot up. "I didn't know that I'd been assigned a babysitter. Did Madison put you up to this?"

Ahh, so her older sister was the culprit who'd given her the invitation, which made sense considering Madison, and her husband Rick, frequented the club in San Diego. "No, but she'd thank me if she knew I'd stepped in. That guy has no clue what to do with a brat like you."

She scoffed. "Oh, and you do?"

As soon as I arched a brow, indicating that oh, yes, I most definitely knew *exactly* how to discipline a little hellion like her, her entire face flushed with realization before she jutted her chin out.

"Well, I can't remember signing anything that said I needed a vetting process or some kind of dom-sub matchmaker, and I'd know if I did because I read that form pretty thoroughly. I did, however, read something about how to let the staff know if a creep is bothering you."

I held her gaze and called her bluff. "Then go ahead. Signal."

Andrea huffed out a deflated breath. "You know, I think it's your arrogance that annoys me the most."

"Oh, you have a list?"

She nodded. "A very long one. I rearrange it sometimes when I'm bored on a rainy day. Nothing like a good burning hatred to keep life interesting."

Andrea threw every one of her words out at me like a challenge, and she had no idea how badly I wanted to grab her and spank her and tease her until she gave in and called me sir and begged me for mercy. She didn't back down from my rebuttals, she just jabbed right back, having no idea what kind of bear she was poking. Our entire interaction had my cock twitching hot and heavy between my legs, had me aching to see just how beautifully she'd submit to me.

"You look good," I told her, because I was in danger and needed to hurry up and end this conversation before things really got out of control. "I'm sure that dress will look even lovelier hanging up neatly in your closet at home."

Andrea frowned at my comment, her forehead puckering as she tried to make sense of what I meant. "Are you telling me to...take my dress off? Because the line is *it would look better on my bedroom floor.*"

Oh, yes, it would. I couldn't argue that. "I'm telling you to go home and change into something comfortable," I replied, trying to reason with her. "Watch some trashy TV. Enjoy some ice cream. You don't belong here."

Andrea bristled and waved her hand to the bartender for her second—and last—drink. "I belong here just as much as anyone else. In fact, I was doing just fine until you showed up and scared that guy off."

"If he was worth your time, he would have stayed calm and handled me instead of tucking his tail and running off."

"I don't think you realize what you look like

when you're being all..." Andrea waved her hand up and down at me. "You *know*."

I grinned, unable to stop the look of amusement before it formed. "Actually, I don't know. Enlighten me."

Andrea shook her head, causing that enticing ponytail to brush across her bare shoulders. "You're insufferable, and I'm here to have a good time. I can handle myself. I'm not a child."

Before I could catch myself, I let my gaze drag down the length of her body, then back up again until I was staring into her vivid blue eyes. "Trust me, I'm very aware of how *adult* you are."

"Great." She gave me an overly perky grin and picked up the drink that the bartender delivered to her. "I'm glad we can agree on something. Now, if you don't mind, I'm off to enjoy whatever the club has to offer."

As soon as she walked off by herself, I saw enough male interest in the room to spur me into action. I pushed off the bar and caught up to her before any other guy could approach her. Gently grabbing her arm, I brought her to a stop, ignoring the look of annoyance she shot my way and the way she stiffened at my touch.

"*What?*" she snapped irritably.

I sighed. "You really *are* going to be stubborn about this, aren't you?"

She stared into my eyes, and as I watched, that defiance ebbed, and she swallowed hard before replying. "I'm here for a reason, Chase, and I'm not leaving until I experience…"

She caught herself before she could finish her sentence, but the flash of insecurities I saw in her eyes softened my attitude toward her. "Experience what, Andrea?" I prompted.

I didn't expect her to give me an answer when I could see that whatever she was holding back was so personal, so I was shocked when she did reply.

"I want to know what it's like…to have a man dom me."

The honesty, the vulnerability, was unlike anything any other woman had ever shared with me. Her reasons for wanting this went deeper than just the thrill of being tied up, or paddled, or any other number of Dom/sub scenarios. This felt like a deep seated need for her, and that was something I could relate to and understand…even if I hated the idea of Andrea experiencing all those firsts with another man.

I knew telling her to leave again was just going to piss her off, make her more rebellious and possibly push her toward an *I'm going to prove you wrong* stance. The last thing I wanted was her to be in the wrong headspace, and I wasn't about to give someone as innocent as her to the wolves prowling around the club.

"Tell you what," I said, softening my tone. "Why don't I show you around, give you a proper tour of the place, and see if any of the men I know who are good, well-trained doms are in tonight and available so you don't end up with an amateur."

Skepticism etched her expression, not that I could blame her, considering my one eighty in attitude. "You would do that for me?"

I nodded, telling myself this was nothing more than a professional courtesy, even while everything else in me balked at the thought of handing her off to any other man. "Yes. To ensure your first time is handled by someone experienced and capable."

She studied my expression a bit longer. "Is this your way of offering a truce between us?"

The corner of my mouth twitched, because it was clear she was calling me out on my standoffish behavior over the past six years. "Yes."

She smiled, so sweet and trusting, all animosity between us gone for now. "All right, then. Lead the way," she said, passing off her unfinished drink to a waiter.

I offered her my arm, and Andrea slipped her hand into the crook of my elbow as I guided her out of the lounge, as if she were my play partner for the night…which she was not. I caught sight of Austin, and almost laughed at the comical look of shock on his face as he watched the two of us exit the room together. I could relate, because if someone had told me I'd be escorting Andrea around The Players Club as well as finding her a competent dom to play with for the night, I would have told them it would only happen if hell froze over.

Yet, here we were, no longer sniping at one another, with Andrea trusting me to select a proficient man to pop her BDSM cherry. Unfortunately, I had ulterior motives in mind. If she wasn't going to leave the club of her own accord, I'd just have to give her a different kind of incentive to make her reconsider.

As I guided her to our first destination, on the way I could have easily identified at least five men that I knew personally who would show her an easy and professional initiation into the world, acquainting her with the basics, and give her a memorable and pleasurable experience.

I ignored every single one of them, along with the looks of interest they sent in Andrea's direction. In fact, I was fairly certain my expression told them to *fuck off*, considering they didn't bother asking for an introduction to the new girl in their midst.

Instead, I took her immediately to the public sex room, since there was always an orgy going on in there. I hoped if anything was going to unsettle Andrea, it would be the kind of raw, unrestrained fucking that went on in this section of the club. I wasn't into that kind of exhibitionism myself. I enjoyed focusing on my one partner too much to share, but I didn't judge anyone's kinks.

Once inside, I heard Andrea's breath catch as she stared at the various positions and stages of undress as I led her along the perimeter of the room, where other people watched the sexual display, or fucked while being voyeurs to all the shameless debauchery unfolding in front of them. Andrea didn't squirm or seem uncomfortable. Just curious. Fascinated, even.

Her maturity impressed me. That was a point in her favor, but wouldn't help me with my end goal with her. I'd have to bring out the big guns.

"This way," I said, redirecting her attention. "I'm not seeing any of the more experienced doms in this area."

There was a door that led upstairs to more

rooms, if you didn't want to pick your way through the bodies to take the grand staircase behind the bar. I opened it and ushered Andrea through and up the carpeted steps to the second floor.

On this level, all the public rooms had windows you could peer into. I stopped us at one of them, where people were already engaged in a scene. A woman was tied up to a St. Andrew's Cross and taking a hell of a flogging, her shrieks loud even with the sound-absorbing walls.

I paused, letting Andrea take in the scene. I was sure she'd hear the screams, see the red, welted, crisscross marks all over the woman's body, and call it a day.

Over on another one of the benches, a submissive was strapped down and being fucked hard and relentlessly, begging for the man to stop, sobbing as her dominant thrust into her like a jackhammer while pulling on her hair and smacking her ass, which was already bright red.

I knew that it was all play—the partner had a safeword she could use if she really didn't want to be so forcefully fucked, or the pain got too intense. The club was a safe place for a lot of people to engage in consensual non-consent roleplay. Even if that wasn't the type of scene we were watching,

37

many submissives would instinctively say 'no' or 'stop' without really meaning it, just out of instinct. Safewords were a way to make sure there was no confusion.

But Andrea probably didn't know that. She was new to this. What she saw and heard was a woman begging for the man to stop, and watching as the person fucking her ignored that request. That had to affect her, make her pause and consider what she was here for.

Andrea's hand tightened on my arm and she made a noise in the back of her throat, and I glanced at her. Her eyes were a little wide, but she didn't look afraid. She looked... intrigued. There was absolutely no fear on her face. No apprehension.

Fuck. Not what I was hoping for at all.

"Looks like Jordan is already busy," I said, making an excuse to move on.

In the next room, which was medical themed, a woman and her submissive were already getting into blood and needle play. *Aha.* Now this would be sure to scare Andrea off.

The submissive's legs shook a little as she lay on the table, strapped down, whimpering as she let her mistress slide needles in under the first layer of skin. It wasn't anything I hadn't seen before, but I could understand why it would be rather intense for a first timer to witness.

I snuck a peek at Andrea to gauge her reaction. She bit her bottom lip as she watched the scene, but again, she displayed no trepidation or aversion to what was happening in the room.

"Is this one of those things you need to be certified on before they let you do it?" she asked curiously.

"Yes," I said, surprised she'd remembered that from the club rules.

We moved on, this time finding a couple engaging in electrostimulation. The woman was tied to a bed, spread-eagle, while her partner used a violet wand on various parts of her body to deliver a stream of electricity, the intensity ramped up high enough that the woman's skin rippled with every touch. The man dragged the tip over one of the woman's nipples, and her back arched as she cried out from the sensation. Beside me, I felt Andrea's entire body jolt in response, as if she'd been on the receiving end of that stimulating voltage.

"It's pretty intense, yeah?" I asked, hoping that this was finally her tipping point that had her running toward the exit.

"Very," she agreed, and looked up at me, her

eyes not filled with the concern or fear I'd been anticipating, but a surprising flash of irritation. "I know what you're trying to do, Chase. You're trying to scare me off, but I didn't come here tonight without being prepared or knowing what I want..."

Andrea's voice faded as a woman's moan caught her attention and she glanced over my shoulder, her eyes widening. I turned, curious to see if something had finally pushed her too far. I followed her line of vision to an open area, where another woman was secured to a St. Andrew's Cross, her dom edging her, alternating between using his hand and a vibrator between her legs to increase the pleasure. He took her right to the brink, then denied her the release, again and again.

"Please," the woman begged, her whole body shaking with the need to climax. "Oh, god, please, I'll do anything, just let me come, *please*..."

He started again, and I could tell by her high-pitched cries she was so close to orgasm—but right at the precipice, the man stopped all stimulation. The woman sobbed in desperation.

Edging was one of my favorite things to do to my partner, and my cock stirred a little on instinct. When I looked back at Andrea and saw her reaction, my dick hardened the rest of the way.

A dark pink flush of arousal colored her cheeks as she stared at the duo with a desire that was visceral. Her pupils were blown wide as she watched, entranced by the scene. Her full lips parted, and I could have sworn I heard a soft, low moan escape her throat. Through the thin fabric of her dress, I could see her hardened nipples, and I couldn't miss the rapid way her chest rose and fell with each breath she took.

Jesus, Christ. She wanted to be dominated, badly, and I understood that craving for a particular kind of sexual kink more than most. Pain was my pleasure, but I also wasn't immune to the exhilaration of pushing a woman to her limits, to seeing how much she could handle before I let her come apart. Imagining Andrea in that scenario, with me in control and her helpless to do anything more than accept what I doled out, made my blood run hot in my veins.

Knowing I was probably going to hell for what I was about to do, I stepped behind Andrea, sliding an arm around her waist and pulling her backside flush to my body. She gasped, her hands touching my arm as she instinctively sank back against me, then deliberately rubbed her ass along the hard length of my cock, tempting and teasing me.

I'd tried my best to make her see reason, but I

knew that Andrea was on a mission and there was truly nothing else I could do to dissuade her from finding another man to give her what I was capable of providing. The thought of anyone else touching her, or fucking her, was no longer an option for me. If she played with anyone tonight, it was going to be me.

I splayed a hand low on her belly, and her head fell back against my shoulder, her hips rolling in a silent plea for my fingers to traverse lower, to slide between her legs and stroke her pussy the same way the man in front of us was making his submissive squirm.

"Chase," she whimpered, sounding a bit delirious. "I want...I need..."

She was so caught up in the lust coursing through her body that she couldn't even get the words out. "I know exactly what you need," I murmured into her ear. "Better than you do. Why don't I take you to a private room and show you?"

She nodded jerkily, and didn't even hesitate to give me exactly what I wanted, which was her. "Yes, please."

CHAPTER 3

Andrea

*C*hase's offer knocked the wind out of me, but as reckless and utterly insane as it might be, I couldn't bring myself to say no. Because in this place, surrounded by all levels of depravity, I didn't want to be rational.

What I wanted, who I'd *always* wanted, was Chase.

Regardless of everything that had transpired between us over the past six years, in this sexually heightened environment there was no mistaking the mutual chemistry, no hiding from the heat coiling tight in my belly just from being pressed up against his hard, muscular body.

Denying that attraction, and Chase, would have been a lie. And for tonight...I was okay with pretending that maybe, just maybe, this wasn't the worst idea I'd ever had. I trusted him to make my first time at The Players Club good for me, that he'd give me everything I'd ever hoped for sexually and teach me what I wanted to know. And because I knew Chase personally, I'd be able to relax and sink into the experience without being self-conscious. And really, that's all that mattered, right?

It didn't hurt that Chase was insanely hot, and his deep, confident voice murmuring in my ear that he knew exactly what I needed already had me wet and throbbing. I felt like I was breathing fire, just watching all these other women on the receiving end of what I craved so deeply. The idea that Chase would be the one to introduce me to that Dom/sub dynamic had me ready to sink to my knees and beg. It was a fantasy I had never let myself entertain with Chase as my instructor, because there'd been no way it would ever come true.

And yet, here he was, offering to show me everything I'd secretly wished for.

Chase stepped around me and extended his hand, his expression not nearly as impassive as it had been in the past. Oh, there was still that reserve about him, that element of control he always exuded, but tonight I saw the flicker of anticipation, along with the sinful promises in his eyes, and I couldn't wait to explore each and every one with him.

I took his hand and allowed him to lead me into one of the vacant private rooms. The moment we stepped inside and he closed the door, all sound from the club was gone. We were truly alone.

I glanced around, taking in the décor. The walls were lined in velvet, a lovely dark green color rather than the stereotypical red. There was a lot of equipment, some of which I recognized from my research, and other pieces that were foreign to me. There was a rack of toys along the wall, a set of drawers that I was sure held even more surprises, and a bed in the middle of the room.

Chase let go of my hand and walked to the monitor on the wall. He touched the screen, bringing it to life. "Your code?"

He wanted to look at my limits. I gave him the digits, and he quickly and efficiently perused the form I'd filled out. Then he returned, slowly walking around me, inspecting me from every angle in a way that felt like a stamp of ownership. I found myself trembling under his sharp, assessing gaze. It was like some kind of switch had been flipped inside of him, and now there was no doubt of his power and authority in this situation, and over me. It was intoxicating.

When he was done making that circle, he stepped back. He clasped his hands behind him in a commanding stance, while those dark eyes of his met mine. "Undress," he ordered.

One firmly spoken word. Clearly, there would be no sweet, romantic preliminaries tonight, but my time with Chase wasn't about the kind of slow, intimate seduction that usually led to sex between a couple. In this room, it was all about pleasure and satisfaction, and this man in front of me was all business.

"Don't make me ask a second time," he said in a stern tone when I took too long for his liking.

I shivered at the veiled threat in his words, as if I didn't comply *right now* there would be consequences to pay. While a part of me was curious to see what would happened if I disobeyed, I wasn't sure I was fully prepared to test Chase just yet.

I reached for the straps of my dress, pushing them off my shoulders and letting them fall down my arms, exposing my upper body to his gaze, which didn't seem fair considering he remained fully dressed. His eyes flicked to my breasts, his expression not giving anything away as he continued to watch as I shimmied my hips so I could push the rest of the material to the floor. My underwear followed, and then my heels.

He picked up my clothes and set them on a nearby chair, then returned. While I stood still he circled around me once again, gently trailing his fingertips over my body, heightening my awareness of his touch. He grazed them across my arms and shoulders, and down to my breasts, murmuring huskily, "what a pretty little thing you are," making me flush from the compliment.

I gasped in surprise as he flicked his finger against my nipple, furling it into a tight, hard bead. Before I could recover from that unexpected sting of pain, his hand was skimming down my stomach. Holding my gaze, he dipped his long fingers between my legs, gathered my clit between two fingers, and gave it a little pinch. I swallowed back a moan, but the muffled sound somehow managed to escape past my lips, anyway.

"Don't hide your sounds from me," he said, my mind short-circuiting at the lazy way he kept tugging on my clit. "I want to hear every moan. Every blissful sigh, every scream of pleasure when I allow you to come. Your body belongs to me, so that means your orgasms are mine to give when I feel you've earned them. Do you understand?"

I nodded, and found my voice. "Yes."

"Yes . . ." He inclined his head, waiting for me to figure out what he wanted.

"Yes, sir," I finished.

His eyes flashed with approval. "Good girl."

His praise shocked me—not just because he gave it to me, but how good it made me feel. How those words softened everything inside of me and made me want to please him even more.

He gave my pussy one last deep stroke, and my knees went weak when he withdrew his hand and sucked the taste of me off of his fingers, then licked his lips as if he didn't want to miss a drop. I felt like I could hardly breathe, I was so turned on.

"Is there anywhere I can't touch you?" he asked. "Anything that's off-limits?"

"You *just* read my list," I said, belatedly realizing how sassy my reply sounded when he smacked my ass with the flat of his hand. I sucked in a startled breath because *damn*, that hurt. Chase clearly wasn't messing around.

"Do not undermine my authority, or backtalk,

unless you want to see where that gets you," he said in a strict, uncompromising tone. "I asked the question because I want to hear it from you, directly."

"You can touch me anywhere you'd like, sir," I said, then rattled off the kinks I'd listed under my hard limits on the form.

"Better," he said, and pushed his white shirt sleeves up a bit higher on his arms, to his elbows, giving me more of all those intricate tattoos on his skin. "We'll start with the standard safewords, which are the easiest for someone new to this dynamic to remember. Green, yellow, red. Do you understand what each of them means?"

I nodded, since it was another thing I'd read in the club's guidelines. Still, I repeated it back to Chase just in case this was another test. My ass still stung from the first smack and I didn't want to add another. "Green, I'm good and can handle more. Yellow, slow down. Red, stop."

"Okay, then let's get started." He strolled over to the area where all the toys and implements were, then crossed his arms over his chest. "Pick three. Whatever appeals to you. We'll start with those."

I drew in a breath and walked over, an air conditioned breeze brushing across my bare skin, which offset the heat I was feeling from the searing way Chase looked over my naked body. When I reached the wall, I contemplated my choices, overwhelmed by all the options. *Three toys. I could do this.*

There were a few accessories that I wasn't quite sure what they did, but everything was clearly high-quality. Even the whips and floggers looked like they'd been handcrafted with the finest leather, and the more personal items were sealed in brand new packaging.

I did want to get spanked, and not just with a hand, so I picked a riding crop. Seemed pretty straight forward for a first time. I selected the cuffs, obviously, because the thought of being restrained and forced to endure whatever my dom administered appealed to those forbidden desires I'd been harboring. They were leather on the outside and fur-lined on the inside, which would at least make them comfortable around my wrists. I also picked a black silk blindfold. I liked the idea of not being able to see Chase while he played with me, and not knowing what to anticipate. Blocking my vison would add a nice little thrill of uncertainty.

Pleased with my selections, I presented the toys to Chase. He took them from me, then walked over to one of the narrower pieces of equipment in the room, which was padded in black leather.

"Bend over this table," he said.

I did as I was told, positioning my body so that I was bent at the waist. The surface was only big enough for me to rest my torso on, which meant my breasts dangled over the opposite side. Standing behind me, Chase lightly scratched his nails down my back and sides. It almost but didn't quite tickle, and I moaned at the pleasurable sensation.

"Such a good, obedient girl."

The sexy murmur of his voice in my ear had me melting with desire as he gently pulled my hands behind my back and wrapped my wrists in the furl-lined cuffs. Then he slipped the blindfold over my eyes, making sure it was securely in place.

"Not too tight?" he asked of the restraints.

"No, sir, thank you," I said, making sure I addressed him formally.

"I should have known you'd be a quick learner." Chase sounded amused, but his praise was genuine. "I like what you picked out. These are a good start." I jolted a little as I felt the crop lightly drag up the inside of my thigh. "But they're a bit tame, wouldn't you say? After everything I showed you around the club tonight, I thought you'd be more willing to jump into the deep end."

"You're the experienced one, not me," I shot back before I could sensor my tone. "If you think I went too easy, then you should have picked out the toys."

I received a snap of the riding crop on my ass, and I gasped as that burning sensation turned into an arousing tingle that spread down to my pussy.

"An excellent idea," he said, and I heard rustling around behind me. "You picked out three toys...I'll pick out three toys. I think that's only fair."

I held my breath, a little nervous as I tried to figure out what Chase was grabbing based on the sounds I heard, but I really couldn't be sure. The blindfold made it feel like my other senses were going haywire, trying to compensate for the loss of sight. It filled me with an exciting, terrifying tension because I had no idea what was about to happen to me.

My legs were gripped powerfully from behind and forced to spread apart, then smooth leather wrapped around both of my thighs. I heard the clink of something snapping into place. When I tried to move my legs, I couldn't because something was pressing against my inner thighs.

My heart began to race.

"Spreader bar," Chase murmured right in my ear, and I could feel the heat of his body as he bent over me. "Now you can't close those pretty legs to escape what I'm about to do to you, no matter how much you want to. You're at my mercy."

He rubbed the flat of the crop between my legs, then tapped the leather tip against my already sensitive clit. I gasped in shock. The impact didn't hurt, but the audacity of it, and the fact that I couldn't stop him, was electrifying. It was like he wanted me to know he owned me tonight. That I was his toy to play with, however he pleased.

His hand caressed down my back as he stepped up behind me. "Now, a little something to fill you up before I do."

I expected a vibrator, or something similar. I was *not* prepared to feel something nudge up against my asshole, slick and cool and solid.

A startled squeak escaped past my lips and I instinctively tensed up, trying to press my legs together to stop the intrusion, but unable to because of the spreader bar. The butt plug he was trying to work into my ass felt impossibly large. I'd never done anal play before. I'd been neutral on that particular kink—it didn't turn me off and it hadn't been a hard limit for me. But now, a sudden instinctive panic gripped me—a fear that the plug wouldn't fit.

"You need to relax," he said, his voice deep and soothing, as was the hand stroking along my hip.

I forced myself to calm down because I trusted Chase. I exhaled and unlocked my muscles as he continued pushing the plug into me. The stretch in a foreign place made the object feel huge, and I groaned in relief when I realized it was finally in place, snug and tight and full in my ass.

But that was only two toys. The spreader bar and the anal plug. Things that had definitely pushed me beyond what I'd ever done before. I couldn't imagine what he'd select for his third device.

I heard his footsteps as he walked around me, until he was standing in front of the table I was bent over. "Stand up straight," he ordered.

I lifted my upper body and when his large, warm hands gripped my breasts, squeezing them, I moaned because the way he fondled the pair felt so good.

"You have great tits," he said appreciatively. "So perky. And your nipples are so responsive." He rubbed and lightly pinched them until they were stiff. "Are you sensitive here?"

"Kind of, sir," I replied.

"Hmm, that's a little too vague for me," he said as he hands fell away. "I'd like to know more definitively, so let's find out just how sensitive they are."

I inhaled a quick breath as something bit down on my nipples, tiny harsh metal teeth digging in. The pain was equivalent of an electric jolt that was connected to every one of my nerve endings, and I panted for breath as my brain tried to process the intense sensations ricochetting through my body.

"Ohmygod," I gasped. My first inclination was to remove whatever Chase had secured to my nipples, but that wasn't possible. "What...what..." The extreme pressure was so all-consuming I couldn't even form a cohesive sentence.

"Nipple clamps," Chase explained as he splayed a hand between my shoulder blades and eased me back down so I was bent over the table again, my breasts swaying freely. "Too much?"

I heard the challenge in his tone and knew for certain he was testing me. He expected me to safe-word out. To say yes, I'd changed my mind.

It wasn't going to happen. The pinch from the nipple clamps was a lot, but not overwhelming. In fact, as the seconds ticked by and I regulated my breathing, I realized that twinge of discomfort kept me focused. Utterly present in the moment. I couldn't think of anything except that rhythmic throb in my nipples and how oddly *blissful* it made me feel.

"I'm good, sir," I said honestly. "I...I like the pain." Even as I said those words, I knew they were true.

There was a moment of silence, as if Chase was processing his surprise that I was actually enjoying this. "Well, then, let's continue. Ten hits with the crop. I want you to count each strike for me. If it's too much, say *red*. If you need a pause, say *yellow*."

I nodded, and Chase gave me a warning tap on my inner thigh. "Use your words, baby."

The pet name thrilled me, not that I'd ever tell him that. "I understand, sir," I said, clasping my fingers together behind my back where they were restrained. "Red for stop. Yellow for pause."

He was quiet for a long moment, lulling me into a false sense of security as I let my body relax. The first smack came out of nowhere, hitting the back of my thigh. The unexpected strike made me clench down around the plug in my ass, and made my breasts with the clamps on them shake. It was so much stimulation, more than just the sting of the crop, and it drove all other thoughts out of my head to make room for more enjoyable sensations to take hold.

"One," I counted out loud, remembering just in time.

"Very good," Chase murmured as he slowly, softly, slid his hand up my back, grounding me before adding another swat in the same vicinity.

"Two," I called out.

As he continued, I realized the key was not to fight the pain, but to embrace it. I breathed in and out between each smack, almost meditating, letting that initial burn ebb into a more euphoric sensation. I allowed my brain and body to adjust to the ache, and I was rewarded with a sublime pleasure that washed over me and added to the intoxicating high.

Between each swat, Chase left me hanging just enough that I was tense with anticipation, but never so long that I was taken out of the moment. I felt so present in my body, so aware of every part of me. Every single one of my senses was heightened, and I loved that I was the sole focus of Chase's attention, in a way that no other man had ever made me feel.

"*Ten*," I gasped out as the final lash struck my sore ass.

"You did so well, sweetheart," he praised in a gruff tone, the depth of his voice infused with lust. "But I'm not done with you yet."

I was gently hauled up to standing, and still wearing the blindfold, my head spun a bit. The clamps were removed, and I cried out in relief as the blood flowed back into my nipples. Chase gently brushed a thumb over one of the sensitive tips, and I sucked in a breath at how hot and engorged it felt.

I realized, dimly, that my pussy was soaking wet, my arousal coating the inside of my thighs. My legs trembled, and Chase pressed himself against my back. At some point, in between strikes with the crop, he'd undressed, and the heat of his skin added to all the other sensations my brain was trying to process.

"*Now*," he murmured into my ear as one of his hands slid around to my throat so that he could tip my head back against his shoulder. "I'm going to fuck that pretty, wet pussy until you come all over my cock. Do you know why?"

My mind raced as I looked for an answer. "Because—because it's yours, sir."

"That's right." His other hand stroked my stomach, and I couldn't stop shaking with desire. "Are you on edge? Hmm?"

"Yes...yes, sir," I stuttered.

He moved his fingers lower and slowly rubbed my clit. I moaned, slumping against him. It felt so good, with my aching breasts, and my ass feeling full and penetrated, and my legs still forcefully spread apart. And Chase, mastering my body like he knew exactly what to do to make me give myself over to him. To submit to his dominance.

It was sensory overload, and I wanted to come, badly. It was almost a surprise how much I needed the release, like an orgasm and sex was brand new again.

I moaned, and just as I was approaching the peak—he abruptly stopped. I whimpered, my entire body trembling at the edge, desperate and needy. I would have done anything to orgasm in that moment. *Anything.*

And Chase knew it.

"Not yet," he chastised, his voice soft but still in command. "Not until my cock is buried as deep inside your pussy as it can get."

He lifted the hand from my throat and peeled off the blindfold. I blinked, the room coming back into focus. The lighting was soft and muted but still too bright for a moment until I adjusted. I was still shaking. I couldn't seem to stop.

Chase released one of my wrists from the restraints, but only to bring my arms around in front of me and resecured the cuff so that I remained under his control. He removed the spreader bar, then bent down and swept me up into his arms, effortlessly carrying me to the bed.

He laid me down on my back with my head on the pillow, then pulled my cuffed hands up and arranged them so that I was now secured to one of the hooks embedded into the headboard.

He stood by the side of the bed, and I turned my head and stared at his naked body, my breath catching in my chest as I took in *all* of him for the first time.

Dark haired, dark eyes, and a honed physique built for sin, Chase was gorgeous. I wasn't surprised to see that he was fit as hell underneath all those clothes. He'd just picked me up like I weighed nothing. And he had a ton of tattoos across his chest and down both arms. They were all stunning, and I wanted to know their meanings, wanted to examine them more closely.

But what had me staring in disbelief was the cock he held in his hand.

His hard, thick, *pierced* cock.

My eyes widened and my mouth fell open in shock. I knew that people could get genital piercings. Hell, this was Las Vegas and I'd even seen a few women with their nipples pierced, which I'd found intriguing. But I'd never seen anything like this, up close and personal. My first thought was that it had to have hurt, right? An insane amount.

Chase smirked. "Yeah, I figured I should take the blindfold off so you're aware of my piercings before I fuck you."

I found myself wanting to reach out and touch him. The fact that I couldn't was both frustrating and arousing. I couldn't kiss him, touch him, lick him— or anything else my mind might conjure. And I was curious. I wanted to know what all those piercings felt like. Not just for him but for me, *inside of me*.

"What are they?" I whispered, still in awe.

"A Prince Albert and a Jacob's Ladder is what they're called." Chase stroked his stiff cock, running his fingers over the silver piercings. "This one's the Albert." He skimmed his thumb over the one that went through his urethra. "This one's the ladder."

I watched as he ran his finger along the line of barbel piercings that went up the underside of the shaft—it seemed pretty self-explanatory to call it a ladder.

"Did it hurt?" I asked him, then grimaced because it was a stupid question. Of course it hurt.

A depraved gleam entered Chase's eyes. "Yes, but I'm a masochist that way. I liked the pain."

Interesting. "Does it feel good now?"

"*Yes.*" His voice was a low growl that made me shiver.

I licked my bottom lip. "How will it feel for me?"

He cocked his head. "Want to find out?"

I swallowed and nodded, feeling a little depraved myself. "Yes."

"Who knew you were such a filthy girl," he said, though he sounded pleased with that knowledge. "Are you on some sort of birth control?"

"Yes."

He gave the Prince Albert a tug, playing with the metal piece. "We've both submitted clean health records to the club. Do you trust me to fuck you bare?"

The thought of having nothing between us made me feel light-headed. "I do, sir."

"Good, because this will feel so much better for both of us without the latex."

He moved up onto the bed, spreading my legs wide so he could kneel in between them. There was still a pleasant ache in my thighs from being forced to hold them apart for so long, and now that I was on my back on the bed, the cool sheets rubbed against my sore bottom from the riding crop.

He hooked his fingers behind my knees, bending my legs back and opening me wide, exposing every inch of my pussy to him and lifting my ass a few inches off the mattress. With practiced ease, he angled his hips, lining up the broad head of his cock against my core without needing his hand.

His dick was bigger in every way than anyone I'd ever been with, and even though I was slick and ready, I gasped at the sensation of being forced open and stretched by his substantial shaft, feeling twice as significant with the plug still inserted in my ass. He groaned at the tight fit as he pushed forward slowly, easing his way inside, and although the sheer size of him burned, it wasn't enough to make me want to stop.

No, I actually wanted more...I wanted, *needed*, to feel every single inch of him as deep as he could go.

And oh, God, the *piercings*. They rubbed up inside of me in a way that I thought only toys could. I gasped, trying not to squirm as he *finally* bottomed out inside of me and gave me a minute to adjust to being stuff beyond what I thought was possible.

"Fuck, you feel good," he said gruffly as he anchored my legs around his waist before he leaned in, braced his forearms on the bed next to my shoulders, and began fucking me.

The first two strokes were slow and easy, teasing me so that I could feel every single one of those barbells piercing his shaft, and to give my pussy the chance to accommodate his size. Gradually, he moved faster, his hips driving a little harder, his cock sinking impossibly deeper.

He looked down at me, his own features taut with restraint. "Remember your safe word, because you might need it," he warned.

I shook my head against the pillow. "I'm good, sir."

He gave me a *we'll see about that* smirk, right as he sped up, slamming into me roughly, stealing my breath from my lungs as he began thrusting in earnest, making me feel as though I was about to be split in two.

I cried out, my hands grabbing onto the headboard slats and my back instinctively arching to escape, but his body was too strong and powerful for me to buck off. He continued battering me with his cock, and soon that initial pain ebbed into something hot and exquisite as my body gradually grew accustom to *everything*.

My breaths came and went in shallow bursts, and my eyes rolled back in ecstasy as pleasure pulsed through me. This man's dominance, his unrestrained aggression, was exactly what I wanted, what I needed, and my body responded accordingly to each relentless thrust, driving me closer and closer to an orgasm. . . only to have Chase slow back down, making me thrash deliriously beneath him as I shamelessly pleaded, *please, please more.*

But as desperate as I was to come, I was even more desperate to hold onto this incredible moment. I had no idea a cock could feel so good inside of me, and I reveled in the fact that I was finally being held down and fucked as vigorously as I'd begged for.

Chase stared down into my face, and I realized that he was watching my reactions. Watching *me.* This was why he had me on my back, cuffed to the bed...so he could see my expressions and enjoy the fact that he was the one controlling my pleasure.

This man was so in tune with my body, sensing when I was about to climax and when I could handle it harder, deeper. He made sure we were in sync, and I felt a sudden rush of something I hadn't at all expected. Not just being helpless, not just submissive, but *taken care of.*

The knowledge made my head spin, but I didn't have the ability to think about it for long. All I could do was *feel* because Chase sped up again and didn't stop, his eyes dark and intense as they held mine, and his jaw clenched. Another orgasm beckoned, and I tensed a little, instinctively bracing for him to stop and not let me reach the peak—but oh, God, he did, and I came harder than I'd ever had in my life.

I screamed his name as I climaxed, desire flashing white hot through my veins, spilling across every nerve ending. My pussy clenched around his cock, and I was pretty sure I squirted. The pleasure pulsing through me was so overwhelming it threatened to break me. The piercings on his shaft inside of me gave me an added level of sensation that shot my orgasm into the stratosphere, and the fact that he'd forced me to hold back on that orgasm until now only added to the intensity.

I was glad my wrists were tied and had Chase's weight holding me down. I wouldn't have known what to do with my body if it hadn't been bound. If it hadn't been in Chase's capable hands.

Chase groaned and buried his face in my neck, and with one last deep thrust I felt him go stiff, his cock throbbing as he emptied himself inside me. The idea of him marking me up by coming in me bare had another hot shiver running through me.

I lay there, panting, all thoughts gone from my mind, my body limp and heavy, sated.

That was everything I could've ever hoped for, and more.

Chase caught his breath before I did and pushed himself up and off of me. His gaze was still intense but gentle as he searched my face while he undid my cuffs and massaged my wrists. Then, he settled on the bed next to me and pulled me onto his lap. I curled up against his warm chest and sighed in contentment.

"How are you feeling?" he murmured, idly stroking a hand up and down my arm.

He sounded—not *soft*. I wasn't sure Chase was capable of soft. But he sounded genuine. So genuine that I just sank into it, and let myself be taken care of by him.

"I'm good, thank you, sir."

"You can stop with the formalities now. The scene is over. This is just aftercare."

I frowned to myself. 'Just' aftercare. Like him holding me was no big deal after the most profound sexual encounter of my life. And maybe it wasn't a big deal to him. Maybe it was just a big deal to me because I'd never experienced anything like this before.

The realization was painfully ironic. This was

the softness that Heath had been so eager to give me. I was craving it now, happy to accept it. But this was in the aftermath of all that rough domination. If Heath had been willing to work with me and give me what I wanted... I would've happily given him *this,* what he wanted.

It was a bit of a shock to lie there and realize that dichotomy, but I didn't say any of it out loud. The last thing Chase wanted to hear, I was sure, was my revelations about my defunct relationship.

So, instead, I lifted my head from his chest and smiled up at him. "That was pretty damn amazing. I always hoped it would be like that with the right person, so thank you for the experience."

A small frown formed on his brow, even as he gently brushed my hair back from where some of it had fallen out of my ponytail, sticking to my forehead with sweat. "You did exceptionally well."

"I would like to do this with you again sometime," I said, the words rushing out of me. I was exhausted right now, but I already knew that I wanted to learn more about this lifestyle. "This is everything I've ever wanted sexually, and I want to learn about the different Dom/sub dynamics. I trust you to teach me."

That frown deepened and he shook his head while lifting me off his lap and setting me aside on the bed while he stood up. "I think it's best if this is just a one-time thing between us."

That momentary warmth and tenderness was gone, and I could almost see him erecting those walls between us again as he put on his pants, those emotional barriers that had kept me at arm's length for the past six years and it infuriated me now that I knew how compatible we were.

If he thought he had the last word on the matter, or that I was going to passively, meekly agree, he was wrong. The only place I ever planned to submit to a man was in the bedroom.

I moved off the bed, too, and walked to where he'd left my things on a chair. "Okay, fine. Have it your way," I said as I slipped my dress over my head and tugged it into place. "But if you won't be the person who will teach me and guide me through this, then I'll find someone at this club who will."

His gaze snapped back to mine, flashing with barely banked anger. "You don't fucking belong here," he snapped.

"Really?" I shot back, stunned at the sheer force of his fury—which, much to my shock, seemed territorial and possessive. "You can honestly say that after everything you put me through tonight, and I loved every single thing, especially you dominating me? Or did you honestly think that you were going to scare me off? With your pierced cock and your nipple clamps and an anal plug? Either you teach me what I want to learn, or I'll find someone who will."

He clenched his jaw and glared at me, mouth-wateringly shirtless and his hands jammed on his hips, as if he could intimidate me into changing my mind. I lifted my chin and stood my ground, glaring right back. I'd never met anyone who sparked the same wild heat in me that Chase did, and I could admit to myself that I'd feel robbed if I only had this one night with him to explore all this new territory. I was insanely attracted to him. I trusted him. But if he wouldn't guide me through this, then I would find another capable dom in this club who would.

Chase looked like he wanted to reach out and strangle me, or bend me over his knee and paddle my ass for being so willful and not backing down. "God, you're so fucking stubborn," he bit out.

I lifted my chin. "And determined," I said, two words that told him I was not going to yield on this decision.

Chase assessed me, more cool and composed now. "All right."

I blinked in surprise. "All right?"

"All right," Chase repeated, sounding exasperated. "I'll teach you. But only so that you can explore with someone safe and trustworthy before you go out on your own."

"Wow, condescending much?" I rolled my eyes at him as I put on my underwear, then slid into my heels. My legs were a little wobbly, but I did my best to hide it. I didn't want him to see how sex with him still had me weak-kneed, even as irritation prompted me to continue. "You know what? Forget it. Not if you're going to act like you're doing me some big gracious favor."

He narrowed his gaze at me. "You asked me to do this and now that I agree, you don't want it?"

That scowl probably made most women cower, probably men, too. But after tonight, there was very little about Chase that could scare me off. Not his sexual inclinations, and certainly not his boorish attitude.

I walked straight up to him and jabbed him in the chest with my finger, which he probably didn't even feel considering all the muscle there. "What I want is someone who will actually be a good sex partner, not someone who's going to keep me at arm's length and treat me like I've got the plague." Done with this aggravating conversation and equally aggravating man, I started past

71

him. "I'm not a charity case. So you can just take your—"

Chase seized my ponytail in his hand, bringing me and my tirade to an abrupt stop. He tugged hard, forcing my face back and up, and then his lips were on mine.

I found myself grabbing onto his arms so I didn't fall on my ass. With his hand holding me in place, he ravaged my mouth in a hot, deep, angry kiss that was filled with fury and passion and so much heat I nearly melted right there in front of him. I'd never, ever, been kissed so aggressively, his lust and hunger and dominance thrilling me.

I almost whimpered in disappointment when he ended the kiss, but managed to look indignant instead. "What...what was that for?"

"I just want to make sure," Chase purred in a low, husky tone, "that you can handle whatever I have to teach you."

If he'd told me to spread my legs in that moment so he could fuck me again, I would've done it without hesitation. "I hope you can deliver on that claim," I taunted him. "You're trying to act like the big bad wolf but so far, I'm not seeing anything all that scary."

Chase's eyes darkened, and a sinful smirk curved his lips. "Trust me. I'll give you just as much as you can handle. Maybe more." Chase let go of my ponytail and stepped back, once again in control. "I'll get your phone number before we leave the club, and we'll arrange another time to meet for our first session."

Elation surged through me, along with a sense of triumph I couldn't deny. "I look forward to it."

CHAPTER 4

Chase

a few days later, and I still couldn't stop thinking about Andrea. The way she'd melted under my guidance, and how she'd embraced everything I threw at her without a hint of hesitation at The Players Club.

Jesus. She'd been a fucking revelation. I'd half expected her to tap out. Hell, if I was being honest, I'd counted on it. That's why I deliberately pushed the scene harder than I normally would have with someone so new. I'd brought out the clamps, the spreader bar, even the damn plug. Not to truly scare her, not to hurt her, but to give her an easy out if she wanted it.

She didn't take it.

Instead, she'd thrived like she'd been made to be my submissive, lighting up under my direction. She'd wanted the aggression, the dominance. *Wanted me*. All of me—the control, the roughness, the dark shit that most women couldn't handle.

The image of her—eyes wide and sparkling with excitement, body arching into mine, voice sweet and breathless when she called me *sir*— burned through my mind, refusing to fade. And when I'd seen her stubbornness flare afterward, when she stood up to me even after everything...*fuck*, that tenacity had hit me harder than anything else had all night.

That passionate spark inside of her? I wanted to see it again. I wanted to coax it out and make her burn for me. I wanted to break her down and build her back up, until she trusted me enough to give me everything. Every whimper. Every moan. Every sweet surrender.

It scared the shit out of me how much I wanted that. How much I wanted *her*.

I tried to end things between us the second she started talking about *more*. More scenes. More lessons. More of us. But the moment she threatened to find someone else to give her what she needed, my blood went cold. No one else was going to touch her. No one else was going to see her come apart, soft and desperate and perfect, the way she had for me.

I clenched my fists as I increased my speed on the treadmill I was running on in the company gym with my co-workers, while struggling to tamp down the vicious, possessive need rising inside me. I wasn't some goddamn white knight. I wasn't wired for gentle, or forever promises. I was the man you called when you wanted your world cracked open and remade from the inside out.

And somehow, she trusted me to teach her, to guide her, to be the one person she could trust to show her pleasure and pain, and give her all the things her body craved.

It honestly messed with my head how much I wanted to be the man she needed. How much I already wanted to ruin her for anyone else.

"What did that treadmill ever do to you?" Kane asked, smirking from one of the same machines beside mine as he wiped sweat off his forehead with a towel.

I grunted but didn't answer right away, pounding out another half mile like I could outrun the mess trying to claw its way out of my chest. It was Monday. Just three damn days since Andrea, and I already wanted her again like a drug addict jonesing for a hit.

I forced myself to slow down on the treadmill, trying to get my breathing under control. "Sorry. Just got lost in thought."

"Yeah, we noticed," Xavier chimed in, spotting my brother Austin on the bench press. "You've been out of it since we got here. You're usually the first guy running your mouth when Kane's form looks like shit."

"Appreciate the support," Kane deadpanned, throwing an empty water bottle at Xavier, who dodged it easily without losing his grip on the bar.

"You looked like you had a good night..." Austin said as he racked the bar with a grunt. "At the club on Friday."

I wiped my face with a towel and gave a short, distracted laugh. "Yeah. Right. The club."

I *had* been thinking about that night. About Andrea. About her trembling under my hands, and looking at me like I could tear her apart with my cock and she'd beg for more.

Just not anything I could say out loud.

"You disappeared with someone pretty quick," Tate said, grabbing a set of dumbbells and giving me a pointed look. "Cute brunette. Short dress. Sweet little...smile."

I glared at him before I could catch myself and Kane caught it, arching a brow.

"Relax, man," Kane said, chuckling. "None of us are trying to poach your girl."

"She's not my girl," I said immediately. Too fast. Too sharp.

They all went still for a beat—just long enough for me to feel it—then went back to their sets like they hadn't noticed. But they had. Of course they had. These were men who made a living off reading people, threats, and dire situations.

"She's an acquaintance," I added, forcing the words out in a casual tone. I shrugged like it didn't matter because I wasn't in the mood for anyone's shit talking. "Just showing her a good time."

Austin glanced up at me from the bench, his mouth twisting like he didn't quite buy that load of bullshit. I didn't let it show that I saw him clocking me. Didn't let him see how badly I wanted to punch something, someone, out of sheer frustration.

"Good for you," Xavier said easily, flashing a grin. "She definitely looked like she had a good time when you were walking her to the door after the fact."

I gave a noncommittal nod and turned back to the treadmill, punching in a harder speed like I could sweat out the guilt gnawing at my gut.

Just showing her a good time. Yeah, right.

I could lie to the guys. Hell, I could lie to myself and pretend that's all it was—that my night with Andrea hadn't felt different and more intimate the second she called me *sir* with that sweet, trembling voice.

Unfortunately, no amount of running or lifting weights was going to change the truth.

I wanted her.

Not just her body. Not just another scene.

Her.

And that knowledge rattled me more deeply than any threat we'd ever faced on the job, because deep down, I knew how my time with Andrea would end. I'd walk away. Not because I wanted to, but because she deserved a man who could give her something permanent and lasting. And better than a guy whose life was built around exit strategies and contingency plans because an emotional commitment wasn't something a man like me had the ability to offer.

She deserved someone who could put her first. Someone whole and stable. And that person wasn't me. Because if I let myself believe, even for a second, that I could keep her...I also knew I'd eventually devastate her. And that was something I'd never be able to forgive myself for.

But give her lessons in all the ways she could enjoy pleasure and pain? Yeah, that I could do.

As if I didn't have enough on my mind, Sutton pounced on me the moment I walked into the office after having showered in the gym and changed into a professional suit for my current assignment.

Sutton was the head of security operations at the firm, hired by my father and Mac to handle the Las Vegas division of Noble and Associates. He was older than the rest of us by over a decade, but still someone I considered a friend when we were off the clock. He had a steady head on his shoulders and I appreciated his experienced perspective on things.

"Chase. Glad you're in." Sutton grabbed me lightly by the elbow and guided me through the building toward his office. "I have an update for you on Rothschild."

"Everything all right?" Harry Rothschild was the man I was currently assigned, and who'd received death threats from a former employee he'd fired. I'd only stopped by the office to check in before heading to his estate to pick him up and provide security detail for the rest of his day.

"Better than all right," Sutton said, as we entered his wing of the firm and his newest secretary looked more than a little anxious at her boss's return. "The police arrested the guy behind the threats."

"Well, damn," I said, surprised to hear that as I nodded politely at Amy as we passed by, hopefully to offset Sutton's more gruff and demanding attitude when it came to his assistants. "What happened?"

Sutton scoffed as he lead me into his office. "Idiot bought a shit-ton of illegal fireworks. His neighbor noticed and called the police, worried that he'd set them off in the neighborhood and damage nearby houses. Once the police arrested him for that, they did a quick search in his garage and found more hostile letters to Rothschild. It appears he was planning to use the explosive material to turn it into a homemade bomb to use on Rothschild in some way."

I scrubbed a hand over my jaw and shook my head. "Jesus."

"I know." Sutton sat down in the leather chair behind his desk. "We're lucky the guy got caught before he could execute his plan. I hope Rothschild reconsiders some of his firing practices after this."

I snorted in derision because that wasn't likely to happen. Harry Rothschild had inherited the CEO position from his father who built the company. He was spoiled from the day he'd been born and had grown into a pretentious prick. I didn't see him wising up and making smarter choices with his employees all of a sudden. The whole time I'd been his security detail he'd thought he was untouchable and had treated me as though I was nothing more than a nuisance.

"At least it's over with," I said, uncaring of how relieved I sounded.

Sutton gave me a small smirk that told me he agreed, then he quickly smoothed it out into his usual stern look. "In the meantime, I don't have a new assignment for you yet, so take advantage of having a few extra days free before something else comes in."

That's how this business worked. I really had no set days or hours. My assignments—depending on what they were—dictated when and how much I worked, so it was nice to have a little down time. "Great, thanks," I said, heading for the door as I tossed a little jab over my shoulder. "You can go back to terrorizing your latest secretary now."

"I do not *terrorize*—"

I left Sutton still arguing with me, gave Amy a reassuring wink on my way out of our boss's office, and pulled out my phone. I was composing the text to Andrea before I even realized what I was doing, and then I had to stop myself.

I'd *just* scened with her a couple days ago. I had planned to let some time pass then invite her to the club again this weekend, but now that I had a couple of days free, the first thing on my mind was how soon could I see her, and play with her.

My phone felt heavy in my hand, the text half-composed. It would be good for me to text her, right? We'd made an agreement, and wasn't it now my responsibility to make sure she received her lessons and had access to what she needed to learn about the BDSM world?

And what you need, that treacherous voice in the back of my head mocked me.

Trying not to analyze just how selfish my own motives were for wanting to see her so soon, I sent the text.

CHAPTER 5

Andrea

It had only been three days since Chase had rocked my world at The Players Club, but I was already eager for another session with him.

Honestly, it was distracting as hell because our next encounter, whatever it might be, was all I could think about. It was the equivalent of an addiction, like the first time I had sex as a teenager, or when I had snuck my first underaged alcoholic drink. That beautiful taste of something forbidden that made you feel amazing, and made you feel *free*. Then, you wanted more because you couldn't get enough of those intoxicating highs.

As much as I wanted to, I didn't text Chase. I didn't want him to think I was too eager or clingy, or trying to make this arrangement between us anything more than it was. I was an adult. I could handle a few days without sex or seeing Chase. But maybe this weekend if I was lucky…

My phone dinged with a text and I looked away from my computer at work to check the incoming message, expecting it to be Madison or Violet. Instead it was from Chase. My heart immediately began to race as I read his note.

Are you free to come to my place this evening after work? I have quite the personal collection I'd like you to see… and maybe try out.

Excitement blossomed in my belly, and just knowing what he was alluding to, my body quivered with anticipation. Biting my bottom lip, I quickly responded. *Let me check my calendar.* I didn't want to sound too eager, but not uninterested, either.

You think you're cute?

I found myself grinning, and also wondering if I was with Chase right now if he'd punish me for being so cheeky. *I know I'm cute. And what do you know, I'm free, lucky you. What time would you like me to come over?*

6pm. See you then. He followed that up with his address.

"Something's got a big smile on your face."

The sound of my co-worker's voice startled me out of my giddy little bubble, and I glanced up at the man who strolled into my office. "Hi, Brandon."

Brandon was a nice colleague of mine, and I liked to consider us friends. We'd worked a lot of hours together lately on a massive campaign for a big hotel and casino. Not unusual, here in Vegas.

Unfortunately, he'd also asked me out last week, and I'd gently, but firmly, turned him down. I didn't want to complicate work by dating someone from the office, and I wasn't looking for a long-term serious relationship after I'd just gotten out of one. Opting for honesty, I'd told him those things.

What I *hadn't* told him was that I also wasn't keen on jumping into the same exact scenario I'd just left with Heath...being with a man who couldn't fulfill me in the bedroom.

Maybe that was unkind of me to assume, but Brandon's docile personality unfortunately reminded me of Heath just enough that I couldn't help but wonder. All that aside, though—no dating coworkers, and no jumping from one relationship to another. Even this thing with Chase wasn't serious. I needed some time and space to figure myself out.

"Oh, just a funny meme Violet sent me," I replied, putting my phone away.

"I think it's sweet how close you two are." Brandon sat down on the edge of my desk, smiling. "How was your weekend? Do anything fun?"

Well, that was a loaded question with an equally loaded answer. "Oh, not much," I said with a shrug. "Violet had to work so I just puttered around the house by myself."

He tipped his head to the side, his brown eyes warm as they met mine. "I always picture you doing something fun, having lots of hobbies. You seem so creative."

"You're sweet." And he was. A little *too* sweet, for my tastes. He was so eager and kind, if not a bit overenthusiastic.

"You know," I said, giving him a smile. "I've been thinking about last week, and I wanted to— well I wondered—there's this lovely woman, I don't know if you met her, Rebecca? She works in the accounting department. Which I know sounds boring but she's actually very interesting. She goes rock climbing and camping all the time, and I wondered if you'd like me to set you up with her."

Brandon blinked a few times, then frowned. He looked upset, in a way I'd never seen him, even when I'd turned him down. "You...you want to set me up with someone?"

"Well, I just thought—"

"I'm not desperate."

The indignant tone of his voice took me aback and I scrambled to make amends. "Right, no, of course not, that's not what I meant. Rebecca's really—"

"I'm not interested in just anyone, you know," Brandon insisted. "I like classy, sophisticated women, and they're hard to find."

On some level, I should have been flattered by the compliment, but honestly I was just more embarrassed that I'd made things awkward. "I'm sorry. Forget I said anything." I waved a hand between us as if to clear the air, then clicked on the graphic I'd been analyzing before I'd gotten distracted by Chase's text. "How about we look at that ad we created again? See if there is anything we can do to elevate it for the client."

Thankfully, that segue back into work cut through the tension I'd caused and we were able to have a productive day. But to be honest, the more the afternoon wore on, the more my mind began to drift. I kept wondering what Chase had in store for me.

I had no idea what to expect this evening, but as I headed home after work to shower and change I decided I didn't want to be too dressed up for tonight, or too casual. I fretted for a while, wanting on some level to impress him. I went through half a dozen outfits while being grateful that Violet was still at work. I didn't want her to see what an anxious mess I was over Chase Noble, of all people.

Eventually, I decided on a nice set of lingerie I'd bought on sale, in a pretty coral hue and a scalloped lace design. Then, I chose a nice but casual summery dress to put over it. Understated on the outside, but sexy and sophisticated beneath. Perfect.

I followed the directions Chase had given me to his place, finding myself at a very luxurious high rise on the outskirts of Vegas with residential condominiums. I rode the elevator up to one of the top floors, and when I arrived at his place and Chase ushered me inside, my jaw dropped a little as I took in the floor to ceiling windows in the spacious living room and a shiny black and chrome modern kitchen.

In comparison to the modest condo Violet and I had purchased together, this place was definitely high end. But of course he'd live somewhere a little more private and exclusive. He worked for possibly the best security firm in the city—one that serviced billionaires, celebrities, and even royalty —and he was a member of The Players Club. No simple one-night-only guest invitation for him.

Despite the luxurious feel of the place, there was something very pristine and almost sterile about it all. I didn't see much color, no splash of artwork on the walls, and I definitely didn't see any personal effects, like photos or other intimate items that really made a house a home.

"I'm glad you came," Chase said, approaching me.

He wore a light gray t-shirt that pulled across his wide chest, the muscles in his arms straining the short sleeves, and a pair of well-worn jeans. His feet were bare...and just like his hands and dick, they were big, as well as symmetric and well groomed. How odd was it that I found them incredibly...sexy?

He put a hand on the small of my back to guide me to one end of the open floorplan to the dining room table. To my surprise, a lovely dinner was set out.

"I hope you're hungry," he said.

"I...am, thank you." I hadn't thought I was, my stomach tangled tight with nerves up to this point, but the pasta and chicken sitting ready to be served looked and smelled delicious.

Confused, I turned toward him. "Can I ask what all this is? I thought I was here for a . . . a lesson." I didn't know how else to describe our arrangement.

He tipped his head, amusement shining in his eyes, which I liked seeing more than his normal gruff demeanor. "What, you just thought I'd strip you naked the moment you walked in the door and fucked you over the back of the sofa?"

My face flushed, because yes, that's pretty much what I'd anticipated. Some kind of immediate sexual encounter, not something resembling a...date.

He shook his head, a slight smile on his lips. "This is all *part* of the lesson," he said, pulling a chair out for me and winking as I sat down. "Outside of a place like The Players Club, or a one-time scene, a good, experienced dom will take care of his partner, including feeding them before any sexual activity. It helps to have carbs for energy, and something in your stomach so you don't get light-headed or dizzy during some of the more intense scenes."

I nodded, filing away that bit of information. A part of me was shocked that he was taking this so seriously, that he was truly teaching me things I didn't know and were important when it was time for me to find a partner of my own.

I swallowed hard at the thought...because right now, I couldn't imagine doing this with anyone else other than the enigmatic man sitting next to me.

"People know aftercare," he went on, uncorking a bottle of wine. "But not enough of them talk about the buildup, the beforehand. This is the kind of thing that creates trust between yourself and your dom outside of the bedroom, or playroom, as it may be."

I laughed lightly. "I assume you have the latter here at your place?"

"Yes." He hesitate for a moment, his expression turning serious. "A bedroom implies intimacy, and it's important to me that my play partners distinguish the difference and know that my playroom is strictly about sex and pleasure, nothing more. My bedroom is off-limits."

My chest tightened a little as I processed that.

Okay, duly noted. The man, for whatever reason, didn't do *intimate.*

"Wine?" he asked, indicating the bottle he'd just opened.

"Yes, thank you."

He served me then himself. "Don't have more than a glass," he advised, setting the bottle aside. "I think this vintage goes great with this meal, but if you have a dom who keeps trying to top your wine, or whatever alcoholic drink you're having, don't trust him. A lot of emotions can happen during a scene, and you need to be sober to really process them."

"Got it," I said, appreciating the insight.

We plated our food, and after a few bites of the delicious meal Chase spoke again.

"So, it sounded like what we did on Friday was your first experience?" he asked curiously. "Or close to it? Have you done any type of BDSM before?"

I shifted uncomfortably in my chair. "No, not really. I tried to introduce toys into my last relationship so we could explore different aspects of BDSM, but my boyfriend freaked out about it." I exhaled a deep breath and met Chase's gaze. "He told me that perverted sex was for sluts and whores."

Chase's jaw clenched, and the intense flash of anger I saw in his eyes startled me. "Clearly, an asshole."

I shrugged, trying to downplay Heath's reaction. "It just wasn't his thing."

"He didn't have to shame you for your preferences," he said, his voice a low, soft growl, clearly pissed on my behalf. "I'm glad you have a clean slate, instead of doing something with him that would have been more damaging."

"How so?" I asked, and ate a bite of chicken.

Chase huffed out a breath. "Sometimes, when people who are in a relationship decide to try out kinks, they don't do things properly, so they aren't prepared for an actual Dom/sub relationship, and they have to unlearn things."

Curiosity filled me. "Like what?"

"Like doing bondage or impact play properly and safely so no one gets hurt. Or thinking that a safeword can only be used when something gets out of control. Sometimes you need to say 'yellow' for example, to take a breather. Or they do things like fire play or wax play without taking classes or being certified, which leads to people being burned or permanently scarred."

I shuddered at the thought as I took a sip of wine. While a part of me was drawn to wax play, which seemed like a more muted way of experiencing an intense level of heat on your bare skin, fire play wasn't something that appealed to me at all.

"So, you really have no hands-on experience, other than our night together?" Chase confirmed.

I shook my head and wiped my napkin across my mouth. "No...I—I've wanted to do this for a really long time. I'm not making that up and I'm not being impulsive."

"I never said you were," Chase replied.

I scoffed before I could stop myself. "You pretty much told me on Friday night that I didn't know what I wanted and I was in over my head."

He visibly winced. "Okay, yes, I thought you were maybe pushing yourself to extremes and didn't know everything that BDSM entails. And going to a sex club for your first time like that, without any prior experience, is pretty fucking ballsy." Chase grinned for a moment, then grew serious once more. "But honestly, you impressed me. If we're going to do this, I want to know exactly what you need, Andrea. I can't give it to you if I don't know what you like or prefer."

I exhaled and set my fork on my plate, appreciating him wanting that honesty and insight, but voicing them wasn't going to be easy. Chase had already done things to me that Heath never would have dared, but there was still that part of me that remembered how Heath would react every time I told him what was on my mind. How he'd recoil and put me down for wanting something outside the norm.

But ultimately I trusted Chase and knew that he'd respect me and my desires, and that's what gave me the courage to share my fantasies with him.

"I really like you tying me up so I'm restrained and you have all the control and power," I admitted, shivering internally when I saw the heat in his eyes at that confession. "And the... sensory deprivation, is what it's called, right? Blindfolding. Maybe even putting noise-cancelling headphones on at some point, or using a gag. I liked the riding crop. I actually enjoyed it more than I thought I would, but I'm into spanking and I think...I've thought about flogging."

He sat there patiently, listening attentively as I opened up and spilled my deepest desires, which actually felt liberating.

"When I pictured a scenario in my mind, I'm tied up and helpless and my partner can fuck me however he liked. Be as rough and aggressive as he wanted, even if I told him to stop, but not using the safeword."

"That's consensual non-consent," he said, giving the act a name.

I nodded. "Yeah, that," I said, hearing the husky timbre of my own voice. Just talking about everything was turning me on, making my body feel sensitive—my breasts, between my thighs. "I'd never had clamps on my nipples, and it definitely hurt, and so did the crop...but I liked the pain. It made everything more acute, but eventually, that pain receded and my body registered it all as pleasure, as weird as that might be."

A knowing look passed across Chase's features as he leaned back in his chair, his fingers idly spinning the stem of his wineglass on the table. "Not weird at all. Pain can transition into pleasure due to the release of endorphins, which block pain and induce feelings of euphoria. It's like an intoxicating hit of dopamine," he explained, clearly having done his research on the matter. "A lot of people get off on pain, including me. Why do you think I got those piercings?"

"I've heard it makes everything feel even better."

"It does," he agreed. "My dick is extra sensitive when it's erect. But the process of getting the piercings, and the pain involved, was hot and arousing for me, too. Not that I could do a lot about it at the time since there is a recovery period after getting your dick pierced." He chuckled.

I bit my bottom lip, thinking about everything he'd just said. How he wanted me to be open and honest about my desires. "Sometime, I...I'd like to see how you handle pain like that."

His eyes darkened and gleamed at the possibility. "I'd be more than willing to show you...sometime. Since we've agreed to do this, whatever it is you'd like to explore, I'd be happy to guide you. Nothing is off-limits, so long as it's something you enjoy."

I appreciated the way Chase talked about all of this, so calm and natural. It helped remind me that this could be normal.

"So, let's talk about limits," Chase said, tipping his head a bit curiously. "You're into bondage, you like the idea of some impact play, and you seem to enjoy a bit of pain. Is there anything that you know for sure you're not into?"

I immediately felt overwhelmed when I thought about all that was out there, my mind racing. "I don't know. There's so much."

Chase's expression softened in understanding. "How about this. Let's stick with the stuff you know you enjoy, and we'll introduce new things here and there and see how you feel."

"Okay." I liked that idea, and smiled at him. "I'm putting a lot of trust in you," I teased.

"Trust me, I know." Chase looked dead serious. "And I don't take it lightly."

With each of us done with our meals, I helped Chase clear the table. I rinsed the dishes while he put away the leftovers, my mind and body already feeling restless for whatever was to come. The unknown, I realized, was a huge turn on.

Chase informed me that dessert would be part of aftercare, and I pouted at him. "That's so not fair."

He smacked my ass and chuckled. "Careful with that attitude. You're asking for a real spanking."

I braced my hands on my hips and gave him a haughty look. "Isn't that literally why I'm here?"

Chase reached out and took my chin in his fingers, tipping my head back so I had no choice but to look into his suddenly dark, intense eyes. "I always knew you'd be feisty," he murmured.

He didn't sound upset about it. The atmosphere in the room shifted, from casual and easy to hot and filled with sinful anticipation as everything transitioned into what felt like the start of a scene.

"What are you going to do about it?" I taunted, suddenly breathless.

The corner of his mouth twitched, and he narrowed his gaze. "You know," he said, his voice a deep rumble of sound. "You've got a lot of nerve coming into my home and disrespecting me. Maybe I *should* do something about it. You definitely showed signs at the club of being a particular kind of submissive. The kind that pushes back against her Dom. A *brat*." He arched a brow as he stared down at me. "Would you like to see what I do to brats?"

His expression looked so fierce, so uncompromising, my stomach muscles clenched and I suddenly felt as though I couldn't breathe. All those times I had begged Heath to be more dominant with me, to *take* me, this is what I'd wanted. I started trembling as a thrilling, exhilarating fear took hold.

I also suddenly felt incredibly rebellious. I'd never given Chase what he wanted easily. I wasn't going to give it to him now.

"Guess I'll find out," I said, and shoved away from him, breaking his hold on my chin. "If you can catch me."

I bolted away and sprinted down the hall.

CHAPTER 6

Andrea

I had to admit, there was a kind of childishness to my actions, like a toddler who made their parent catch them because they didn't want to take a bath. But there was a hot thrill in the pit of my stomach, and a smile I couldn't wipe off my face as I heard Chase running after me. I knew he would catch me. That was never a question. But I wanted him to work for it.

I had no idea what the layout of this condo was. I turned a corner and was faced with multiple doors. I passed a slightly open one that seemed to lead into a bathroom, then entered the second one and rushed inside, closing the door as quietly as I could after me, realizing this must be some kind of guest room.

I laid down on the floor on the side of the bed away from the door and tried hard to keep my breathing quiet. I definitely didn't want my panting and gasping to give me away like in all those horror films.

Footsteps passed by the door, and I bit my lip to smother a grin, allowing myself to relax as everything went silent.

Less than a minute later, hands grabbed my ankles, pulling me away from the bed. I shrieked in surprise, somehow managing to dislodge his hold and jump to my feet, only for Chase to grab me from behind, his strong arms banding around my waist. I automatically struggled and tried kicking at him. The low, dark chuckle in my ear made me shiver as he held me effortlessly against his hard body.

I could feel the thick shape of his aroused cock against my ass and I tried not to arch against that tempting heat. I was supposed to make him work for it, dammit!

"The bathroom connects to this room and the hallway," Chase breathed in my ear. "But nice try. You thought you were clever."

"Smug asshole," I muttered.

"Yeah, sometimes," he replied, well, smugly.

I kept squirming, but I liked that I couldn't get away. His grip was like iron until he released me to turn me around, then hauled me up over his shoulder before I realized his intent. Without any effort at all, he carried me out the door as I continued to fight him, pummeling his backside with my fists and trying to kick my feet.

"Settle down," he said in a growly voice, then smacked my ass with the flat of his hand.

I sucked in a breath, even as I relished the slow burn spreading across my skin. "Make me."

"Oh, I intend to," he said as he carried me down the hall to another room.

I lifted my head to look around as we entered. This one was done up in black and chrome like the rest of the house, but I instantly noticed the bed— the equivalent of a double sized mattress—had large black leather cuffs hanging from the posts. It didn't have the usual pillows and sheets, either, but was a thick leather pad—which I assumed made it easier to clean.

He flipped me onto the bed, making my head spin for a second as I gained my equilibrium then took in my surroundings. There other sex furniture in the room, and even a cozy looking love seat with a blanket draped over the back cushions. A rack of paddles and crops and floggers hung on the wall, along with a large wardrobe with double doors, which I assumed held more toys.

I watched as he took off his t-shirt, tossing it onto a nearby chair, leaving him just in his jeans. My greedy gaze took in all his elaborate tattoos, the width of his shoulders, and those muscled abs I wanted to lick with my tongue.

Instead of crawling over to him and doing just that, I slid my hands over the leather of the bed—it was butter soft and very comfortable. "Is this the part where I beg for mercy?" I grinned at him.

"Oh, you'll be begging all right." Chase's voice was so *casual*, his confidence so completely assured, that I couldn't stop the rush of moisture that flooded my pussy.

Then, his expression grew serious. "As we continue with these lessons, I want you to do me one favor."

I tipped my head and gave him a sassy look. "Depends on the favor."

"Don't stop being a brat unless you really, actually, want to submit." His gaze held mine. "I want to earn your submission."

I searched his gorgeous face and realized he was completely sincere in his request, which I found fascinating. The idea of a man, *this man* in particular, feeling as though he needed to earn my acquiescence was humbling, and exhilarating. He didn't want me to make things easy on him, and that was something I could do.

"Okay," I said with a nod as I scooted closer to the edge of the bed. "In that case—"

I jumped up to sprint out of the room again, but this time Chase was ready, reacting with quick reflexes that shocked me. He managed to grab my hair, not by the ends but his hand gripping the strands close to my scalp, making me yelp in surprise. He used that leverage to drag me back down onto the bed in a display of strength and agility that had me gasping.

"Now, I definitely like a little predator play," he said, smirking down at me and holding me in place with that hand still in my hair. "But that's not what I have in mind for you today. I want to introduce you to a few more of my toys and see how you do."

"What makes you think I want to do whatever you have in mind?" I shot back.

This all felt so delightfully...not normal, exactly, but *comfortable.* I didn't have to worry that I was being a bad sub or not giving him what he wanted, because I was doing what I always did when I was with Chase. I pressed his buttons. The only difference now was that he was allowing himself to react to my willful behavior. And Chase, to my shock, seemed absolutely delighted every single time I said or did something defiant.

He really likes that I'm a brat, I thought, startled.

It made me feel powerful, even though I was the submissive person here.

Finally, he released my hair, but his presence at the side of the bed gave me little room to bolt again. "Does this dress come off easily?"

I nodded, shocked at how quickly he helped me to sit up, then pulled the dress up and over my head in one smooth move.

He stared at me, at the seductive lingerie I wore, the heat in the eyes searing my skin. "Holy fuck," Chase breathed out.

I flushed all over. I'd never had a man look at me like that—like he wanted to absolutely devour me.

"You're such a goddamn tease beneath that sweet, demure dress," Chase murmured. "I fucking love it."

Confidence surged through me out of nowhere and I jutted my chin out. "What makes you think you get to do anything other than look?"

Chase growled and moved onto the bed, straddling my hips and pinning me down with his weight. I arched up, gasping and thrashing, trying to buck him off just for the sheer pleasure of testing his stamina. He grabbed my hands, but I was no match for his grip and strength. I couldn't get away from him even if I really wanted to. I squirmed, helpless, and whimpered as this whole power dynamic made my pussy throb.

"You're gorgeous like this," Chase murmured huskily, his gaze on the way my breasts were half spilling out of my lacy bra as he gently pulled my wrists up. "I can't wait to see you all trussed up on a proper St. Andrew's Cross...but for now, I want to see how much pain—or pleasure, depending on how good or bad you are—those breasts and pretty pussy can take."

My chest heaved in anticipation as he secured my wrists to each corner of the bedframe. The cuffs wrapped around my wrists almost like a soft grip themselves, keeping them firmly held in place. There was no way I could get out of them or even move my hands all that much.

Chase grinned down at me when he caught me testing the restraints, satisfaction gleaming in his dark eyes. "Yeah, you're not going anywhere."

He moved off me, then the bed, walking down to where my feet were. He grabbed my legs and pulled them apart, and I saw that the lower corners of the bed had cuffs as well, which he secured around my ankles. They were adjustable for height, and he tightened them a bit so my legs were spread without being stretched to the point of discomfort. I squirmed against the cuffs, testing them. They didn't budge and there was no way out.

"Such pretty lingerie," he murmured, trailing his hand along the inside of my thigh then teasing my pussy with a light stroke of his fingers over my panties. "I guess I'll leave you in it, this time. Instead of ripping it off you. Of course if you don't behave, I might change my mind. Now, why don't we start with something basic."

"Fat chance," I muttered defiantly.

The corner of his mouth twitched with amusement. "I'm tempted to blindfold you again. Gag you, even, so I don't have to listen to your smart mouth. But I want you aware so you can use your safeword if you need it."

"I'm *so* scared," I said sarcastically.

Chase merely arched a brow and selected a flogger from the rack on the wall, with a dark wooden handle, beautiful dark green leather strips, and black, wooden beads tied off on the ends. "I had this custom made," he said, returning to me and lightly trailing those cool beads against my warm skin.

I shivered, feeling my nipples pucker against my lace bra. Everything felt unexpectedly soft, and somehow, Chase dragging the strands along my thighs and stomach felt even more vulnerable than my ass. Very slowly, he trailed them up and down my body like a soft, sensual caress. I relaxed, sinking into the soothing sensation.

He flicked his wrist and the leather strips smacked my thigh. I gasped, clenching instinctively for the pain. Chase chuckled as the strands landed so much softer than I'd expected. It was a tease compared to the riding crop. *He* was teasing me, I realized.

Chase lightly slapped my other thigh with the flogger. One-two, one-two, one-two, in a mesmerizing, soothing rhythm. The arousing sensations lulled me once again, my limbs going lax.

Smack. A little harder this time, and the beads tapped in quick succession against my pussy. I shrieked in surprise, my legs trying to draw together but stopped by the cuffs. I panted up at him, my eyes wide. "Whha—oh my God."

"Just breathe," he murmured in a low, coaxing voice.

He returned to the previous unhurried rhythm,

but now those sensations gliding along my skin were far less tranquil because I had no idea when a gentle stroke of leather and beads would turn into a proper sting. Just when my body would relax, soothed and almost floating in a strange headspace I'd never felt before, the next hard slap would land and I'd cry out, shoved back into the present, every nerve ending alert.

From the side of the bed, Chase watched me avidly, hungrily, his wrist rotating and twirling the flogger with an impressive ease and skill that had me beyond aroused. I knew he could reduce me to a sobbing wreck with this, but the tease was actually worse. I shivered, my awareness heightened, as I waited and *waited* for the next blow.

"Now that you've had a little taste of what this flogger can do," Chase said, a sinful grin curving his lips. "Why don't we ramp things up so you can pay for your bratty attitude earlier? Or, you can be a good girl for me and call me sir."

I glared up at him, knowing he wouldn't want me to give in that easily, nor did I want to. "Not happening," I fired back.

Crack. The flogger snapped against the upper swells of my breasts, the part that was exposed by my bra. I cried out, shocked at the small red welts rising on my skin. My pussy clenched. Whether it was the pain, the surprise, or the fire in Chase's eyes as he stared down at me, I was consumed with lust.

"Are you going to be a good girl for me now?" Chase asked, looking every inch the uncompromising dom as he wielded the flogger.

I clenched my jaw and shook my head.

Crack. He flogged my breasts again. I screamed, arching, and tears leaked from the corner of my eyes. Then, I moaned, because it hurt so good.

He kept at it, hitting my breasts, then my thighs —and then my pussy with the leather strands and beads. I was delirious with the need to come, completely at his mercy in all the ways I'd always imagined, from a man who knew what I could take and wasn't going easy on me. Occasionally Chase would pause and ask if I was good or needed a break, and I always refused him.

I understood safewords now like never before, as he used the flogger on me and pleas of *no* and *stop* tumbled out of my mouth. It was an instinctive reaction, but just hearing myself saying the words and Chase ignoring them only elevated all the exquisite tension building inside of my body.

I felt intoxicated with desire, and beyond frustrated that despite the way those beads and strands of leather licked and slapped at my covered pussy, it wasn't enough to make me orgasm. It was a frustrating form of edging that had me making inarticulate sounds in the back of my throat.

"Are you going to be good now?" Chase asked me again, when I felt as though I was on the brink of madness.

"Yes," I gasped out, panting for breath and desperate to climax. "Yes, sir, I'll be good."

"There we go," Chase praised me as he set the flogger aside then returned, skimming his fingers down my stomach to the waistband of my panties, idly tracing the elastic band. "I'm proud of you for enduring so much. You deserve a reward for that."

"Yes, please...sir, *please*," I begged.

He slid his hand into my panties and inhaled sharply, his nostrils flaring. "Fuck, you're drenched."

I whimpered as he rubbed my clit slowly, methodically. "Sir... please..."

"Did that flogger make you all wet, sweetheart?" Chase asked me, still stroking and teasing me. "Did that pain feel so fucking good and make you want to come?"

I nodded frantically, unable to form words.

Chase knelt on the bed at my side, pushing two thick fingers deeper into my body to fuck while he ground his palm hard against my aching, sensitive clit. "Go on then, baby. You can come all over my hand. You were a good girl and good girls get to come."

As if his permission had been what I'd been waiting for, my back arched as much as my restraints allowed and I embraced the orgasm slamming through me. I gasped for breath then moaned as my pleasure soaked body shook uncontrollably with the force of my release.

"Jesus . . .you're so fucking perfect," I heard Chase say, his words making me smile despite how weak I felt. "So damn beautiful with all those red marks on your skin."

As I drifted back down from my orgasm, I turned my head and watched as he ripped open the front of his jeans. He wasn't wearing underwear, and his stiff, massive cock immediately sprang free. He groaned, and using the slick moisture from my orgasm as a lubrication, he began stroking his cock in his fist.

The sight mesmerized me. Not just the piercings on his straining shaft, but the expression on his face. The need and lust and hunger, all for me.

He rose up on his knees, and with his free hand he traced the welts on my breasts with his fingers, his eyes dark and hooded. He stroked his cock faster, his breaths quick and shallow and uneven...

watching him jack himself off was the hottest, most erotic thing I'd ever seen.

"*Fuck*," he finally growled, his jaw clenching as he came in hot spurts all over my stomach, marking me in a way that made me feel like I belonged to him. Like I was *his*.

Chase sat back on his heels, his cock still twitching in his hand as he rubbed his thumb over the sensitive head and shuddered one last time.

Once he recovered from his own orgasm, he smiled down at me with pride in his eyes. "You did so well," he murmured, and I soaked up the genuine compliment. "How do you feel?"

It took me a few seconds to find words, but there was really only one I needed. "Amazing."

CHAPTER 7

Chase

H oly shit. I couldn't remember the last time I'd enjoyed a scene so much. There was a certain connection and effortless chemistry with Andrea that was rare, making it easy to just be myself with her. To maintain all the control I needed, to be the dominant partner, and just watch her fall apart so beautifully for me.

I would have loved to stretch things out, to push her even further to test her pain threshold, but considering this was her first introduction to a flogger, my main concern was making it the best experience for her as possible. There was plenty of time to try other things on her, and to fuck her again properly.

I released her arms and legs from the restraints, massaging them as I uncuffed each limb, then helped her out of her lingerie and used a warm washcloth from the adjoining bathroom to clean her off. The image of her post-orgasm, her skin red from my flogger, my cum coating her stomach, was one that would stay with me for a good long while.

Andrea was pliant as I gathered her up into my arms and carried her over to the loveseat in the room. I set her down, wrapping her in a blanket to make sure she stayed warm while I stripped out of my jeans, put on a pair of casual sweatpants, then went to the kitchen to grab a bottled water and the dessert I'd promised her: chocolate lava cake.

When I returned, I set the items down on the table next to the sofa, then picked her up and settled her on my lap. She pulled the blanket tighter around her and cuddled against my chest. I made sure she drank the water and fed her the cake, and ate a few bites myself.

Andrea hummed in pleasure, which made me smile...something I did a lot around her, I was starting to notice. She didn't talk for a bit, but I didn't mind. A lot of submissives went nonverbal after an intense scene. There was no awkwardness between us. In fact, being with her felt very relaxing and natural, in a way that was surprisingly effortless.

Once the cake and water were finished, I set that aside and pulled her close, idling stroking her hair, enjoying the way her body softened against mine and she sighed in contentment. Some people seemed to think that aftercare was just for subs, as a way to ease them back into reality and reset their equilibrium after an intense scene, but with Andrea, I—shockingly—found I appreciated this quiet time just as much. It gave me the chance to really feel how relaxed and satisfied she was, and to revel in the knowledge that I was the one responsible for her current blissed out status.

After a while, Andrea stirred against my chest and lifted her head, smiling up at me. "That was…" She searched for words and settled with, "Wow."

I completely understood. "It's a lot, isn't it?"

She nodded, but then frowned up at me. "I wanted…your cock."

I chuckled as I alternated between running my fingers through her soft, silky hair and massaging her scalp. "Greedy girl. I didn't want to overdo things tonight."

She bit her bottom lip, her eyes shining with a glimmer of desire. "It was definitely hot watching you jerk yourself off and come all over my stomach."

I loved that she enjoyed the filthier aspects of sex.

"How did you get so good at this?" she asked, her finger idly tracing the line work on one of the tattoos on my chest. "I know you're teaching me, but I'm a sub. How do you teach a dom?"

I shrugged. "Finding other more experienced doms to watch while they worked with their subs, and to practice BDSM with those doms watching and guiding."

"What got you into the lifestyle?" she asked curiously. "I mean, for me I read romance novels and I started to just gravitate to the ones with heavy BDSM in them. Then I started seeking it out online, reading about all the different aspects of BDSM and fantasizing about what I wanted."

My jaw clenched before I could stop the reaction. My reasons were deep and dark and not something I'd ever shared with anyone ever before. My gravitation toward dominant tendencies were based in a form of PTSD and that fear of losing control again, as I had in the military. I had no desire to dredge up those unsettling memories, so I kept my explanation short and simple.

"I served in the Navy for six years. Once I was discharged I was different." An understatement, considering how that one horrific incident in the military had changed the course of my life in ways I'd never anticipated.

"Different?" Andrea glanced up at me, tipping her head to the side. "What does that mean?"

Her expression was so open and guileless as she stared up at me, and I saw the questions there, as if she knew I wasn't giving her the whole truth... which clearly, I wasn't. But how did I explain to someone so bright, so full of life, that control for me wasn't just a preference, it was a necessity to keep the darkness at bay?

I exhaled slowly and looked away, fixing my gaze on the bed across from us, anything but her. "It's not something I talk about," I said gruffly, but here I was, giving this woman more insight than I'd given any other play partner in recent years. "Control...dominance...it's not just something I enjoy. It's something I *need*."

She didn't interrupt me. Didn't prod. Just

listened, quiet and still as she remained curled up in my lap like a complacent kitten.

I glanced down at her, meeting her soft, curious gaze. "When I was in the military, I lost men under my command," I told her, the words scraping out like shards of glass. "It was supposed to be a clean, in and out op, but we were given bad intel. One wrong decision from me and...those men died."

My heart raced at the memories, and I forced myself to keep breathing normally even though I could still see their faces in my mind. Could still hear their voices crackling through the comms... until they were abruptly cut off by gunfire and missiles detonating.

I swallowed hard and continued. "When you're in charge, when others trust you to lead them into hell and bring them out whole, you don't get to make mistakes. But I did, and it cost lives."

She sucked in a startled breath. "I'm so sorry, Chase," she whispered, her gaze holding mine, like she was seeing the pieces of me I usually kept hidden behind dominance and bondage and rules.

"When I was discharged, I wasn't the same man," I went on. Now that I'd shared the worst, I wanted her to understand how it all tied into the person I was today. "Everything felt out of control. My thoughts.

My emotions. My fucking body sometimes. The only way I could breathe was by maintaining control of *something*, and BDSM gave me that. But it's not just about power. It's about trust. Structure. Safety and rules. For my partner, yeah, but for me, too."

She reached up and glided her fingers along my jawline, her expression filled with compassion. "But sometimes, it's okay to lean on someone else, Chase."

I shook my head, because that was no longer an option for me and the last thing I wanted was her to think she could change what was so irrevocably shattered. "I don't know how to do messy, emotional shit anymore," I said, my voice low and gruff, a warning for her to keep her feelings out of this arrangement of ours. "I don't know how to *let go* without something unraveling. I'm not the type of guy who does hearts and flowers and romance, Andrea. I'll wreck your body with precision and pleasure, but everything else inside of me is fucking broken."

She dropped her hand back down to my chest and splayed her palm right over my rapidly beating heart. "You say you're broken like it's a permanent condition. Like it disqualifies you from being loved. But you still *feel*, don't you? You're still standing, still fighting to be present every day. That doesn't sound broken to me."

A laugh escaped me, raw and bitter. "Maybe not to you. But it feels like I've been holding myself together with duct tape and discipline for years."

She gave me the sweetest smile. "Then let me help you peel off the tape. Slow. Gentle. One piece at a time."

Fuck. She didn't know what she was offering to a fractured man like me. Or maybe she did. And that possibility terrified me more than anything else because I refused to disappoint anyone else in my life.

I brushed the backs of my fingers along her cheek and her gaze met mine, lips parting. Before I could think about my actions or stop myself, I tipped her head back and touched my lips to hers. Andrea sighed into my mouth, kissing me back as our tongues touched and tangled and the connection deepened. The kiss was tender, far more affectionate than I had ever meant it to be when I was a man who didn't do kind and caring. Sex I was good at. Emotional shit, not so much.

I pulled back and cleared my throat, desperate to put some kind of distance between the two of us. "How about a nice, warm shower before you head out?" I suggested.

If Andrea noticed the quick way I moved on from that intimate kiss, and our too serious conversation, she didn't comment on it as I led her into the adjoining bathroom. Tonight had been a fantastic play session, but Andrea was nothing more than a temporary distraction.

Or so I tried to convince myself.

CHAPTER 8

Chase

*A*fter a too long day out in the sun for a security detail, I all but collapsed against the bar as Austin slid into the seat next to me, holding up two fingers to the man standing behind the counter. "Macallans, neat, *please.*"

The bartender raised his brows at us but brought us our drinks as requested. My brother and I knocked them back, ordered another, and then two tall glasses of ice water to go with it. I wasn't out in the blazing Vegas desert heat anymore but my body still seemed to think I was. My throat was parched and I was thirsty as hell.

"Remind me the next time we're asked to work an outdoor concert that I tell Sutton 'hell fucking no,'" Austin muttered, sounding just as exhausted as I felt.

"You and I both know you'll say yes, because it's your job and dad would kick your ass for getting mouthy with Sutton," I pointed out.

We had a certain level of leeway on assignments but not *that* much. Everyone hated working concerts, especially the ones out in the open heat, but we all drew the short straw eventually. You couldn't evade it forever. Luckily Sutton tried to spread those kinds of jobs out so that we all worked our fair share.

Austin groaned after downing over half of his iced water in one go. "Just let me live in my fantasy for a moment."

"I don't want you to live in *any* of your fantasies," I said, my tone wry. "They tend to cause me trouble."

Austin sent a smirk my way. "Oh, c'mon, I'm not *that* bad."

I side-eyed my brother. "Whatever you gotta say to help you sleep at night."

My phone buzzed and I glanced down at the display. I'd had it on Do Not Disturb all day so that I wouldn't be distracted during work, and now I scrolled through my latest texts.

There was one from Andrea—a link to another set of lingerie to go with the others she'd sent my way over the past few days. Very cute, beyond sexy, and very reasonably priced, on sale.

I typed out a reply. *If I didn't know any better, I'd think you wanted something.*

I just think it's smart to know what to buy me in case you really do rip my underwear off next time. Who knows how long shipping could take? Might want to order in advance.

I grinned despite myself. *You have no idea how many spankings you're earning yourself.*

We'd been texting on and off all week, just like this...as if our too serious discussion that night at my place had never happened, which I was grateful for. It had been forever since I'd had enough of a relationship with a sub to flirt with her like this. Usually I met someone at the club, had fun once, or we only met up at the club and didn't talk outside of it.

But my...*situationship* with Andrea just felt natural. The times we'd bumped into each other before we'd hooked up at The Players Club, we had always been prickly. Okay, so, *I'd* been prickly. I'd known I wanted her and that I wasn't good for her, so I'd been a bit of a jackass. But she'd snarked right back at me, and now this felt like a natural next step in our dance to move from slightly antagonistic banter to proper flirting.

Austin nudged me with his elbow, redirecting my attention back to him. "Your three," he murmured.

Realizing what he meant, I glanced casually over to my right and saw a blonde woman with legs for days sitting alone at one of the high-top tables in the middle of the bar. She was toying with her half-empty martini glass and glancing my way, a sultry smile on her lips.

She was gorgeous, no denying that. From the way she sat alone and the heels and short skirt she wore, not to mention the way she was openly eyeing me, I was pretty damn sure she was here hoping to meet someone for the night. Exactly the kind of woman I'd usually go for.

I took another sip of my drink, glancing back at Austin. "I'm exhausted, man. I don't have the energy," I lied. The truth was...the only woman I wanted was Andrea.

"Yeah, that's something I've never heard you say, *ever*," Austin retorted in shock. "Who are you and what have you done with my brother?"

I rolled my eyes. "ha ha."

127

My phone buzzed again with another text from Andrea. I didn't smile, but something must've happened to my face, some slight crinkling in my eyes or shift in my jaw, because Austin's gaze flew to my phone. "Who're you so chatty with?"

"No one."

"Uh huh," he said, trying to peer closer. "No one, he says, while furiously typing away, ignoring his brother, and not interested in the pretty woman who clearly wants him to fuck her. Don't make me snatch your phone."

"Like you could even manage it," I teased him, but this was my brother. We'd been close, up until I left for the service. Afterwards...I did my best but I knew Austin could tell I held personal things back from him. I also never wanted my brother to feel I shut him out because of anything he did, when it was all *me*.

"It's Andrea," I told him, surprising myself with my own honesty.

Austin's brows rose. "Andrea—Andrea *Corbin?* Madison's Andrea?"

"Could you not say it like that?" I didn't need the reminder that I was fucking the woman of someone in our close circle of family and friends, and the implications of how potentially disastrous that could be if things ended badly. "And yes, *that* Andrea. We've been—"

"Holy shit," Austin said, interrupting me before I could finish. "I assumed the two of you hooked up that night at The Players Club, but are you two now a *thing*?"

"We're not a thing," I insisted, but I also wasn't sure how to describe our situation. *I'm giving her BDSM lessons* felt like the setup for a porno, and I decided to just simplify our arrangement. "We've hooked up. A few times now," I finished.

Austin stared at me in disbelief. "And the two of you are texting on the regular? That's shocking, especially for you, considering your fuck 'em and leave 'em motto."

I set my drink on the bar top, trying to down-play things. "I knew she was interested in me when we first met, all those years ago...and I was kind of a jerk in response."

Surprise and curiosity flitted across Austin's face. "Why?"

I exhaled a deep breath. "She'd just turned twenty-one, and our age difference felt like a lot, back then." Not to mention I'd just been released from the Navy and was dealing with all the mental and emotional shit from losing my comrades.

"I get that," he replied, nodding. "But it doesn't feel like such a big age difference now, does it?"

"No." And she wasn't innocent anymore, either. Or at least she didn't want to be innocent. She was ready to jump into the deep end of the BDSM pool without floaties, so to speak. Eager and willing to learn anything I threw her way. "She's been quite a...challenge." And that wasn't a complaint because I liked a bit of provocation in the bedroom.

Austin chuckled. "That's good. You need someone who'll keep you on your toes."

He was just talking sexually. That's it. But my throat still closed up. God, I kept Andrea at arm's length for a *reason*. And now, I was like a teenager, sixteen again, convinced all I wanted was sex but secretly unable to tell the difference between that and love, like all kids.

"I'm not looking for a relationship," I said firmly, as if saying it out loud could convince myself of that fact with Andrea.

"For crying out loud, Chase, it's not the fifteen hundreds," Austin said, his tone wry. "You don't have to marry a girl because you're sleeping with her. I think it's great that you've got someone you can see regularly that you genuinely like and enjoy. They always say it's better when you have a regular scene partner."

I nodded and Austin clapped me on the shoulder. "Just let go of your precious control for once and enjoy yourself. You deserve it."

I forced myself to smile, to give my brother what he wanted to see. "In that case, you won't be upset if I ditch you to go see her?" I teased him.

"And abandon me? You—" Austin stopped, realizing I was joking. "Wow, you really had me going there for a second."

I ruffled his hair like we were kids again. "Get us some food to go with all this alcohol or we'll have splitting headaches tomorrow."

Austin grinned and signaled to the bartender. I let my smile slip once he looked away. He didn't understand. 'Just let go,' he'd said, like my problem was that I had a Type A personality or something.

If only it were that easy.

CHAPTER 9

Andrea

"*T*he guy went absolutely berserk and so of course we had to call security," Violet said, telling me all about the latest incident at the casino where she worked.

I held obediently still as she painted my fingernails and I listened to her story. We were having a lazy night in, and I wanted to have my nails painted dark red to match the fun lingerie I was going to wear to see Chase tomorrow. He'd invited me to the club again as his guest, and I couldn't wait to see what he had in store for us.

"You wouldn't believe it," Violet went on,

shaking her head. "The guy was kicking and screaming as they carried him out, like a kid that had a toy taken away. As if he thought he made a big enough scene they'd just give him his money back."

"He lost a few hundred grand at *your* poker table," I pointed out.

"He sure did. Which don't get me wrong, it sucks. But he bet the money and lost it, all his own doing. Now, he's banned from the casino and I'm pretty sure there's some embarrassing videos of him online somewhere."

"That's crazy," I said, and meant it. "I don't understand how you handle it all."

Life at a casino seemed wild. I knew how to play poker and Blackjack and all that—you couldn't live with Violet and avoid a card game forever—but I'd only gambled at a casino once. I lost a hundred dollars, which had been enough to freak me out and swear off gambling forever. Especially considering my father's own addiction to gambling that had not only destroyed his life, but had put myself and Madison in debt after he'd taken out numerous loans and credit cards in our names.

Violet paused a moment to look up at me and grin. "What can I say. I like the excitement."

"Easy for you. You keep a cool head. Me, I'd be freaking out."

"Not my fault you have no poker face whatsoever, unlike *moi*." She rolled her eyes at me. "God help you if you ever had to lie to the police."

"Why would I need to lie to the police!?" I never understood how Violet's crazy mind worked.

"When you help me pull off a daring casino heist, *duh*, why do think I work there?" Violet said playfully as she capped the nail polish bottle. "Okay, let that dry."

She stuck her toes out and grabbed a sparkly green color for herself to start on them while I gently blew on my fingernails.

My phone buzzed and Violet immediately smirked. "Chase again?"

"Maybe." I couldn't check my screen from here and I didn't think my nails were quite dry enough yet to risk grabbing the phone. "I'm seeing him tomorrow."

"Lucky you," she said, swiping her big toe with the polish. "I'm so jealous that you get to have sex on the regular with a hot guy, while I have to resort to my battery operated boyfriend. So not fair."

A knock came at the door and Violet groaned.

"I can't get up like this." She waved a hand toward her foot.

"My nails are close to being dry. I'll get it." I'd just be careful with my fingers on the knob. "Coming!"

I headed to the door and peered through the peephole. I wasn't as surprised as I probably should've been to see Violet's younger half-brother, Christopher, standing on the other side.

Ugh.

I opened the door. Christopher grinned at me. He looked a little disheveled, the way he always did, with his dark blonde unkempt hair and wearing a wrinkled t-shirt and a pair of old, faded jeans. He stood in a slouch, with his hands shoved into the front pockets of his pants.

"Hey, Andrea, good to see you."

"Christopher, hi," I replied, forcing myself to be polite when I was already irritated because there was only one real reason why he'd stopped by. "Here to see Violet?"

"Not that I don't love seeing your pretty face too, Andrea, but uh, yeah," he said, trying to look past me. "Is she here?"

Christopher was the kind of guy who could be charming when he wanted to be. When I'd first met him, I was charmed too, although not attracted. That shine had worn off quickly as I'd gotten to really know him over the past few years.

"C'mon in." I opened the door further for him to pass by, and for Violet's sake, I tempered my annoyance. "You want anything to drink? We ordered pizza but it hasn't gotten here yet."

"I'm all good, thanks," he replied, then smiled too enthusiastically at his sister. "Hi, Vi!"

"Chris, hey!" Violet stood up as Christopher approached her and gave her a quick hug. "Nice of you to stop by. Are you sure you don't want some pizza?"

He shifted anxiously on his feet. "I, uh, really can't stay long...I just need a couple extra twenties if you have them?"

*And there it was...*I turned away so that neither of them would see me roll my eyes. Christopher and Violet had different fathers, but shared a mom, and he was always in some sort of trouble. Violet said it was just growing pains, that he was only twenty, and that being there for each other was what siblings did, especially considering the difficult way they'd grown up—with two absentee fathers and a mother who was always off chasing some man to take care of her. My own father had been one of those guys.

I admired Violet for being such a great big

sister. Violet, for the most part, didn't let anyone too close, but she was so caring when it came to Christopher, and it reminded me of how Madison had raised me when Dad wasn't around, which was most of the time. Dad was nothing more than a drunk or a gambler, often both at the same time, and I wasn't sure I would've even finished high school without Madison's guidance and support through some of the most difficult years of our lives.

But this—this wasn't about cooking meals or helping with homework or taking him shopping for proper work outfits when he interviewed for jobs. Christopher just showed up, asked for money, sometimes stayed for dinner, and left until the next time he was strapped for cash.

I just couldn't help but worry that he was using her.

"Of course, whatever you need." Violet waved her hand and glanced at me. "Can you grab my purse, Andrea?"

I fetched her handbag. Violet always carried a ton of cash on her from tips and bonuses. I worried sometimes that she'd get mugged, but unlike me who was hopeless at self-defense, Violet took kickboxing and carried a butterfly knife and knew how to protect herself.

Violet counted out the cash. "Are you sure you're okay, Chris?"

"I am, it's just hard times, y'know," he said, taking the money and stuffing it into his jeans pocket. "Not enough shifts at work to cover the rent with my roommates...our landlord's an asshole..."

"I get it." Violet fondly ran a hand through his hair and smiled. "You know I'll always be there to look after you, or help you when you need it."

"Thanks, sis." Christopher gave Violet another hug, then left.

"His excuses are getting better," I noted, not holding back the sarcasm in my voice.

Violet gave me a sharp look. "Knock it off."

I folded my arms across my chest. "He only ever shows up when he wants money, Vi."

"He's a good kid," she said defensively. "And once you get behind financially, it can take a while to get caught back up. I see it all the time with people who blow their money at the casino. It takes one night to lose it all and months or years to build it back."

I didn't want to turn this into an argument. Violet was going to see the best in her brother, and that was that, so I changed the subject.

"All right, you said it was your turn to pick the movie tonight, so, what'll it be?"

Of course she chose a horror flick, and in order to distract myself from all the jump scares, I thought about meeting with Chase at the club the next evening. I was sure a good play session would take my mind off my worries for Violet. I was probably being paranoid. Violet was responsible with her money, tough, street smart, a badass. She could put her foot down with Christopher if she needed to, and she wouldn't give him more than she could afford to give.

Speaking of paranoid...

The following night, as I walked to my car to leave for The Players Club, an odd sense of unease trickled down my spine. I looked up and down the street, but it was too dark and I couldn't see anyone. And yet...I had the strange feeling I was being watched.

I tried to shake off the sensation as I headed to the club...except my anxiety escalated when I realized that someone seemed to be following me in a dark vehicle, but from a distance. As soon as I neared the gated community in Summerlin, the car veered off in a different direction, much to my relief.

I was beyond grateful when I saw Chase

waiting for me out in the courtyard when I arrived, since as his guest he'd have to escort me into the club.

"Hey, you." Chase's easy smile turned into a frown as his gaze searched my expression when I reached him in front of the main entrance. "Everything okay?"

I forced myself to put on a happy face. "Umm, yeah, I'm fine."

"You sure?" He tipped his head, his stare more direct now. "You look tense."

He looked genuinely concerned, and considering Chase worked in security, I decided to tell him the truth. "I just had this weird feeling, getting into my car to come here. Like someone was watching me. And then I thought a car might be following me, but they went a different direction as soon as I reached the gated community." I laughed, trying to shake it off. "I'm probably just being overly sensitive. Violet's half-brother stopped by last night and he always puts me in a weird mood."

Chase straightened, his demeanor serious. "You feel unsafe around him?"

"Around Christopher?" I snorted and shook my head. "No, just pissed off most of the time. I'm sure I'm just imagining things."

"But maybe you're not, so trust your instincts," he said, his tone gruff. "If your gut is telling you that someone is watching you, then be aware and vigilant of your surroundings. And if anything else strange happens, then you tell me immediately, okay?"

I resisted the urge to salute him. "That sounds like an order, *sir*."

His eyes darkened as he stared down at me, gaze narrowed. "Trust me, it is. And one you don't want to ignore. I also want you to text me when you get home from work from now on."

I held up a hand to stop him. "Okay, that's a bit much. You aren't the boss of me, and I'm not one of your clients."

Chase's jaw clenched. "I want to make sure that you're safe."

I sighed, not pleased with his over-bearing attitude. "Chase, I thought someone was watching me. And that could be true. It's nice to know that you don't think I'm crazy. But it could've just been a nosy neighbor watching from their window, and the car thing…they could have been headed to Summerlin, too. There was no direct threat, and I don't think I need to start reporting my whereabouts to you every day."

"I've seen how quickly these situations can

escalate—"

"There is no situation!" I said, raising my voice loud enough that the valet glanced our way. I exhaled a breath and lowered my tone. "Here I was worried I was overreacting but you've got that covered." I folded my arms across my chest. "I'm fine."

"You might not be," he said, determination flashing in his eyes. "Consider this an order from your dom."

My jaw dropped open, and it took me a moment to respond. "Oh, no, you don't," I snapped. "You don't get to use the dom card outside of our playtimes. What's next, you telling me what I can and can't eat? Who I can or can't see in my free time? You don't control me, mister." I poked a finger into his very hard, very solid, very unyielding chest. "Let's get that clear right now. If I'm not in a scene with you, you don't get to tell me jack shit."

Chase looked at me for a long moment, a quietness settling over his body. It made him look intimidating, threatening even, and a hot anticipation pooled in the pit of my stomach.

Chase wasn't some mafia boss and he wasn't truly dangerous. But right now? I felt like he could be, at least for a scene. And that illicit fantasy playing out in my mind, of him overpowering me, got me embarrassingly wet.

"You think I can't control you?" he asked, his voice as dark and menacing as his expression. He grabbed my elbow in a firm, unshakeable hold and guided me toward the front doors to the club. "We'll see about that."

Oh, shit. I felt like I'd just taken a leap off a cliff without realizing it—but I also suspected I was going to enjoy the fall.

CHAPTER 10

Chase

*a*ndrea told me she felt like she was being watched, and suddenly my head was full of worst-case scenarios. One thought circled repeatedly in my mind, over and over: *I can't lose someone else.*

The military warned us when we were recruited, I did want to give them credit for that. Not right away, of course. First they sold us on how it would pay for our education, give us valuable skills that would ensure us quality civilian jobs for the rest of our lives, how we'd be heroes, how we would be proud of ourselves, how we could always hold our heads high knowing we had pushed ourselves to limits most people couldn't even imagine, and conquered.

But later on, towards the end of Navy WARCOM training and right before we were shipped off for our first assignment, that's when they warned us. *You might not all make it. You will lose friends.*

I didn't think anyone could prepare you for just how close you would become with the people who served with you, the others in your unit that were a part of your daily lives. 'Brotherhood,' they called it, but that word didn't really encompass everything that connection entailed. I had a brother and I adored him even if I'd never let the little shit's head swell by telling him. I'd die for Austin. What I'd had with my WARCOM team... it was something unquantifiable. A bond forged through shared hardships, loyalty, and absolute trust. It was knowing with absolute certainty that the person standing next to you would risk their lives for yours, and you'd do the same without hesitation.

So yes, they had warned us. But I didn't think it was possible to really prepare someone *enough*. Especially not when those same fears spilled over into my civilian life and my job as a security specialist, as a man trained to protect clients who were purposefully targeted.

Andrea's words made every possible bad scenario flash through my mind, of how things could change on a dime when a possible threat wasn't taken seriously. The thought of something bad happening to her ramped up my anxiety in ways that shocked me, when I was far more level-headed with the clients I was hired to protect.

I can't lose someone else. I can't lose someone else. I can't lose someone else. The words cycled through my head like a mantra, and she thought she could be a brat about my worry? My genuine concern? She was about to learn otherwise.

Andrea wisely remained quiet as I checked us in and led her up to one of the private rooms I'd secured for the night. Most of the time I tried to get a private room, but with other women, if I ended up playing with them in an open area, I never cared. But with Andrea, I was possessive and territorial...I wasn't about to let anyone see her like this but me.

"Strip," I ordered once the door closed behind us, my tone sharp and uncompromising.

As if sensing how tautly wound I was, she didn't fight back. No snarky remarks. She did as she was told, quickly removing her sexy little dress and then the red, lacy, barely there lingerie she wore beneath. If I was in a better mood I would have stopped her, would have taken the time to appreciate the way those scraps of scarlet fabric looked against her pale complexion, how the sheer panties gave me a teasing glimpse of her pussy and the push up bra framed her perfect breasts.

As soon as she was completely nude, she walked toward the bed. I intercepted her before she could settle herself there, grabbing her arm and leading her to the St. Andrew's Cross in the room. She gave me a curious glance, but again, she didn't balk or resist as I quietly and efficiently secured her wrists and ankles against the wooden planks so that she was restrained and standing spread-eagle, locked into position, unable to move. Naked and vulnerable and breathtakingly gorgeous.

I tucked a finger beneath her chin and tipped her head back, forcing her to look at my face and see the displeasure etched there. "You have no idea the control I have over you," I growled furiously. "But you're about to find out. You're going to learn to *obey*."

Andrea's breath came quick and fast, her eyes wide as she stared at me, but not in fear. No, her complexion was already flushed with arousal, her nipples as hard as pebbles, and I had no doubt if I slid my hand between her thighs she'd already be soaked. I ran my fingers down the side of her neck, feeling her tremble. *Christ.* Just seeing her like this got me so unbelievably hard.

I wanted to take out my stiff cock and stuff her so goddamn full that she couldn't move, couldn't breathe without feeling me *everywhere.* I wanted to impale her to the hilt, hear her scream my name as I drove inside her body like a goddamn madman. On any other day I might have done just that. Maybe gagged and blindfolded her, put some noise cancelling headphones over her ears so that all she could sense, all she could feel, was my fat cock and blunt piercings wreaking havoc inside that pretty pussy.

But not tonight. I exhaled a deep breath and made myself tamp down those baser desires. This wasn't about instant gratification. This was about teaching her a goddamn lesson.

I grabbed a bullet vibrator and set it up to rest directly against her clit, strapping it onto her thigh to hold it in place. Using the remote control, I turned it on just low enough to tease and torment and edge her, but not nearly high enough to make her orgasm.

Andrea's eyelids immediately fluttered. "S-sir..."

I was pretty sure she knew immediately that she wasn't going to come anytime soon. I watched her for a minute as she attempted to grind her hips against the smooth head of the vibrator, small little movements, her gaze growing heavy-lidded and hazy. Her mouth hung open, tiny noises emerging from the back of her throat.

Dark desires rose up inside me, and I grabbed a leather flogger and went to work on her body, ignoring her shocked cries as I snapped the leather strands against her breasts, her stomach, her thighs, marking her pale skin with bright red stripes. I didn't go easy. There was no soft, gradual build up like last time. My ministrations were not gentle or even tempered as I yielded the flogger like a whip, each strike a painful punishment I wanted her to feel to the depths of her soul.

She gasped as each blow landed, her head rolling back on her shoulders as she struggled against the snap of leather and the tease of that vibrator against her clit. My dick throbbed as I watched all those beautiful pink welts rise up on her skin, as I flicked my wrist and continued delivering each sharp, stinging sensation, again and again.

Smack, smack, smack.

To be honest, I expected her to protest. Or even use her safeword to end the pain I was inflicting. Instead, Andrea just...surrendered. Submitted to me and my dominance and control over her mind and her body. She moaned and whimpered, her flushed expression delirious with pleasure, and I realized that she was in subspace. She was completely mine, letting me do what I wanted to her body, what I needed to make *me* whole.

The sound of leather slapping against her skin was rhythmic, almost hypnotic, releasing my own anxiety with each strike, calming me and clearing that dark, awful fear that had lodged in my chest, until I was no longer staring down the end of a long, black tunnel. Until I felt like I could breathe normally again.

I set the flogger aside. Andrea's body was trembling, her gaze completely unfocused, her breathing slow and deep. She looked fucking gorgeous strapped to the cross, completely restrained, her body a canvas that she'd let me use to assuage my own turbulent emotions and compulsion for control.

She deserved to be rewarded for her patience, for her strength, for giving me, her dom, exactly what *I'd* so desperately needed. Because she'd known, based on that conversation we'd had that night at my place. She'd listened, and understood, and I couldn't truly recall when, if ever, a session like this had ever been so cathartic for *me*. It was a revelation that made my head spin.

I pick up the vibrator's remote control, turning it up a notch. Andrea jolted and moaned, loudly, her gaze clearing as the device buzzed against her clit.

"Do you want to come?" I murmured.

It took her a moment to respond, and to my shock, she shook her head.

"No?" I could see her pussy clenching and dripping, her inner thighs coated with slick arousal. I had no doubt she wanted to come very, very badly.

"I want...what you want, sir," Andrea slurred. "I'm yours, to do with as you please."

Her complete acquiescence pleased me. "Yes, you're fucking *mine*. I control you," I said, wanting to make my point about who was in charge. Who made the rules in this relationship, however temporary, and that she would obey them.

"Yes," Andrea agreed. She looked up into my eyes, her gaze locking on mine. "I'm—I'm yours, you control me."

"Say it again."

"You control me," she moaned, her body arching against the vibrator.

I turned the device off and removed it, and Andrea sobbed, clearly wanting an orgasm more than she was willing to admit. No worries there...I just planned to make sure it happened as she was coming all over my cock, while I was balls deep inside her pussy.

I pushed a lever and tilted the cross so that she lay horizontally, now at the perfect angle for me to fuck her, even with her still restrained. I pulled my stiff cock out of my slacks, realizing to my shock that I'd leaked all through my underwear and onto the fabric. I hadn't even noticed, I'd been that deep in my own dom subspace.

In that moment, it was like all sensation rushed back into my body and I was suddenly so hard, so aching for release, that it physically hurt.

There were different types of pain. Most people who weren't experienced only knew the pain from impact play of spanking or flogging, or something similar. But when you really immersed yourself into a scene, you learned all the different beautiful sorts of pain that existed, including the torment that came from being denied a climax. Feeling good for so long, but not quite good enough, that the desperation of it all made it hurt.

I fucking loved when it hurt like this.

Moving between her spread legs, I took my dick in hand and slid the head along her slit before burying every inch of my shaft inside of her with one long, driving thrust, the violent impact of our bodies joining making me groan, and Andrea scream. I hadn't given her much of a chance to adjust, and I knew it had to be a stretch and bit of a burn to accommodate me, even with how soaked she was, but the way her body clenched around my cock felt so fucking amazing.

"Love... love..." Her voice was breathy, and it took her a few tries to get the words out. "...your cock. Feels so good. Oh god it's so good..."

I knew from past subs that the piercings on my cock could be too much, hitting too many sensitive places all at once if I didn't take things slow and easy. But in this moment, that wasn't an option for me. I wanted, *needed*, Andrea too much. She moaned and cried out as I fucked her roughly, ruthlessly, her pussy clenching tight and hot around my shaft every time I drove deep.

I leaned over her, grabbing onto her hair and tugging hard, forcing her head back and her body to arch beneath mine. She whimpered as I slammed into her, and I growled deep in my throat, feeling the exquisite pressure and friction of all my piercings rubbing along her inner walls.

Her lashes fluttered open as she looked up at me, her eyes glazed with the kind of ecstasy I understood all too well. "Does it hurt?" I rasped, shifting the angle of my next thrust so I dug in a little deeper, scraped those metal barbells a little harder in all the right places.

"Yes," Andrea gasped. "Hurts so *good*."

"Fuck yeah," I growled in agreement.

Her skin had to be incredibly sensitive and sore from the flogging. I reached down with my free hand and deliberately raked my nails along her thigh where I'd flogged her, just to see how she'd respond.

Andrea screamed and immediately orgasmed from the pain.

Holy *fuck*.

Another savage thrust and I came instantly as her pussy went painfully tight around me. I couldn't possibly hold back. Bliss ruptured from my core, snaking outward. The orgasm ripped through me, hot and sharp, tearing a deep, guttural groan from me. I felt such a clarity, a beautiful mix of pleasure and pain in that moment, like everything toxic had drained out of me and all that was left was a wonderful, peaceful haze.

This was why I dommed—chasing not just the journey and adrenaline rush, although I did love that, but this moment in the aftermath, when every worry, every dark thought in my mind, faded away. It was one of the few times I truly felt relaxed and at peace.

When I recovered from my orgasm, I reluctantly pulled out of Andrea and she made a small noise. I stumbled a bit as I released her from the cross and cleaned her up. I hadn't been this exhausted by a scene in a while. My head was clear but also pleasantly empty, which to me was pure bliss. I wanted to just lie down and sink into the moment but didn't have that luxury just yet.

Andrea was wobbly on her feet for a moment as she stepped off the cross, but once she got her bearings she grabbed my arm to get my attention. "Chase. Hey."

I looked at her. She was obviously tired, just as exhausted as I was after that mind and body altering scene, but her gaze was sharp and clear.

"What can I do?" she asked softly.

I frowned at her, not understanding what she meant. "What?"

"What do you need," she clarified, sliding her hand down my arm until she was holding my hand. "For aftercare."

I shook my head, feeling out of sorts from this role reversal. "I'm the dom here. I'm taking care of you."

The corner of Andrea's mouth curled upwards. "Right, because I'm the only one who was just went through something extremely intense." Her mocking tone gentled, as did her expression. "Sir, please. Right now, I'm your submissive. Let me *serve* you. I'm yours. What do you need?"

I stared at her, shocked by what she was offering. Usually, after a session like what just transpired, I wanted to be alone. To just collapse and rest, and coast on the wonderful empty feeling in my mind as long as it lasted.

But I honestly couldn't remember ever having a session like this, where one woman had given me every fucking thing I'd needed—from the control and dominance, to her submission, to the emotional release of letting go of all the shit in my head—with someone I truly trusted. And now this, Andrea asking *me* how I was doing, telling me that she would serve me and give me whatever I needed.

"Come home with me," I said, knowing I was about to break all my rules with her, but after tonight, I couldn't bring myself to care. "You need a hot bath, for your muscles. Mine is like a hot tub."

Her beautiful blue eyes searched mine, far more intuitive than I would have liked. "Is that what *you* need?"

I need to hold you, I thought, shocking myself with that truth. "Yes." With her, there was no point in lying.

Since we'd driven separately, I followed Andrea to my place. Because of what she'd told me earlier when she'd arrived at the club, I kept an eye on our surroundings, on every car that followed behind us, even though it was all normal evening traffic and no one actually tracked us from Summerlin all the way to my condo. Once we arrived, I took her hand in mine and we headed up to my place. We didn't talk as I led her to my en suite and drew us a bath, and we both stripped back out of our clothes. Once the tub was filled with the steaming water, we climbed in and I drew Andrea toward me.

With a soft, content sigh, she rested her back to my chest, her head on my shoulder. It felt good to be in the hot water. It helped my muscles relax, helped me feel weightless and continue that pleasantly empty and drained feeling. The slight weight of her in my arms, knowing she was completely safe here with me... it helped more than I wanted to admit.

Beneath the water, I idly stroked my hands along her arms, her breasts, her thighs, soothing the welts on her skin and just needing to touch her in a gentle, caring manner—without the expectations of sex. She dozed off and I continued caressing her body, thinking about what had just transpired at the club. I could have gone too far for her back there, I could admit that now. But she'd taken everything I'd doled out, without resorting to using her safeword. She'd *enjoyed* it.

The fondness I felt for her was overwhelming. Like I could actually feel for once how soft and fragile my organs were inside my chest.

The idea of someone hurting Andrea was—it was unthinkable. Fuck, I was in so much trouble and already way over my head with her. I never should've started this agreement with her, because deep inside I'd known this would happen. But I couldn't have let someone else do this with her, either. My possessiveness and desire warred with my self-preservation.

I suppose in the end it wouldn't matter, because terminating this pact between us wouldn't be my choice. Tonight, I'd given her just a taste of the darkness inside me. When she saw all of how broken I was, how I'd never be the man she deserved, Andrea wouldn't want me anyway, and this would end.

It was for the best. I knew that. But holding her in the deliciously hot water, feeling her soft trusting body in my arms, watching her peacefully sleep...

I also knew the end was going to hurt, and not in a way that I enjoyed.

CHAPTER 11

Andrea

I followed Violet through the grocery store with my cart while she tossed the items we needed inside. My body was still pleasantly sore from yesterday's activities, pink streaks still lightly scoring my body beneath my clothes like a badge of honor. The scene, although intense, had been one of the hottest things I'd ever done with a man—and exactly the kind of dominance I'd craved.

The act, meant to punish and establish who was in charge, had also been so incredibly intimate because it had been *with Chase*. He hadn't just been dominant. He'd been...*raw*. Vulnerable with me, even.

I'd loved every moment, but I didn't know what to make of Chase's state of mind while he'd wielded the flogger. It wasn't like he'd been out of control. It was more like he was so *in* control—until he'd finally allowed himself to let go while he'd fucked me. He'd taken me hard, almost brutally, trembling like something inside of him had cracked open—I'd been so attuned to him that I'd felt it. By giving him complete dominance over me, I'd unknowingly opened a door for him to feel something deep, messy, and real...whatever that was for him.

I'm sure I wasn't privy to everything in Chase's past. But there was one thing I did know...last night wasn't just sex. It wasn't even just kink. No, it had been a therapeutic release for him. He'd needed that moment. Not just physically, but emotionally. Desperately.

I thought I'd been the one surrendering, but maybe he'd been the one to finally let go...

"Hey." Violet playfully snapped her fingers in front of my face, startling me out of my thoughts. "Earth to Andrea."

I shook my head and refocused. "Sorry. What's up?"

"Did we like the chicken or the pork pot stickers? I can't remember."

"Chicken," I said absently.

"What's on your mind?" Violet asked as she grabbed the right bag from the freezer section. "You looked like you were a million miles away."

"Nothing. I just...I don't know," I hedged, then confessed where my mind had been. "Just thinking about Chase and last night." I'd told Violet about the intense scene at the club, along with everything else that had happened leading up to Chase flogging me. Me being stubborn and mouthy and him proving who had the upper hand.

What I hadn't divulged was just how much I'd wanted to truly belong to Chase in those moments when I'd given myself over to him. Now that I had distance and perspective, I was a little worried that my response to him wasn't all based on being high on subspace during the scene, but that my feelings for him were changing and evolving in a way that went beyond this arrangement we'd established.

"You're good, right?" Violet's eyes glimmered with concern. "I mean, Chase seems like a great guy."

"He is a great guy," I said, but despite the intimacy of our time together last night, Chase made it clear where he stood. That he wasn't a forever kind of guy, and, well … I knew deep down that I *was* a forever kind of girl. That eventually I'd want to get married, have a family of my own. "He's teaching me all the things I want to know about my kinks and fantasies and BDSM, but I don't want to be that girl who falls for the unattainable guy who's made it clear he's not in the market for a serious relationship. You know how that always goes. Awkward."

To my surprise, Violet laughed. "Right, because the man who apparently only cares about the sexual part of your arrangement texts you constantly, and goes overboard with the safety checks because you had one weird moment of paranoia," she said, describing Chase's behavior.

I frowned, because I was trying not to read too much into those things. "Still, I don't want to set myself up for—"

WE ROUNDED the corner of the aisle and not paying attention to where I was going, I nearly ran my cart into someone. "Oh my God I'm so sorry!"

The person came to an abrupt stop in front of our cart, and I realized with a twist in my stomach that it was Heath. My ex.

"Andrea?" Heath blurted out. "Wow, hi."

"Hey." Staring at him now, I wondered what I'd truly ever seen in him. He was good looking enough, but when I compared him to Chase, I realized that he wasn't—hadn't ever been—enough of my type and I'd just been settling. "What are you doing here?"

Yes, everyone went grocery shopping, but Heath lived in Henderson, one city over from Vegas. This store wasn't at all near his neighborhood.

"Having a lucky day, apparently, running into you," he said, not really giving me the explanation I wanted to hear. "How've you been? You look great."

"Oh, thank you," I said, trying to be polite when this unexpected encounter had me a little off kilter. "I'm doing all right. How are you?"

"I'm hanging in there," he said with a smile, ignoring Violet completely, whom he'd met a few times and who was openly eyeing him suspiciously. "I was actually just thinking about you— about us—the other day, and—"

I glanced down at my phone like I'd just received a text. There was no way I was going to have a conversation with Heath about potentially getting back together, or anything else for that matter after the way he'd treated me. "Shit, we're really running late," I said, cutting him off. "Violet and I need to get going. I'm sorry."

He frowned at the way I'd quickly dismissed him. "Well, call me sometime. I'd love to catch up."

Yeah, that wasn't going to happen. "It was nice seeing you," I lied instead. "Take care of yourself."

Violet grabbed the end of my cart and tugged it along. "See ya," she threw over her shoulder at Heath, her tone dripping with sarcasm.

"Don't be antagonistic," I chastised her once we were out of earshot.

"He was being creepy," she said defensively, and she wasn't wrong. "He doesn't even live near here, right?"

"No, he doesn't," I said, glancing over my shoulder because I felt like he was still watching me from somewhere in the store. "Let's just get out of here."

Violet quickly grabbed the last of the groceries we needed from the produce section. We did self check-out and hustled out of the store. My nerves didn't really start to calm down until we were safe at home. I put the groceries away, while Violet seemed fixated on her phone.

"What are you up to?" I asked, putting the bags of salad into the refrigerator.

"Checking out Heath on social media," she replied, then grimaced. "Oh, eww."

"What?" I couldn't help myself and looked over her shoulder at what had prompted her negative response.

Heath's last post was a repost of one of those photo quotes that people shared around. It said, *why do women always rush to get their hearts broken by abusive assholes, while the real gentlemen wait patiently for a recognition that never comes?*

My stomach pitched. I couldn't help but think that post, and those words, were directed at me—at what I had wanted in bed. Heath seemed to think me wanting a dominant partner meant I wanted to be abused.

Violet shot me a concerned look. "You look like you're going to throw up."

I pressed a hand to my belly. "I feel like I might," I said, and voiced the thoughts I'd just had out loud to her.

Her lips pursed. "Well, if it is directed at you, *he's* an asshole as well as a creep. BDSM isn't abuse and wanting that power dynamic in the bedroom doesn't mean you want to date a jerk. And Heath's not much of a gentleman if he posts shit like this."

"Very true," I muttered.

"Do you know what a real gentleman does?"

Violet continued, a triumphant smirk on her lips. "He tries to protect you when you feel unsafe," she said, clearly referencing Chase.

"Oh my God." I groaned. "Violet…"

"I'm just saying!"

"Chase and I are just scene partners. Nothing more." I had to keep telling myself that, just to keep my own emotions out of the equation.

Violet rolled her eyes. "Good God, you make it sound like you're in a play together."

That *almost* made me giggle. "Ha ha."

"Well." Violet put her phone down and crossed her arms over her chest. "No matter what, I'm glad you broke up with that idiot. You clearly dodged a bullet with him."

Yeah, I could definitely agree with her on that.

CHAPTER 12

Chase

The major upside to working with as many wealthy clients as we did was that they often gave us guys some pretty great perks. Like tickets to a sold out concert, or an evening out at a Michelin star restaurant, or front row seats to a sporting event. People tended to be grateful, and generous, when they knew you were the one saving their life and keeping them safe, and so gifts were pretty normal and commonplace.

This time, Ford had been given a group gift card for one of those indoor skydiving places, so a bunch of us guys from the office were going. Sutton bowed out because he was the enemy of fun and Kane was on a job so couldn't attend, which left two slots open.

If any of you know anyone who would be interested in joining on Sunday, let me know! Ford told the group chat.

When no one replied, my mind went to places it shouldn't have, and before I could change my mind I sent a message back to Ford. *Is it okay if I invite a friend and her sister? Or do you want this to be a guys only event?*

Hey, I'm all good, as long as they like skydiving!

I hadn't seen Andrea since that night at the club. We texted, and even though she'd followed through on my request for her to message me when she got home after work, I saw this as the perfect excuse to see her outside of the club and establish more of a friendship between us, so that when we went our separate ways, we'd at least have that to fall back on. Or so I told myself.

I asked Andrea if her and Violet would like to join us, and she replied fairly quickly, and enthusiastically.

We'd love to! I'll admit I'm a little nervous, but Violet is totally into that kind of thing. Nothing rattles her. I think she's a little bit of an adrenaline junkie.

I found myself grinning stupidly as I replied back. *Then she'll fit right in,* I assured her.

When we all met up at the skydiving place that Sunday, I couldn't stand how adorable Andrea looked as she bounded toward where I was waiting for her, outside of the event, her high ponytail swishing from side to side as she beamed at me. She was wearing practical, form-fitting clothes that would work well for the activity, and I couldn't help but notice how well her jeans fit her curves, not to mention the way her t-shirt outlined her breasts.

Next to her was the woman I assumed was her half-sister, Violet, who looked like a throwback from the 50's in a pair of high waisted pants that ended mid-calf—pedal pushers I was pretty sure they were called—and a halter style top with a polka dot print. The cute outfit totally contradicted the *don't fucking mess with me, tough chick vibes* radiating off her.

She and Andrea did look similar in terms of their facial features, though Violet's hair was more blonde than brown, unlike Andrea's. Their height was about the same, but I was good at reading people and there was a definite edge to Violet that I immediately sensed. The word *rebellious* came to mind. And maybe even cut-throat if the need arose.

While Andrea came across as guileless and trusting, gregarious even, when she wasn't being a brat and pushing my buttons, her sister appeared far more guarded and gave me the impression that she wasn't someone who took shit from anyone. Her gaze was sharp and assessing, sizing me up in a way that was direct and unapologetic as the two of them approached me.

As soon as the two of them finally reached me, Andrea introduced me to her sister. I shook Violet's hand, we did the whole "nice to meet you" spiel, and I wasn't surprised that she had a strong, unflinching grip to go with that tough exterior attitude.

"Thanks for inviting us," Andrea said, looking up at me with the sweetest smile that did stupid things to my heart rate.

"Of course. But wait until you meet the other guys before you actually thank me," I teased, opening the door and ushering the women in.

"I've been dying to meet you all," Violet said, brushing past me with a little side-eye. "See the guy Andrea's told me about and make sure he's good enough for my sister."

Andrea elbowed her sister in the side. "Vi, stop," she hissed in mortification.

"What?" Violet gave her a wide-eyed innocent look that was far from angelic. "What are sisters for if they can't look after one another and make a man sweat a little?"

I barely held back my chuckle. I could appreciate Violet's protective tendencies. Was I good enough for Andrea? For our short term agreement, yeah, I could give her everything she wanted and needed to navigate her way through a BDSM lifestyle...and that's all that really mattered.

The other guys were already inside, and I quickly introduced each of them: Austin, Tate, Xavier, Archer, and of course Ford who had the gift card.

Austin already knew Andrea and was happy to chat with her. The others were polite, but I could see they were intrigued by the fact that I'd invited not just one woman, but two to this outing. I was sure I was going to take shit for that later, when the girls were gone.

We checked in, changed into our flight suits and attended a quick orientation. Most of us guys were experienced and had been there before, so it was mostly for the girls' benefit. They stood up front with the instructor, and while they learned the basics of indoor skydiving and asked questions Ford came up beside me.

"So, who's the person with Andrea again?" he asked in a low voice, sounding confused.

"Violet, her half-sister."

His brow furrowed a bit more. "I thought Madison was Andrea's sister. Austin told me about her."

"Yeah, so Andrea and Madison are full sisters, same parents," I said, telling him what I knew. "I guess their dad wasn't the best and, uh, fucked around in more ways than one. Violet happened. But the two of them are really close, no resentment or anything. They actually live together."

"That's great it worked out that way." Ford shifted his gaze to Violet, and I didn't miss the interest etching his expression.

"I'd tell you she doesn't bite, but I actually think she might," I warned him. "She looks the type."

Ford smirked. "Never been afraid of a little challenge."

"Yeah...good luck with that one," I said, suspecting he'd need it with Violet if he decided to pursue her.

"Okay," the instructor said once the orientation ended, leading us to the skydiving chamber where we'd all take turns. "Who wants to go first?"

"Ladies first?" Austin goaded in a teasing tone.

"Hell yeah," Violet said enthusiastically, grinning as she stepped forward, already putting her helmet on. "I'll volunteer as tribute."

"I told you. Total adrenaline junkie," Andrea said to me with a laugh as the instructor helped stabilize Violet in the vertical wind tunnel, where strong gusts of wind created a sensation of floating in mid-air. "I'm nervous, but I'll go next. This looks really fun."

"Trust me, I think you'll enjoy it."

She glanced up at me. "Have you ever done this before?"

I nodded. "For real, actually."

"Oh my God, of course you have." Andrea rolled her eyes, but she was still grinning at me.

I grinned back, feeling something shift inside of me. Loosening and relaxing in a way that felt dangerously close to falling for her. Jesus, I was becoming a fucking sap where Andrea was concerned.

Ford came up to the two of us while we watched Violet learn to control her body position within the airflow.

"So, how long have you and Chase been... friends?" Ford asked Andrea conversationally.

I appreciated Ford's tact. I hadn't introduced

her as my girlfriend to everyone, since, well, we weren't dating and girlfriend signified exclusivity, which we'd never established—though I had to admit I'd probably fucking break any man's arm who dared to touch her in any kind of intimate way. But I honestly didn't know what other damn word to use for what we were. *Hey this is the girl I'm doing BDSM with* just sounded crass, so *friends* it was.

"We met back when we both lived in San Diego," Andrea said as Violet whooped and hollered during her turn and Austin shamelessly egged her on while Tate filmed on his phone. "We're all kind of interconnected in a friend and family sort of way. My sister, Madison, works for Chase's mother, Jillian, at her interior design firm."

Ford grinned. "Ahh, the brilliant women behind all those specialty fantasy rooms at The Players Club. I gotta say, I'm kind of partial to the medical themed one. I've never tried it out, but I'm definitely...intrigued."

Andrea blushed adorably. "Not really my thing, but I'm sure there's some woman out there who has a kink for that."

"Your turn, Andrea!" Violet called as her time in the wind tunnel ended.

Andrea exhaled a deep breath as she glanced up

at me, sudden anxiety flickering in her eyes. "Okay, wish me luck."

"You don't need it," I assured her. "You got this."

She grinned at me and then hurried over to the instructor. Violet walked over to Ford and me, removing her flight suit right in front of us while Ford stared at her as if she'd just done a strip tease for his eyes only. Violet arched a brow at him as if to say, *what the fuck are you looking at?*, and he quickly glanced away.

I swallowed back a chuckle. I could see the immediate push-pull between these two, and it was comical.

We watched as the instructor positioned Andrea, and she let out a shriek when he released her and the gust of wind lifted her up, suspending her in the air. She glanced my way, grinning, and I gave her a thumbs up sign.

"So, you and Andrea have been seeing a lot of each other," Violet said, her tone direct.

I met her gaze, just as direct. "Wow, I knew this interrogation was coming, but you really don't waste time, do you?"

"Nope." She crossed her arms over her chest, which was great for Ford's benefit since it enhanced her cleavage in the low cut halter top she wore. "You know, Vegas was founded by the mafia and people say that organized crime still has a pretty big hold on this city. They used to drive people out into the desert all the time. All that empty red ground is really full of unmarked graveyards. Basically impossible to find the bodies once you're out there."

I arched a brow at her. "Are you insinuating that you have mafia friends who'll take care of me if I hurt her?"

She made a scoffing sound. "Why would I ask the damn mafia to do something that I can do perfectly well myself?"

Ford had a coughing fit to cover up his laughter. Violet looked over at him and deadpanned, "Something funny?"

He cleared his throat. "No, no. Not funny at all." Ford looked fucking delighted by her.

Oh, boy. "I like and care about Andrea," I told Violet honestly. "Even more, I respect her, and I would never do anything to hurt her." Which was precisely why I would never enter into a proper relationship with her. She deserved far better than what I could give her.

Violet pursed her lips and nodded, seemingly satisfied. "All right. That's a pretty good answer."

"Thank you," I drawled, just a little sarcastically. "Anything to spare my life."

She rolled her eyes in a way that definitely reminded me of Andrea. "No wonder she likes you," she muttered. "Smartass."

"You're a bit of a smartass yourself," Ford chimed in.

She shifted her attention to him, her expression annoyed. "I didn't realize this was your conversation?"

Ford smirked, completely unfazed by her caustic tone. "I mean I could pretend to be deaf if you want me to."

Andrea's time in the wind tunnel ended, and I decided this was my chance to leave Ford and Violet to their...whatever that was.

"Hey!" I said as she jogged toward me, her face flushed and her eyes bright from the adrenaline rush she'd experienced. "You looked like you had a blast."

"I did. That was amazing!" Andrea fell against my chest, her hands gripping my t-shirt as if to help stabilize herself again. Breathless and exhilarated, she had the biggest smile on her face. "Holy shit! I'll have to do the real thing!"

I chuckled. "That can be arranged."

"Yeah?" Andrea looked beyond excited by the prospect of jumping out of an actual airplane.

I nodded. "Sure."

She looked so elated and carefree, and I had the strongest urge to just kiss her. So, I framed her face in my hands and I gave in to the impulse, reveling in the sweet, surprised gasp that brushed across my lips as our mouths touched, then melded completely.

Austin was now in the skydiving tunnel, making a big scene about it, so Xavier and Tate were focused on him—Tate filming on his phone and Xavier encouraging his antics. I could hear Ford and Violet still bickering behind me, so I couldn't be sure if they were paying attention to us, or not.

It was a stupid thing to do, to blur the lines like this with a public display of affection. I didn't want to play with Andrea's heart or confuse her. But I couldn't help myself, and honestly, giving into my desire for her was so worth it, just to feel the way her body went slack against mine, the soft little moan of pleasure she made against my mouth, and the dazed, joyful look in her eyes as I pulled back.

"Sorry," I murmured, not really feeling apologetic at all as I gently brushed stray strands of hair away from her face. My fingers lingered longer than necessary, drawn to her like some magnetic pull I couldn't seem to fight. "Happiness looks good on you."

Andrea smiled at me, and for a moment the whole damn world soften around the edges. That smile—bright, genuine, *mine*— pulled me under like a riptide. I nearly kissed her again, but then she whispered, "It looks good on you, too."

My heart seemed to knock against my ribs as I stared down at her beautiful face. I had no idea what to do with that—didn't know how to take something so simple and honest and believe it. Happiness wasn't something I was accustomed to or wore well. It wasn't something I trusted to stay beyond a fleeting moment.

The next day, Monday, I sat in one of the security firm's offices, trying to concentrate on the paperwork I needed to fill out for an upcoming job, but my mind kept drifting back to that exchange between us. Every line I was supposed to fill out blurred with the echo of her words.

It looks good on you, too.

The truth was, she made me want to believe it. And that terrified the hell out of me. Because if happiness did look good on me, it was only because she'd put it there. And I didn't know if I deserved to keep it.

"Contemplating how you need to call your mother?"

I jolted in my office chair and looked up,

watching as my father, Dean Noble, strolled into the room, still seeing him as the larger than life man I'd admired growing up, and still did. "Dad!"

"Hey, kid." He grinned at me as I stood up and rounded the desk to give him a hug, which he returned, then clapped me on the shoulder as we parted.

"How are you?" I asked, surprised to see him here in Vegas, when he normally spent his time at the original San Diego security firm. "And I *do* call Mom, which I'm pretty sure you hear all about."

"I do," he said, and laughed. "But you know how it is. You could call your mother every day and it wouldn't be enough for her. You and Austin are still her boys and she misses you both. How are things?" he asked, his gaze more serious now.

"Everything is good," I assured him, knowing he still worried about me after learning what had happened during that last mission overseas, before I'd been honorably discharged. My father had also served in the Navy and knew how harrowing things could get, and he also understood how those devastating memories lingered even years after being out of that element.

But my mental well-being was the last thing I wanted to discuss with my father, and I quickly changed the subject to him. "What are you doing here?"

"I'm in town for a few days, just to go over some company changes with Sutton."

"Is mom with you?" I asked curiously, since she did occasionally accompany him on these quick Vegas trips.

My father arched a brow. "If what you're really asking is if we'll be at The Players Club while I'm here and cramp your style, rest assured she is not with me this time."

I didn't miss my dad's smirk, though he'd been the one to gift me with a membership to the club when I'd left the Navy, having sensed that I had the same dominant tendencies that he did. He was also one of the few people who had insight to my PTSD and knew just how therapeutic elements of BDSM could be.

As much as I loved and adored my mother, I couldn't deny that I was relieved that she wasn't in town this time. Nothing more awkward than running into your parents at the sex club they owned with Mac, my father's business partner—with Andrea as my date.

"Her and Stephanie are in talks with the new owners of the Playboy mansion to remodel some of the bedrooms with their fantasy designs," my father said, the pride in his voice unmistakable. "So, if that deal gets signed, she'll be busy in LA for quite some time."

My jaw nearly dropped at the prestigious opportunity. "Holy shit. That's impressive."

"Yeah. I'm proud of her." Dad clapped me affectionately on the shoulder, again. "I'm glad you're doing okay. And I'll make sure your mom doesn't bother you about your love life for at least another month. But you know her, she'd love to see you boys settled down with a good woman, and grandbabies in her future."

I almost choked at that and avoided my father's shrewd gaze. When people said I was intimidating, I always told them I learned it from him. But even though I was tempted to tell him about Andrea, I knew it wouldn't matter because nothing was going to come of it and I didn't need a lecture about potentially hurting her, and how that might affect the dynamic between my mother and Madison, since they worked together.

I knew my mom worried about me, too, and just wanted both of her sons to be happy. That was just her sweet, caring nature. She and dad were stupidly in love—it was kind of gross as a kid, but now that I was an adult I envied them their strong, loving relationship. Before all the shit had gone down in the Navy, I'd hoped that someday I'd find someone I still loved and was crazy about after all those years together, like my own mother and father.

Now I knew better. That wasn't in the cards for me.

I hated to disappoint my parents, but at least they respected my privacy enough not to really pry. And it was always good to see my dad again, even if it brought back that ache, to think of my parents' marriage and what I'd be missing out on. At least I had my family, and I knew they always had my back.

It wouldn't do to get greedy.

CHAPTER 13

Andrea

I frowned at the layout of designs spread on the conference table in front of me, contemplating what was missing from the overall message Brandon and I were trying to convey. While we mostly created social media campaigns these days, sometimes it did us good to print everything out and move it around, like we were arranging spreads on a magazine. Just staring at a computer screen for so long, you started to feel a little cross-eyed, and I'd found that changing the medium could jolt me out of an artistic rut.

"I think we made this one pop too much," I said, tapping a section that was brighter than the rest, my brows still furrowed. "It's too pink. We need to tone it down a bit. It's hurting my eyes."

Brandon laughed and made a note. "Sounds good. You know, I think that's the first time I've seen you wear a frown in weeks."

I looked up at him in surprise. "What do you mean?"

"Just that you seem really happy lately," he explained.

"Oh, do I?" I said, trying to downplay the fact that I truly was more relaxed these days.

Regular sex, the exact kind I'd always craved—along with Chase himself—was the reason. But opening up to Brandon—who I knew was still interested in me and had even hinted again about a date—wasn't something I felt comfortable doing.

He tipped his head, studying me too intently. "Yeah, you win the lottery and not tell me?"

He was clearly prying in a joking manner, trying to dig for more information that I wasn't willing to share. "No, just in a good mood lately, I guess," I said, injecting a light tone to my voice while keeping things strictly surface-level. "No reason to be in a bad mood. Everything's going well here, we haven't had any weird client emergencies or complaints..." I forced a casual shrug and added a laugh, one that sounded too loud in the quiet of the room.

Brandon leaned back against the edge of the conference table, arms crossed, gaze lingering. "I love your laugh," he said, his voice low and easy.

I stiffened, my smile faltering for half a second before I caught myself. The praise was probably meant to be harmless, but there was always this undercurrent with him. Always just a little too familiar. A little too personal.

"Well, I'm glad that you're feeling so happy, whatever the reason," he added when I didn't reply, his eyes on my face. "You deserve to always feel that way."

Ugh. There it was again—that tone. Like he was trying to stake a claim to something that had nothing to do with him. "That's sweet, thank you," I murmured, because what else could I say? I hated that I felt the need to feign appreciation just to avoid tension between us, but inside, I was cringing.

There was nothing romantic between us. Never had been, never would be. And I wished, so badly, that he'd quit with the compliments. The hopeful looks. The not-so-subtle hints. It wasn't flattering anymore; it was exhausting.

I wanted to tell him in a firm, uncompromising tone, *please stop*. But I couldn't, not without risking offending him. We worked together. One wrong word and suddenly I'm the "difficult" one. Or worse, I make things awkward for the whole team.

So instead, I returned to rearranging the printouts on the table—professional, polite, and internally begging for the moment to pass.

Thankfully, our senior PR manager called Brandon away to work on a different campaign for the afternoon, leaving me blissfully alone. Knowing I was going to meet Chase at the club tonight after work kept me in high spirits and by the time five o'clock rolled around, I was ready to leave the office, and my earlier encounter with Brandon, behind.

I'd brought a change of clothes with me so I didn't have to stop at home, and I slipped into the ladies room to swap out my more staid office attire of a pencil skirt and blouse for a figure flattering dress and seductive lingerie beneath. I replaced my sensible flats for sexy heels, and I made up my eyes with more dramatic liner and shadow. As the final touch, I swiped a daring red hue across my lips, just to tempt and tease Chase.

On my way, I texted as I headed out of the office building and to my car.

I'm already at the club. Don't keep me waiting long.

I grinned at the subtle, seductive threat in his words, knowing no matter how quickly I got there, he'd still insist it wasn't soon enough, and a delicious punishment would ensue. I couldn't wait.

When I arrived at my vehicle, I came to an abrupt stop, my heart sinking. My front left tire was completely flat, leading me to believe I'd most likely driven over a nail or something equally sharp on the way to work and the tire had spent all day deflating. *Shit.*

I called Chase first thing, knowing this was going to take a while to get fixed and I didn't want him to worry.

He answered immediately. "Hey, what's up?"

"I have a flat tire," I said, bummed that our night together was going to be delayed. "I need to call roadside assistance to change it out for me."

"Don't bother. I'll come and do it for you."

"What? No," I said, shaking my head, even though he couldn't see me. "You're all the way at the club."

"Which means I'll get there about the same time as roadside assistance would anyway," he said in a reasonable, but adamant tone. "Once I take care of

189

the tire, you can drive the car to the club with me behind you."

I bit my bottom lip. I really didn't want to encourage Chase's overbearing protective streak, but the idea of him coming to help me was actually really, really nice.

I sighed, and relented. "All right. But we're not making this a habit, you rescuing me like I'm a damsel in distress, okay?"

He chuckled. "I would *never* make the mistake of calling you a damsel in distress," Chase said, amusement in his tone. "I'll be there in about thirty minutes."

We hung up, and standing out in the parking lot made me feel like an idiot, especially with the Vegas sun beating down on me—yes, even at five thirty in the afternoon—so I waited in the lobby where there was air conditioning, sitting in the empty reception area.

I received a text from Chase letting me know he was a few minutes away from my work when I heard someone exit the elevator and glanced up to see who it was.

"What are you still doing here?" Brandon asked, looking surprised to see me there. "I thought you left a bit ago."

"I tried," I said, giving him a smile as he walked toward where I was sitting. "My tire has a flat."

"Oh, shit. That sucks." He shoved his hands into the front pockets of his slacks, tipping his head to the side. "Would you like me to give you a ride? Or —do you have a spare? I have a jack in my car, I could just—"

Telling myself he was just trying to be helpful, I kept my tone light, but resolute. "That's so kind of you, really, but my—" I caught myself before I said the word *boyfriend* "—friend is already on the way." I kept the gender of said "friend" vague.

A small little frown formed between his brows, and I didn't miss the way his gaze took in my dress, heels, and the sexier makeup I'd applied after work. "It's getting late, so I'll stay with you."

Again, I had to temper my tone. "I appreciate your concern, but that's really not necessary."

He sat down in the chair next to mine. "I insist."

What the hell did I say to that? The lot had mostly cleared out, as had the building, so I told myself he was just being a gentleman. To avoid small talk, I pulled out my phone and texted Violet to let her know what was going on. She'd just arrived at work for the night, but had about ten minutes free before she started her shift, so I chatted with her while I waited for Chase to arrive, which happened shortly thereafter.

Chase parked his car next to mine, and I stood up, and so did Brandon, walking with me outside. When he saw Chase get out of his vehicle, I visibly saw Brandon stiffen.

"So, that's why you're dressed the way you are," he said, finally addressing my attire, a derogatory tone to his voice. "I didn't know you were seeing anyone," he added, jumping to his own conclusions about Chase and sounding low key pissed off that I hadn't divulge this bit of information sooner.

Not that it was any of his business. "I prefer to keep my personal life and work life separate," I said, even though I didn't owe him any explanation. I stopped him before we walked any further, not missing the irritation in his gaze. "Brandon, I know you don't want me to say this, but seriously, you will find the right person for you. You're a great guy and I know someone is going to see that."

Before Brandon could respond, I headed toward Chase. I didn't know how much more obvious I could be without getting hurtful and I honestly didn't want it to come to that.

I grinned as I walked up to Chase, focusing on him instead, just as his own appreciative gaze took in my sexy outfit as I approached him. He looked drop dead gorgeous in a black dress shirt and black slacks—very much the alpha male. He'd rolled back the sleeves of his shirt, exposing those sexy forearms and the beautiful artwork inking his skin. His hair, I noticed, was a bit disheveled, as if he'd spent the entire drive shoving his fingers through the strands because of his worry.

"Hey, you," Chase said, gently laying a hand on my hip as he kissed me—a light touch of his lips, but clearly a deliberately possessive gesture—then glanced back at Brandon. "Who is that?"

Yeah, Chase didn't miss a thing. "A co-worker who didn't want me to wait for you by myself, since most everyone else is gone for the night."

Most people would have responded to that with something like, *oh, that's nice.* Not Chase. His gaze narrowed as he stared after Brandon as he walked to his own car, sizing up the other man, watching him the entire time—as if he was silently letting Brandon know that he was staking a claim on me, which I found secretly hot. Once Brandon was in his vehicle and pulling out of the parking lot, Chase finally returned his attention back to me.

His concerned gaze searched my face. "You okay?"

I tipped my head. "Yeah, why wouldn't I be?"

He gently tucked a strand of hair behind my ear, and I wondered if he realized how sweet and intimate that gesture was to me. "It's annoying as hell, getting a flat."

"It is," I agreed with a sigh. "I'd probably be more upset if I was late to something I couldn't change, like a concert. Thank you for being flexible."

"Of course. We have all night." Chase walked up to the back of my car, with me following behind. "Okay, let's get this tire switched out for you."

I popped the trunk so he could retrieve the jack, tire iron, and spare. He brought all the items to the front of my car, then squatted down to inspect my tire as he prepared to pull it off. I saw the moment his entire body froze, his jaw clenching tight as he grit out, "*fuck*."

"What?" I asked, confused by his response and peering closer from over his shoulder. "What's wrong?"

Chase glanced up at me, something sharp in his gaze, and then he rotated the tire a bit so I could see what had captured his attention. "Someone sliced the tire with a knife," he said quietly.

Shock rippled through me as I saw the long,

thin gash. There was no way that had happened from me driving over something like a nail.

"You couldn't have been driving the car when this happened. It's too deep and the tire would've deflated immediately. Someone did it while your vehicle was parked here."

Chase stood back up and looked around, inspecting the parking lot, then the building in front of us, his gaze locking on the security camera aimed our way. "Where's the security office? I want to inspect the video feed from today to see who the fuck did this."

The knowledge that someone had intentionally slashed my tire made me feel as though I was going to throw up. "I-I'll show you."

Chase accompanied me there, anger vibrating off of him as he asked to view the surveillance video, only to be told, sheepishly, by the security officer on duty that the security cameras trained on the parking lot had crapped out about a month ago and hadn't been replaced. The rage that burned in Chase's eyes when he realized there was no recorded evidence of who might have damaged my tire immediately wiped that stupid look off the other man's face.

"Your boss is going to be hearing from me," Chase said to him, his voice cold and cutting and furious. "This security system is going to get a major upgrade soon or I will personally make the lives of everyone in charge here a living hell."

Normally I would have pulled Chase aside to calm him down, but honestly, I was too busy trying not to cry. Someone had slashed my tire, but why? Who would want to strand me like that? Who would dislike me that much?

I wrapped my arms around my mid-section, remembering that feeling of being watched a few weeks ago and felt even more nauseous. Was someone really after me?

Obviously we weren't going to the club that night. Chase reported the incident to the cops and an officer came by to take our statements and took pictures of the deliberately damaged tire.

"They can't do anything right now," Chase said, his tone scathing. "But a paper trail is vital when the time comes to press charges."

He sounded so confident that he'd find whoever did this. I was less sure. I didn't have any enemies that I knew of—and it was even scarier to think that it could even be someone I didn't know, just some random person who'd selected me as their next victim. I'd watched enough crime documentaries with Violet to know these things occurred...but you always thought they happened to someone else.

I had forgotten that we're all 'someone else' to someone else.

I stood off to the side as Chase changed the tire once the police officer left. I wasn't sure what to do now. Just go home, I supposed, but when I thought about doing that, I remembered that feeling I'd had of being watched outside of our place.

A horrible shiver crept down my spine. I didn't know what to do with this emotion—this feeling that I wasn't safe.

"We're heading to your place to pack a bag," Chase said once he'd swapped out the tire and put everything else away in the trunk.

I stared at him in confusion. "Pack a bag? For what?"

He jammed his hands on his hips. "First you tell me that you think you're being watched and followed, and now this. You're staying with me until we figure out what the fuck is going on, and that is *not* up for debate."

His tone brook no argument, and for once I had no desire to disagree. Relief swept over me because I realized I wasn't alone in this situation. I had someone who wanted to protect me, and who had the skills to do so. I had no doubt that Violet would beat the shit out of someone in a heartbeat for me but she wasn't used to dealing with this kind of unknown threat. Chase was an expert. This was literally his job.

And I trusted him with my life.

CHAPTER 14

Chase

I could barely stop myself from shaking with rage when I saw what someone had done to Andrea's tire. Intentionally. Deliberately.

Worse than that, I couldn't stop the sick feeling that churned in the pit of my stomach as worst case scenarios swirled through my brain—like someone lying in wait to grab her in broad daylight in a parking lot. Maybe that hadn't been their intention. Maybe they were just trying to scare her...but if they *had* been planning something more nefarious and had been foiled only because she'd called me and went back inside the building to wait for me instead of remaining by her car...*fuck.*

The useless security cameras made me want to strangle someone. If they'd had footage then I could have seen the perpetrator.

I questioned if anyone had come in asking about the security system lately, but the guard had no clue. That also made me uneasy. This person, whoever they were, must have figured out the cameras weren't operating. Either that, or he'd known that working or not the cameras possibly had a blind spot where Andrea's car was. None of it sat well with my gut instinct, that someone might have been planning this for a while and this wasn't a random act of violence.

And if they knew where Andrea worked, then chances were they knew where she lived, too. Following her home at any point was easy enough to do. Violet wouldn't be safe at their place, either, if someone found their way inside for Andrea and her sister ended up being collateral damage. I'd make sure there was security out in front of their place for Violet, but Andrea was staying with me, so I could know and see for myself that she was unharmed.

As soon as she realized that she'd been targeted, I'd seen the unmistakable fear lurking in her eyes, and I'd do anything to ease her anxiety and trepidation. I wanted her to feel safe and protected —always.

I hated that this situation was out of my control. All I wanted to do was find this mysterious person and put hands on them, make sure that they never so much as laid eyes on Andrea again—*oh*.

That was the queasy feeling in my stomach, I realized. Complete and total helplessness. I felt helpless to protect Andrea, unable to fight back against someone who operated from the shadows like this.

Andrea put her hand on my chest, her touch gentle and soothing. "Chase, please—breathe for me, could you?"

I realized I wasn't breathing properly, my jaw clenched and my hands balled into fists at my sides. I forced myself to relax, to refocus on the woman in front of me. The fear in Andrea's eyes took on a new shape...she wasn't so much scared for herself. She was worried for *me*.

"I'll stay with you for a bit while we get this sorted out," Andrea said, trying to calm me. "If that will help you feel better."

"I want you to be safe," I gritted out. That was the only thing that would give me any peace of mind.

Andrea nodded. "All right, then."

I followed her back to her place so she could pack. When we arrived, Andrea called Violet and left her a voicemail explaining everything so Violet wouldn't be surprised that some of Andrea's things were gone. By the time Violet got home from work later that night, I'd have a security detail sitting outside of the condo, keeping an eye on the place.

While Andrea gathered her clothes and toiletries, I inspected the entire house and walked around the perimeter, then checked out the front area, inspecting the neighborhood. Andrea had said she'd felt someone watching her one night. I doubted that was the only night that person had been there—it was probably just the only time she'd felt their presence.

I didn't see anything suspicious, but I did note that it seemed a lot of Andrea's neighbors were still out for the evening, no cars in parking spots. On the one hand this could be a good thing if I set up a security camera. It would be easy to spot if someone came around who shouldn't be there. On the other hand if everyone worked long or odd hours then there wouldn't be any witnesses to notice something strange.

I arrived back at Andrea's and waited in the living room. It was a small place, but homey. There were art prints up on the walls—Monet and Van Gogh, but then also some vibrant, tattoo-like designs of animals and abstract landscapes that seemed to be by independent artists.

Andrea vs Violet's tastes, clearly.

They'd painted the walls a nice dark teal color that actually would look good on my walls in my condo. I'd left everything white the way it had been when I moved in. I didn't have time to decorate and I didn't really care to. There wasn't a point when it was just me. But I had to admit that I enjoyed this splash of color.

There was a bookshelf with various novels. The dark romances were obviously Andrea's. In front of the books were framed photographs of Andrea and Violet, a few that seemed to be Violet in childhood with a younger boy, and then a few of Andrea with her sister, Madison.

I spied a picture of Andrea that looked from around the time I'd first met her. I'd been convinced she was too young and naïve for me back then, and I stood by that now, looking at the photo. But I'd wanted her, no matter how bad of an idea it would've been.

There was a thump in the bedroom and Andrea cursed at her luggage, and I grinned. I was actually glad I'd waited to give in to the attraction between us. Andrea was now able to handle me and my darker desires in a way I'd never expected. We complimented one another in a way I didn't think we would have if I'd given into temptation before.

Andrea came out with her luggage, rolling it on wheels. "Okay, I think that's everything."

I gave her a crooked grin. "It's not like we're going overseas. If you need anything else, we can come back."

"We?" Andrea gave me a shrewd look.

"I'm not letting you spend time here alone until I figure out who is trying to scare you," I said, a growl entering my voice. "I think it's best that I drive you to and from work, as well."

Andrea held up a hand. "Okay, wait. You are *not* going to drop everything to be my escort. You have actual work, paying clients—"

"And your life is in danger." I jammed my hands on my hips. "You think I'm going to take that lightly?"

"Chase." Andrea left her luggage to walk toward me, then placed her hands on my shoulders. "I need you to listen to me and not take this the wrong way, all right? You are freaking out. I'll admit I'm scared, too. But you are—you look like you're going to do something stupid. It's like you're—I don't even know." Unable to find the right word, she shook her head.

Unhinged? I wanted to supply for her. Because yeah, a part of me definitely felt that way when it came to her safety.

I took a deep breath. Then another.

"I admit I might be...too cautious." I wasn't going to say *freaking out,* even if Andrea might be right about that. I wasn't going to give her any excuse not to take this seriously, even if I might have been overreacting. I wouldn't let her underreact. I wouldn't let her think everything was fine. I wouldn't let her brush me off, I wouldn't lose her like—

This isn't like that. Andrea wasn't a soldier in war, thank God, and I wasn't going to go down that road with her. I wouldn't let myself. She was right, I was spiraling because of my fears. I had to get a hold of myself.

"But if I'm so cautious," I continued, forcing myself to remain calm, and reasonable, "it's because I understand how quickly these things can escalate. But I also understand why you might think we don't have to resort to DEFCON 4 yet. But it's the way I operate and I need you to take what I say seriously, because if you don't, by the time you realize that your life truly is in danger, it might be too late. I refuse to take that chance with you."

Andrea's expression softened, her hands sliding down to rest on my chest. "I do take it seriously. I'm sorry if I've made you think I don't. You do make me feel safe and I—I really respect your opinions on this. I just don't want you so—so worked up, that's all." She frowned up at me in concern.

I wanted to tell her that I wasn't worked up, but that would've been a laughable lie. I kept my mouth shut.

Andrea sighed. "Look, I'll stay with you. And I'll even let you drive me to and from work if that's what you insist on doing. But only for a week. If nothing's happened for the next week, then will you consider loosening up a bit? Like letting me drive to work by myself and come back home? I can't live with you indefinitely."

I forced myself to nod and agree, because what she was asking for wasn't unreasonable. By the time a week passed I hoped to have caught the fucker who was doing this to her, and the fact that she gave in at all felt like a victory.

"I can do that," I said out loud, when I realized Andrea was waiting for a verbal response.

Andrea smiled at me, looking as relieved as I felt.

CHAPTER 15

Chase

I'd never had a woman in my home before, not really. I had women over, obviously, but they'd never spent the night and they definitely hadn't stayed for days, so having Andrea in my space was new territory for me.

I put Andrea in the spare room that she had, ironically, run into the other night when I was chasing her. The idea of her sharing my bed with me on a nightly basis made my palms sweat. Not because I didn't want it, but because I wanted it too damn much. I wanted to be able to wake up and see her safe next to me, to feel her presence even in my sleep.

That kind of shit was dangerous. I was already in over my head as it was.

Andrea didn't seem upset with me setting her up to sleep in the spare room. I'd had some women in the past who'd hoped for more from me in spite of my clarity from the beginning that it would only ever be sex, but Andrea just thanked me for the extra towels for her bathroom and remarked on how comfortable the mattress was.

It was nice, to have someone who respected our relationship and my boundaries.

Knowing she was under my roof, I slept better than I anticipated. I did wake up twice and stepped out into the hall, briefly peering into the guest bedroom. Both times Andrea was sleeping soundly, curled up on her side almost like a cat, her dark hair spread out on the pillow behind her.

When I woke up in the morning, it was to the smell of bacon frying.

Usually I was up pretty early, but waking up twice—and all the stress from yesterday—must have exhausted me more than I'd realized, because when I glanced at the time on my phone I saw that I'd slept in by an hour. I never set an alarm, never had to after leaving the military, just naturally waking up the way I had when on tour. Same time every day like clockwork until it was ingrained into me.

I got up and resisted the immediate temptation to look for Andrea, instead hopping quickly into the shower. When I stepped out, I felt more refreshed, more ready to face whatever would be going on in my kitchen.

Andrea was already dressed for work, although she wasn't wearing makeup yet and her hair was still damp from her own shower. She was wearing a light green dress, cute but still office-appropriate, and in the warm light coming in through the floor-to-ceiling windows behind her...

She looked so fucking beautiful, it made me forget to breathe.

Andrea looked up and smiled at me, and my heart tried to stage a jailbreak from my ribs.

"Hey, you!" she exclaimed, startled to see me. "I thought you'd be up way earlier than I was. Lifting weights or working out, or something."

I tipped my head to the side. "You found the home gym, huh?"

"I don't know why I'm surprised you have one." Andrea served up bacon and eggs onto a plate. "Hope you don't mind the basics for breakfast."

"No, this is great, you really didn't have to." I

actually couldn't remember the last time I'd really cooked for myself. I was capable of doing so, but with it being just me, it was easier to grab something on the way to work. And for dinner, I ordered takeout all the time from one of the many delicious restaurants Vegas was known for. It was a city full to bursting with the best of those, after all.

"You're letting me stay here, so it's the least I can do as a guest. I cook for Violet all the time. She works such weird hours and I think she once burned water." Andrea handed me the plate. "Coffee's brewing. You know you've got a big gym downstairs in your building that you could use, right?"

"I don't like working out around other people." Lifting weights was meditative for me. Sometimes I did it on nights I couldn't sleep to clear my mind. I didn't want other people around for that.

Andrea shrugged and let the subject drop, pouring coffee for herself and for me. She added an unholy amount of sugar to hers.

"No coffee beans were harmed in the making of this drink, so why are you killing the taste with all that sugar?" I asked.

She flipped me off but was fighting a playful

smile. "Shush. Just because you're a masochist who likes it black…"

I flashed her a wicked grin after taking a sip of the dark brew. "What can I say, I love pain."

"No, you don't get to make this sexy," she said, pursing her lips at me in a way I found adorable. "Taking your coffee black doesn't make you a fun person to fuck. It just makes you a sad and self-loathing heathen."

I almost snorted my coffee out my nose laughing.

It felt unusually natural to have her puttering around my kitchen. Andrea acted comfortable in it, like she belonged there, and I couldn't deny that I enjoyed her presence, and even our easy, flirtatious banter.

I stared at her, plate in my hand, for a few seconds too long before I realized what the hell I was doing and went to sit down at the kitchen table.

We ate breakfast quickly. We didn't have a lot of time to talk since she needed to finish getting ready for work, but it wasn't the kind of awkward silence that needed to be filled with idle conversation. It was nice, actually. One of the things I appreciated about my friends, including my brother, was how they could chat and joke and laugh, filling my life with joy even if I was in a quiet mood, which was most of the time. They distracted me from the dark places in my head.

It was unexpectedly nice to be with a woman that I could just sit in comfortable silence with. No need for talking to fill the space. Just enjoying the morning and each other's presence.

Shit. I was getting in way over my head with Andrea, yet I couldn't stop those feelings stirring to life inside of me.

I drove Andrea to work and she didn't make a single snarky comment about my need to do so. As much as I loved her sass, I appreciated her taking this situation seriously.

We pulled up in front of her office, right at the front door. I didn't want her even walking through the parking lot on her own. The sun was out and it was a bright morning, but I wasn't about to take any chances with her safety.

"Thanks for the ride." Andrea smiled at me and leaned over, placing a soft kiss on my lips before I realized her intent. "I get off at five, so don't be late. I'll be starving."

She winked at me, playful as ever, and hopped out of the car. I watched her head into the building and resisted the urge to bang my head against the steering wheel.

Jesus Christ. I was so fucking sunk.

Annoyed with myself, I drove off to work. I parked, stepped out of the vehicle, but was only just closing the car door when the shot rang out.

On instinct, I dropped to the ground like a stone, my body laid out tight and flat to the concrete, trying to make myself as small a target as possible with the car as a shield. My heart hammered so hard in my chest I thought it would burst free.

I sucked in a breath, but the scent of blood and sand was all I could smell, the memory still so fresh in my mind. A gunshot—I tried to pinpoint the direction. Where had it come from? Who was shooting at—

It's not a gunshot. That initial panic cleared as I realized it had been a car backfiring. But telling my body this information didn't matter. There was still blood and sand in my nose. I couldn't inhale properly, the sand in my lungs choking me, the sound in my ears still ringing...

I attempted to breathe. In and out. I desperately tried to claw my way out of the past so I could remember the countless breathing exercises I'd learned over the years when something triggered my PTSD. My therapist told me that the trauma I'd endured in the military wasn't just something I'd magically heal from. And my response to high frequency sounds—like this one, or gunshot or fireworks—would never be the same as a person who'd never experienced what I had.

"Chase?"

My brother's voice sounded like it came from incredibly far away, echoing in my head as if I were in a tunnel. I pushed my body back up so I was crouched beside the car and raised my head, which felt like it weighed a ton.

"Chase, hey." Austin hunkered down to my level in front of me. "It's me, Austin."

Relief swept through me as I tried to pull his face into focus. My reaction to a car backfiring had been embarrassing enough, but I was grateful that it was Austin who'd witnessed the episode, and not someone else. He'd been with me one other time when the same thing had occurred and knew how to handle me, and the situation. Thank God it hadn't happened in front of Andrea.

"Can I touch you?" he asked, aware that any quick movement, if my mind wasn't clear yet, could make things worse, instead of better.

I nodded, realizing I was shaking all over. I hated this, I hated it more than anything, my mind and body in a panic that I couldn't control or escape, a prisoner in my own head. It was fucking mortifying.

Austin took me gently by the arm and helped me up to standing, then put a hand on the small of my back to walk me over to a nearby bench. "Well, this sure is a fun start to the day, huh?"

His tone was casual, relaxed—joking even—but not like he expected me to reply. Considering what a smart-ass my brother was the majority of the time, he surprised me by being calm and level-headed when it truly mattered the most.

Once we sat down, he continued more seriously. "Can you do me a favor, give me five things you can see?"

I despised grounding techniques, but I'd learned that they did help to clear the fog from my brain after this kind of incident, diverting my attention from the anxiety still lingering inside of me.

"The cars," I gritted out. "You. The trees along the edge of the parking lot. The building with the firm in it. Some of the casinos down the strip."

"Great, that's great."

On a regular basis, Austin could drive me nuts, but he had a way of praising me during my panic attack that didn't make me bristle, but relaxed me instead.

"Four things you can hear?" he asked.

I briefly closed my eyes to concentrate on the sounds around us. "The cars, the birds, the wind, and you."

"Three things you can touch?"

"The bench, your shirt, my feet on the ground," I replied, feeling my anxiety easing.

"Two things you can smell?"

"Car exhaust and Mexican food." There was some kind of taco truck down the street selling breakfast burritos, most likely.

"And one thing you can taste?"

"Bacon." It lingered in my mouth—and I realized that I tasted my breakfast, and not blood.

"That was really good." Austin glanced down at my chest, like he had to make sure I was still breathing.

"My eyes are up here," I joked dryly.

My brother smirked at me, relief in his eyes. "If you're feeling well enough to crack jokes, that's a good sign." Austin put his hand on my shoulder. "Keep breathing for me, okay? And don't give me that look."

That look of annoyance, but it was mostly directed at myself. I slumped back against the bench. My panic attack might've been over but my heart was still racing.

"I'm sorry," I croaked out, embarrassment creeping in now that I felt more grounded. "You shouldn't have had to deal with this shit."

Austin frowned. "It's no big deal. Nobody else saw, and I'm your brother. I'm glad I was around to help you."

I nodded. My stomach still felt shaky.

"Are you steady enough to walk into the office and get some water from the break room?" Austin asked. "Maybe splash some water on your face in the bathroom? Nobody'll notice a thing."

Yeah. Nobody would notice. I was good at hiding my inner turmoil, most of the time. But then something like this would happen—again, I was grateful that Andrea hadn't witnessed my extreme reaction to a car backfiring.

I hated feeling weak, so out of control. Paralyzed, even. The idea of Andrea seeing me like this, someone she relied on to protect her so easily triggered...it was possibly the worst thing I could imagine.

CHAPTER 16

Andrea

I ordered my lunch from Grubhub, instead of leaving work to go out and get something to eat. I knew that was a bit paranoid of me after all that I'd lectured Chase, but I knew in my heart that even if he was being overly protective, he was right. Something was wrong. I wasn't going to take the chance that walking down the street to grab a sandwich was what doomed me.

When I received the text that my order had arrived I went downstairs to retrieve it. The security guy at the lobby desk smiled tentatively. He must've heard about the dressing down Chase had given his co-worker yesterday.

"Got your things right here, Andrea," he said.

I frowned. "Things?"

"Your food and the flowers."

Flowers? I turned and there in a lovely crystal vase was a bouquet of lilies. There was a florist card tucked in the foliage that only said *for Andrea*. No name of who'd sent them, no other note. Chase didn't strike me as a hearts and flowers type of guy, and even so he would have signed the card had he sent them to me.

A chill slithered down my spine. It could be a total fluke, but...I had one single tattoo, on my shoulder, that I had gotten in memory of my mother. It was three lilies tied together by a ribbon, representing my mom, Madison, and me. Lilies had been my mom's favorite flower.

It could be a coincidence but...I couldn't help but feel the choice had been deliberate. Which meant that whoever had sent me these flowers knew me well enough to have noticed my tattoo, and knew about it. That didn't narrow down the list *too* much since it could be seen whenever I wore a dress or a top that revealed my shoulders... but it was still narrowing it down enough that it made my stomach churn. Of course, my first thought went to Heath, who'd seen the tattoo up close and personal many times.

"Thank you," I said to the guard, gathering up my delivery bag and the vase.

I took the flowers up to my desk and hid them underneath, near my feet, so nobody could see them and question me about my "admirer. I was glad it was lunch time so almost everyone else was in the break room or had run out to get their own meal.

It was a struggle to eat my lunch, but I made myself. I knew if I didn't I'd just be sick with nerves *and* sick with hunger later.

When Chase arrived to pick me up after work, I told him to come up to my office and get me.

"Everything okay?" he asked, concern etching his features as he walked up to my desk.

He looked so handsome, but more than that, he looked steady. Alert. Prepared. Someone who would never let me get hurt. I clung to that. "I got these today."

I showed him the flowers and unsigned card, and mentioned the correlation to my lily tattoo.

Chase's jaw clenched. "I agree, this is most likely someone who knows you pretty well, rather than a random stalker, and is probably from the person who slashed your tire."

"It could be someone who heard about the tire and wanted to make me feel better," I said, clearly grasping at straws so I didn't have to think about the worst case scenario.

He arched a dubious brow. "If it was, they would've said so in the note."

I knew he was right. I just didn't want to entertain the idea that this person was escalating. The difference between the slashed tire and the flowers disconcerted me, too. It was like hot and cold. The type of person who would give you a ton of affection one moment, love bomb you, and then whip around and hurt you in some way.

"Let me take the flowers, and I'll check out the florist, see what I can find," Chase said, picking up the vase so I didn't have to carry it to the car. "I'll drop you back at my place on the way, so you don't have to deal with it."

I nodded, relieved and grateful. "Thank you." It felt like there was a net closing in around me but I couldn't see where it was, or who was pulling it tight to trap me.

The drive to Chase's condo was quiet. He made sure I was settled before he left to do his investigating, and I realized I was more anxious than I cared to admit. I needed something to take my mind off things while he was gone.

I changed out of my work attire and into a pair of yoga pants and a tank top, and since I had this big place with a glorious kitchen all to myself, I came up with an idea. Chase seemed to enjoy the breakfast I made for him this morning, so why not make us dinner? When I went to throw some stuff away in his kitchen trash, I'd seen nothing but takeout boxes, and his fridge and freezer had only a few ready-made meals.

I scoured his pantry, surprised to find an unopened box of penne pasta, canned chicken breast, and cream of chicken soup, along with frozen vegetables in his freezer, and shredded cheese in the fridge. Enough to make a chicken noodle casserole.

Growing up as poor as we'd been, my sister and I had learned to take the most basic of ingredients and make them into something savory and edible. In fact, it had become a game between us...who could create the cheapest, best tasting meal with the least ingredients. This casserole had been one of our favorites. It wasn't anything fancy, but it was the equivalent of comfort food, which I suspected both Chase and I could use right now.

Pleased with my plan, I boiled the pasta, then mixed everything else together and layered it into a metal pan I'd found in one of the lower cupboards, then popped it into the oven, timed for forty-five minutes.

Unfortunately, I hadn't expected that Chase's fancy kitchen with all the weird buttons on the appliances would have some surprises in store for me. Everything was so sleek in black and chrome, all the buttons activated by touch rather than being physical buttons and dials like I was used to. I didn't suspect anything was wrong, though, not until I smelled something burning way, *way* too soon and realized I'd turned on the broiler instead of the oven.

"Shit!" I yelled, grabbing a magazine about muscle cars from the coffee table in the living room and waving it back and forth in the kitchen to disperse the smoke so that the ceiling alarm wouldn't go off.

I heard the front door open, then Chase call out, "Uh, Andrea?"

"Don't worry, nobody's dead!" I assured him, trying to make light of the situation.

Grabbing two mitts, I yanked open the oven and retrieved the casserole, now blackened and burnt to a crisp on top—completely unsalvageable. A lump formed in my throat and I realized with horror I was in danger of crying.

"It's just the chicken noodle casserole I was making for dinner."

I thought Chase would be annoyed with me—I did just burn something in his oven and his place now reeked of smoke—but instead he laughed and went to open the windows to help clear out the awful smell.

"Sorry, the damn contraption's more complicated than it should be, I know," he said, seemingly unconcerned. "I barely use the oven. I probably would burn something too."

"I turned on the broiler rather than the oven," I said, unable to keep the distress out of my voice. "I'm so sorry, I hope the pan isn't ruined." The edges were singed with sauce and cheese.

"If it is then I can buy another pan, not that I can recall when or if I'd ever even used *that* one." Chase leaned against the counter as I put the pan in the sink. "I'm sorry to tell you this but the florist was a dead end. The order was placed online with their website and paid for by a gift card."

I nodded, prying the casserole—which was charred through a couple of layers—out of the pan and throwing it into the trash. My stomach twisted at the thought of wasting so much food. My vision blurred and I did my best to swallow back my dismay.

"I'm not going to lie to you," Chase continued, completely unaware of how upset I was. "It's concerning that it was done this way. It means this person is smart enough to know that someone might try and track them through their credit cards, or check to see if the florist has video surveillance in their shop. And it also means the person has probably done this, or something like it, before. Enough to be aware of some of the pitfalls."

I nodded again, because my throat was too tight to speak. I knew I should care about what he'd discovered, and I did, but I was too busy caring about this stupid casserole. I could probably salvage the metal pan if I left it to soak…but, fuck, all that food wasted…

Chase laid a hand on my arm. "Hey, Andrea. Look at me?"

Shit. I couldn't. I knew if I did I would do something embarrassing like cry.

Chase's other hand came up to grasp my chin and gently lift my face up to his. I couldn't help it, my vision swam with more tears. The stress and fear of everything going on right now in my life, now compounded by this…

"Whoa, hey, it's okay. I'll keep you safe," Chase

promised, misinterpreting my reaction. "Nobody will hurt you. I promise."

I shook my head. "I'm—it's—" I gestured uselessly at the inedible casserole in the trash.

Chase frowned. "The food?" He sounded completely confused.

"I'm sorry." I wiped at my cheeks as tears fell and tried to explain. "I know it's probably ridiculous to you, but we never had enough money growing up. Madison had to work her ass off for us to afford groceries and the idea of wasting food, because I was so careless, is just—"

"Hey, hey, it's okay." Chase tugged me against his chest and held me tight.

I sank against him and felt how solid he was. His warm, strong arms around me was grounding, like a weighted blanket.

His hand gently stroked over my hair. "You don't need to apologize."

I gave a harsh, wobbly laugh and pulled back just enough to look up at his face. "You've been in literal war and I'm traumatized over a burnt casserole."

There was a pause and I saw a flicker of understanding in his eyes before he said, "I get it. Trauma comes in all forms. You never knew where your next meal was coming from. You couldn't afford to waste food. Madison's...what, five years older? So you were just a kid. That's traumatizing, Andrea. You don't need to apologize for things in your past that affect you even now."

I stepped back, wiping my eyes, but Chase guided me to sit down on the couch in the living area, then went to the kitchen to get me a glass of water while I tried to breathe through my upsetting emotions and calm down, knowing I wouldn't have reacted like this if I was at home with Violet. It was just—I didn't know if Chase would laugh it off or be upset and that apparently sparked the rest of my spiral.

Chase sat down next to me and handed me the water, and I took a few sips.

"Tell me more about your father," he said, surprising me.

I blinked at him since that was the last thing I expected him to say, or even talk about. "You really want to know?"

His dark eyes held mine. "I wouldn't have asked if I didn't."

His expression was earnest, telling me he wasn't inquiring just out of obligation. His interest was genuine.

I set the glass on the coffee table in front of me

and gathered my thoughts. "Dad wasn't the best husband," I said, giving Chase a sad smile, because I knew what great parents he had and I envied him that. "Madison remembers more about it than I do, before Mom died, I mean. Obviously Violet happened, so dad was far from perfect. But after Mom died it was like… I don't know. When I was a kid I told myself it was grief, that's why he went off the rails, with all the gambling and drinking and debt. But now I think it was Mom who kept him on the straight and narrow. Made sure his paychecks went towards our bills instead of something else."

I swallowed hard, and continued. "After she passed, Dad started drinking heavily and gambling constantly. We were always in debt. We didn't usually know where our next meal would come from. I was always scared we'd lose our home. The moment Madison turned eighteen, she fought for custody of me. I—I didn't understand, at the time, how hard that must've been for her to fight in the legal system like that. We were so lucky we had a compassionate lawyer and Madison was granted guardianship of me. From then on money was steady because she worked several jobs to keep food on the table and a roof over our heads, but it was still tight."

"And you couldn't afford to waste any of it," Chase said slowly.

I nodded and my heart gave a little jolt in my chest when Chase took my hand in his, holding it so affectionately. "But dad wasn't done with us. He opened credit cards and lines of credit in both of our names and plunged us both into serious debt, something we didn't discover until he'd died and we started getting notified by collection agencies. It was awful, knowing we had this huge debt hanging over us that wasn't even ours, and no way to pay it off."

Chase looked furious. "I can see why something like that would be triggering."

"We got lucky though...actually, *Madison* got lucky when she met Rick," I said, feeling my cheeks warm a bit as I remembered the unconventional way my sister had opted to make extra money. "She, umm, turned to escorting to pay those bills. Rick was the first man she met, and he offered her an insane amount of money to, well...be his date for a week. It was enough for us to pay off the debt."

A crooked smile tipped up the corners of Chase's mouth, reflecting amusement at the way I'd delicately described my sister's situation. "And look at how well that turned out."

"Ricks a great guy, and perfect for my sister," I said, happy that Madison had someone who absolutely adored her. "He honestly changed our lives for the better, but how I grew up, what our father did to us..."

Chase gently squeezed my hand. "Andrea, listen to me. I can't undo the years of pain that you went through. Though God knows I fuckin' wish I could. But I promise you, you are never going to go without anything you need ever again. Food, money, a place to live, whatever it is, I'll always take care of you. You will never, ever, have to go without. I swear it."

My mouth fell open in shock.

Chase flushed slightly, as if he belatedly realized how overly protective his words sounded. He cleared his throat. "I'm sorry. You're an independent adult. I just want you to know that you're not alone and you can turn to me if you ever need anything at all."

Chase sounded so earnest and sincere, like the idea of me being hurt caused him pain too. And I knew he'd take care of me, especially right now, with an unknown threat hanging over me. He had the smarts and skills to protect me, and the money and stability to provide for me until he caught whoever was stalking me. But I wouldn't ever have thought he'd openly offer me something like that. Because really, at the end of the day we were just fuckbuddies.

But *this* didn't feel like I was just his side piece. *This* felt like so much more.

Chase gently brushed his hand against my cheek for a moment before standing up, diffusing that intimate moment between us. "I'll order us some pizza. We can just have a quiet night in, put on a movie, forget about the day. How's that sound?"

"Sounds great." I smiled at him, foolishly wishing he meant all of those previous words the way I wanted him to—not as a protector or provider, not just some temporary shelter from the storm—but as a man who *saw me, chose me,* and might actually stay when it was over.

But Chase Noble didn't do forever. Whatever this was between us—hot and tangled and addictive—it wasn't supposed to come with promises or tenderness.

And yet, here he was, providing both.

It would be so easy to take what he was offering and pretend it was enough, but I knew myself. I was already falling for him—*hard*—and when Chase eventually walked away, it was going to hurt like hell. Because no matter how safe his promises sounded, I couldn't deny the truth.

I wanted all of him.

And I was terrified I'd never be enough to make him stay.

CHAPTER 17

Chase

*I*t only took a few days of living with Andrea for us to establish a routine.

That second night, Andrea fell asleep on the couch cuddled against me while we watched a movie. At first, I carried her to the guest room again, but when I tried to put her down, she'd given me the most unhappy, disappointed look on her face and I hadn't had the heart to abandon her. She'd had such a hard day—her stalker making their presence known again and then burning the casserole, drudging up those terrible memories— and I just couldn't bring myself to leave her alone.

I took her to my bed instead and held her, because I'd had a fucking rough day, too, and needed that comfort just as much.

Three days later and it all just felt natural. And comfortable. Like this was where Andrea belonged...in my bed. In my life.

I'd never had any kind of relationship like this with a woman before. Andrea was there in the morning, smiling at me, and at night we tended to just have a quiet evening in, watching movies or playing two-person board games or reading together on the sofa. I think I surprised her by being someone who preferred that kind of low key solitude, like the fact that I was into BDSM meant I also was into skydiving every single weekend and clubbing. And sure, I did enjoy a fun adrenaline rush as much as the next person, but I was also in my thirties with a demanding job, and the last thing Andrea needed right now was even more excitement.

Even though I'd assured her that I could buy a new casserole pan and there was no harm done to the oven, and I could definitely afford more pasta and cheese, Andrea still seemed to want to make it up to me, cooking dinner the last few nights. I hadn't had something homemade in ages, and I appreciated the effort because everything she made was delicious. But I also didn't want her thinking she had to make my meals, because she was a guest in my home.

If I was being honest with myself, she didn't feel like a guest. She felt like she belonged here just as much as I did.

And that thought process was incredibly dangerous.

It would've been easier to push the situation out of my mind if I'd had a serious assignment to distract me, but my current one was babysitting Naomi Starr, an A-list actress who was in Vegas for a movie premiere, and I was the unlucky guy who'd been tasked as her security detail for the past few days. Today—which she'd had off from making any appearances—she'd spent shopping at all the high end luxury stores. Nothing going on threat-wise, just me having to make sure that paparazzi and zealous fans didn't encroach on her personal space while she just wanted to exist like a normal person. But it was a dull, boring, mind-numbing task, which meant I had too much time to think about Andrea, and our situation.

When I was able to head back into the office later that day, I stopped by the tech department to check in with Tate, our IT guy for the most part. I'd given him all the information Andrea had provided to me about her ex-boyfriend, Heath, so Tate could run a check on the other man and see if there was any evidence of him possibly tampering with her tire, or sending her the flowers.

"Anything to report?" I asked him, hoping like hell he'd discovered something incriminating.

"Still searching," he said, his eyes on the computer screen in front of him, while I stood on the other side of his desk. "So far, I haven't been able to find anything concrete. I mean, I agree with you it's weird that Heath went out of his way to go to the grocery store he knows Andrea uses, but I haven't noticed anything on his social media or his credit card purchases that raises a red flag. I thought it would be clever of him to buy himself the gift card for the florist say, a month ago, and then use the gift card for the flowers now, but he hasn't bought anything from any florist, gift card or otherwise."

I jammed my hand through my hair in frustration. "Maybe he somehow paid cash."

"Which we both know is impossible to trace," Tate said, finally reclining back in his chair and glancing at me.

I nodded. Heath was my most likely suspect right now. He'd already expressed an interest in getting back together with Andrea and I thought the grocery store run-in was concerning. And, he had intimate knowledge of her Lily tattoo.

Sure, it might've been just low-level creepy to try and stage a natural meet-cute, to prompt Andrea to think about them as a couple again and feeling like it was fate. It was alarming how many times people would do that in real life, attempting to craft their own rom-com moment with the object of their affection instead of just being an adult and texting or calling to ask the person out.

Even though Heath was number one on the list, I also hadn't ruled out the possibility that this was some random person who'd fixated on Andrea after meeting her once or seeing her somewhere— it did happen, unfortunately—but overwhelmingly the stalker, the abuser, the attacker, was someone the victim knew personally.

"I'll keep digging whenever I have the chance," Tate said, pulling me out of my thoughts.

"Thank you." Andrea wasn't a paying customer, and Tate was doing me a huge favor by looking into Heath for me, and I appreciated his time.

I felt restless and wound tight as I drove to Andrea's work to pick her up. It hadn't yet been a week so she was still letting me drive her to and from work, but if nothing else happened in that time, I knew she'd insist on more independence. I didn't want to keep her on a leash, at least not outside of the bedroom, but I couldn't shake the feeling the danger wasn't over. Those flowers were proof enough, even though I wasn't sure Andrea would agree, they were sufficient to prolong my chauffeuring duties.

I parked up in front of her building and Andrea came out, smiling at me as she made her way to the car. She was wearing a tan, form fitting skirt that ended just above the knee, and a white blouse that buttoned up the front, and low heeled sandals. There was nothing overtly sexy about the outfit— it was actually quite modest—but I'd seen the pale pink bra and panty set she'd put on that morning. My dick twitched in my pants when I recalled thinking about bending her over the nearest flat surface, hiking that skirt up to her hips, and fucking her from behind before I dropped her off at work, so she'd feel me for the rest of the day.

Alas, we'd been running late, but that erotic fantasy flooded my mind again. That tension inside of me shifted, and I suddenly felt very keyed up, in an entirely different way.

Since moving Andrea into my condo, we hadn't messed around at all, despite sleeping in the same bed. I didn't want Andrea to feel like she had to have sex with me just because she was staying at my place, and I didn't want to pressure her to play when she was going through this ordeal. But it had been a while since we'd done anything fun and we'd originally planned to go to the club together when we found her tire slashed...

An idea formed, and it made me wonder just how daring Andrea was willing to be.

She slid into the car, still grinning at me. "Hey, you. Good day?"

"Boring," I admitted. "Yours?"

"Boring, as well." Andrea laughed. "That's a good thing, right?"

"It is." At least under these circumstances.

Once she had her seatbelt secured, I pulled away from the curb and brought up *part* of my idea to her. "I was actually wondering...I've been wanting to touch up the shading on one of my tattoos on my arm. Want to come with me?"

Andrea's eyes lit up. "I'd love that, actually. I've wanted to ask you about them but...I know it can be personal."

The way she just automatically respected my boundaries and understood how private I was, was part of why I wanted to let her in, in a way I hadn't allowed anyone else, no matter how attracted I might have been to that person.

"Actually, I'd like to tell you about them sometime," I said, meaning it. "You want to grab a bite to eat and we'll head over to his shop?

She nodded enthusiastically. "Sounds good to me."

We stopped for a quick burger at a fast food joint, then headed to Stained Skin, the tattoo shop that my friend, Mike, owned. He'd inked all of my recent tattoos, and definitely all of my more elaborate ones. I'd met him at The Players Club while we were both getting a drink in between play sessions. I'd been shirtless at the time, and Mike had commented on one of my existing tattoos. We'd chatted, and when I wanted a bigger piece of artwork, something that required a lot of detail, I'd called him up.

It helped that Mike was a club member. He understood me, and what I enjoyed. More precisely, he understood what pain did to me, and there was no judgement for it because he was a bit of a sadist himself.

Andrea looked around the tattoo parlor with interest when we entered, staring at the various examples of art on display.

"You interested in something?" I asked Andrea after I'd checked in with Heather, the young woman who manned the front of the shop.

I knew she had the one tattoo. I'd never asked

about the meaning, although she'd explained it to me after she'd gotten the flower delivery. Another reason I suspected her ex-boyfriend. He'd know about her tattoo and the meaning behind it as well.

"Maybe," Andrea admitted, staring at the old school designs in fascination. "I really love tattoo art, those kinds of vintage styles."

I remembered the vibrant, traditional art prints hanging up in the home she shared with Violet. "Wait, are those your prints that are up in the house?"

"What? Oh, yeah." Andrea grinned, realizing what I meant. "Did you think those were Violet's?"

"They seem her style."

"I can't blame you, considering her vintage and Rockabilly fashion choices. But no, actually, those are mine. Violet likes classical art, early 20th century stuff. The Monet and Van Gogh prints are hers."

My mind was blown. "Seems like both of you are full of surprises."

"Aren't we just?" Andrea winked at me.

Speaking of surprises, I knew exactly what was going to happen with this tattoo—not just the shading, but Andrea's part in it, and those wicked thoughts filtering through my mind already had me on edge in the best way possible. My cock twitched seeing her so playful and coy with me, because I was about to push her boundaries again. See what she was really up for.

"Chase!" Mike emerged from the back, a big and burly guy who was actually taller and broader than me. "Good to see you!"

"You, too." I gave him one of those "bro" handshakes then introduced him to Andrea.

Mike grinned after she greeted him. "Damn, you picked a gorgeous one this time."

"Oh, am I the latest?" Andrea teased me, but I definitely saw a hint of vulnerability in her eyes.

The last thing I wanted her to think was that anyone else had ever shared something *this* intimate with me. "I've never brought someone with me when I've been inked before," I told her, and saw her visibly relax, and her facial features soften. "Mike's a member at The Players Club." Which accounted for his comment because he'd seen me with many women there.

"Oh, I see, well, maybe we'll run into you there." Andrea gave him a sassy smile and she looked confident again, much to my relief. She'd need to be confident for what I had in mind.

I exchanged a look with Mike that he clearly understood, because he led us to the furthest room in the back. Small, but private and insulated. Perfect.

"Have a seat," he said, indicating the black leather chair. "Heather had you down for some added shading on your right bicep, is that right?"

"Yep." I removed the dark blue dress shirt I'd worn to work, then took a seat while Mike put various supplies on a silver tray.

Andrea peered at the artwork in question, a sunset over the ocean. "What's the meaning of that one?" she asked, now that she knew I was open to talking about my tattoos, all of which were black and white, no color.

"This one I did to remind myself of the beauty in the ocean," I said, watching as her gaze tracked over more of my tattoos. "After my time in the Navy and being at sea, I kind of struggled to find the good parts of that environment. To remember how it's teeming with life, and power, and how we're... kind of insignificant, at the end of the day. The ocean will still chew you up and spit you back out if she chooses."

Andrea gave me a soft, teasing smile. "Calling the ocean a 'she' like a true sailor."

Time to address my idea... "So, have you ever heard of cockwarming?"

Andrea blinked at me, and the unexpected shift in topic. "What?"

"Cockwarming," I repeated, holding her gaze, fascinated by the flicker of something very curious I glimpsed in her eyes. "Do you know what that is?"

Mike looked amused but said nothing, settling onto a stool next to my chair and keeping his head down as he prepped his tattoo machine.

Her face flushed a pretty shade of pink. "Um, yes, I've heard of it before, in my romance novels," she said hesitantly, and glanced over at Mike. "But I've never...well, done it before."

"Eyes on me, Andrea," I said, exerting that same low, authoritative dom voice I used during our playtime together.

Her gaze snapped back to mine, her eyes wide and startled, as if realizing where this was heading. That yes, I'd just established that we were entering a scene. I couldn't help the smirk that lifted the corner of my mouth. I'd respect if Andrea declined this very explicit request, but I had a feeling that my feisty girl would rise to the challenge.

"You know I like the pain," I said, my voice deep and low.

She bit her bottom lip and nodded, her breathing changing, slow and deep.

I tilted my head toward Mike, who was going about his business, acting like I wasn't about to get my cock sucked while he worked on my arm. "This is the guy who did my piercings. He knows how I react to that pain. I figure why should I sit here and get hard and not be able to do anything about it...when I have you here? You can kneel between my feet and keep my cock nice and warm in that pretty mouth of yours while I get tattooed."

Her darkened eyes went to Mike again, then quickly back to me, as if remembering my earlier order. "Even in front of...him?"

She swallowed hard, and despite seeming unsure in the moment, the way her nipples had hardened against her blouse told me just how much the idea aroused her, which was why I pushed a little harder.

"Yes. In front of him." My cock already felt heavy between my legs, throbbing at the possibility of fulfilling one of my own depraved fantasies. "It's no different than if we used an open room at the club."

Andrea seemed to mull that over in her head. I was already so fucking hard I was straining the seam of my black slacks, just thinking of indulging the pain and the pleasure of Andrea all at once. Getting tattooed was almost meditative in its pain for me, and to also have my cock enveloped in her warm, soft mouth at the same time…

I waited for her reply, the anticipation killing me. And then I saw it, that straightening of her shoulders and that determined, steely look in her eyes when I issued a dare. I couldn't help but grin. I knew she'd never back down from a challenge, and I fucking love that I was going to be the first to teach her this kink.

She lifted her chin. "Fine, but I want a cushion to kneel on or my knees will be killing me."

I chuckled. "Fair enough. I'm sure Mike has something that will work."

Mike finally acknowledged that he was listening in with a laugh. "I have just the thing."

He retrieved a thick, black leather pad for Andrea to kneel on, and she positioned herself between my spread legs. I could feel my heartbeat in my cock just from looking at her like this, the perfect submissive about to obey my orders.

Slowly, teasing me with a confidence she hadn't had when we'd first gotten together, Andrea undid my pants and pulled my cock out. Her fingers tightened around my shaft as she waited for me to guide her.

"Cockwarming means just that," I told her.

"You're keeping my cock warm in your mouth. No sucking me off."

"Yes, sir," she said, a bit cheekily.

Mike finished prepping the area. "Ready?" he asked me.

"Ready."

Andrea lowered her mouth over the head of my cock the moment the needle touched my skin. I groaned—how could I fucking not—and struggled to stay still as the beautiful pain and pleasure hit me at the same time. I breathed deeply and evenly, sinking into both simultaneously. She had only part of me in her mouth at first. I was thick, my girth stretching her lips wide to accommodate me.

Andrea's palms rested on my thighs, giving her too much leverage to push away if things got too intense, which I decided wouldn't do.

"Clasp your hands behind your back," I said, and her gaze flickered up to me, a frown furrowing between her brows. "You know I'm about having *all* the control, baby," I said, and almost laughed at that flash of defiance I saw in her eyes that just made me fucking harder in her mouth.

She obeyed, and I gave her a moment before I placed my hand on her scalp and gently pushed her head down, slowly but firmly, forcing her to accept more of me. It was her first time taking my dick this way, and instinctively she resisted, trying to rear back.

I tightened my hold. "More," I growled the command, and to my shock she relaxed, allowing me further inside, giving me her complete submission.

I felt her tongue drag along the underside of my shaft, sliding along those barbell piercings as I worked my length deeper, until I was finally settled in the back of her throat, as far as I could go.

Like a pro, she held perfectly still and began breathing through her nose. I closed my eyes, letting my head rest against the back of the chair as I immersed myself in the experience and Mike worked on my arm. I gently petted Andrea's head to reward her for her good behavior, and threaded my fingers through her hair, every once in a while catching a sweet little moan that vibrated in the back of her throat and down along my shaft.

She didn't suck, didn't try to bob up and down. Beautifully obedient, she didn't move, just kept my cock enveloped in the softest, wettest kind of heat. Occasionally, she swallowed, causing the muscles in her throat to constrict around my cock and it felt so fucking good.

The pain of the needle scratching along my skin, and the pure bliss of having Andrea at my mercy, warming my cock as much as I wanted, had me floating in this perfect mental haze, thinking of nothing but the dual sensations. Everything about it was fucking sublime.

Mike pulled away and I heard the tattoo machine shut down. I kept my eyes shut and didn't move as he wiped away the residual ink on my bicep, cleaned the surface again, then blot the area dry.

"All right, Chase, whenever you're ready, you're good to go," he said, and I heard him stand. "I'll give you two a bit of privacy, so take as much time as you need...recovering. There aren't any other clients scheduled after you."

I didn't miss the amusement in his tone. Mike was smart enough to know I wasn't done with Andrea. He also knew I wasn't one to share and exited the room, leaving the two of us completely alone.

Finally, I opened my eyes and glanced down at Andrea, who now seemed perfectly content to keep my cock nice and warm in her mouth, seemingly in a meditative trance of her own. She was so goddamn perfect.

"Such a good fucking girl," I rasped, giving her the praise she deserved.

Her lashes fluttered open, and she looked up at me with her mouth full of my cock, the adoration in those eyes stopping my heart mid-beat because it wasn't something I truly deserved. Her cheeks were flushed with desire, her expression so compliant that I had to resist the urge to just fuck her throat, with her gagging on my dick.

I wanted to fuck her pussy more. Wanted her to feel every rigid inch of my shaft inside of her and know that she belonged to me. The need rising up inside of me was overwhelming, and I ran my fingers through her hair one last time, giving the strands a firm, unrelenting tug as I pulled her mouth free of my cock.

"Stand up and turn around," I said, helping her to her feet and facing her away from me, suddenly desperate to get inside of her.

She gasped as I yanked up her skirt and shoved her underwear down. That scrap of fabric dropped to her knees, catching there, and I hissed with satisfaction when I saw that her lace panties were soaked.

I smacked her bare ass, and she sucked in a quick, startled breath. "Did you wear something nice in case I fucked you today?"

She glanced over her shoulder at me, biting her plump bottom lip, her expression deliberately coy. "Maybe," she replied, her voice a little rough after having my cock down her throat.

"Pity they're all ruined now." I shoved them down until they were pooled around her ankles before sliding my hand up the inside of her thighs, groaning as slick moisture coated my fingertips. "Jesus, look at how wet you are, all from just holding my cock in your mouth. You're my dirty little slut, aren't you? So cock hungry you're dripping with it."

She made an inarticulate sound and pushed her ass back toward me as I grazed my fingers along her slit from behind. "Do you want my cock in your pussy?"

"Yes, please, *sir*," she all but begged.

"Good. You're about to get it." Taking hold of her hips, I guided her back toward my lap. I lined us up, then brought her down hard on my cock, impaling her to the hilt in one hard, claiming stroke.

Andrea cried out, her breath breaking apart as her body clenched around me, hot and tight and utterly perfect. My own groan ripped from my throat, low and wrecked, because nothing—*nothing*—felt like this. Like her.

Her hands gripped the armrests of the chair, head falling back against my shoulder as I slid my feet between hers and shoved her thighs open, holding them apart. And still, she didn't resist. She leaned into it, into me, like she trusted that I'd hold her through the unraveling about to happen.

The floor-length mirror in front of us was meant for clients to admire their ink. Tonight, it was for something else entirely. The reflection of us—of Andrea panting and flushed, squirming on my cock, her breasts rising and falling with each broken moan—was raw and unfiltered intimacy.

"Open your eyes," I ordered, my voice rough with restraint. "Look at us. Look at *you*."

I reached up, unbuttoning her blouse, dragging the sleeves down her arms, then peeling her bra cups away until her breasts were bared. My fingers pinched her taut nipple, while my other hand trailed down to tease her clit, slow and precise.

"Look at how fucking beautiful you are when you let go," I said, watching as my cock moved in and out of her. "Look at how well you take me. Like you were made for this—*for me*."

Andrea sank back against my chest, moaning my name like a prayer, like it was the only thing tethering her to the moment. "Chase," she gasped.

"Chase… Chase…" Her hips rocked against me rhythmically, desperate and unrestrained.

"Feels good, doesn't it?" I murmured against her temple.

"It's so—so much," she breathed. "I can't think. I just…I feel you everywhere."

Satisfaction rippled through me. "You want more, don't you?"

"Yes," she choked out. "I want it . . . I need it."

"Then grind down on my cock," I growled against her ear. "Take whatever you need."

Andrea whimpered and obeyed, hips moving in slow, greedy circles that made my vision blur. I gripped her waist, guiding her pace, restraining the wild part of me that wanted to slam her down and *take*. She was so open, so willing—and fuck, I was losing control fast.

"You feel that?" I murmured, pressing my mouth to the fragrant curve of her neck. "That stretch deep inside of you? That fullness that's making you shake? I own that, and you."

She shuddered against me, gasping when I flicked my thumb over her clit again, hard and deliberate. "You're mine like this," I said, meaning it. "All soft and wet and eager. You give me every fucking thing without even realizing it."

Her body arched, caught in that exquisite balance between pleasure and surrender.

"I want you addicted to this," I continued, feeling her pussy clamp tighter around my cock. "To *me*. I want you thinking about this—about us—every damn time you close your eyes."

Andrea's breath hitched, a soft sound of need escaping her lips. "I already do," she whispered.

That knowledge wrecked me, and my control snapped.

I slid my hand up her chest, fingers settling around her throat, not tight, just enough for her to feel my presence everywhere. "Eyes on the mirror, on us," I commanded as I thrust up into her in a relentless rhythm. "Watch how perfect you look when you take me. Watch how good you look when you're *mine*."

She did, her gaze locked on our reflection as she unraveled on my cock, her orgasm sweeping through her, taking me with her right over the edge. In the mirror I watched her fall apart, pupils blown wide, cheeks flushed, her lips parted as she moaned my name. Her head tilted back, resting on my shoulder, and I bit gently at her neck, savoring the taste of her skin, the scent of her arousal, the way she came apart for me.

Every gasp, every tremble, every moan—it

wasn't just sex. It was something far more intoxicating. And I knew, deep down, when this ended, it would possibly destroy us both.

But right now? Right now, I couldn't stop. Didn't want to.

She was mine, and I'd never felt more alive.

CHAPTER 18

Andrea

"*A*s we go into the next quarter…"

One of my department managers continued to drone on, and I was seconds away from losing my mind. These mandatory monthly meetings slowly sapped my soul, every time. Nothing truly important was ever discussed. Anything that actually mattered could have been sent in a two-line email, and everything else was just a frustrating mix of back-patting and pointless filler.

My phone buzzed against my thigh where I had it wedged between my leg and the chair I sat in.

Smothering a grin, I surreptitiously tugged it out so I could look at the message that had just come through. Yep, another dirty text from Chase.

We'd had that interesting little hiatus from our sex life when I first moved in with him—understandable, considering how stressful the situation had been initially. But that cockwarming scene at the tattoo shop that Chase had instigated had been so deliciously unexpected, and so fucking hot.

Now, we were back to having regular sex again, thank God, and it was even more amazing than before. It felt like Chase had finally gotten the message in that tattoo shop that I would rise to any challenge and he wasn't going to scare me off with what turned him on and what he wanted.

I'm in a meeting, I reminded Chase. *I could get in trouble.*

That's fair, Chase replied. *You can ignore my texts, that's your choice. But if you do, I'll punish you for it later.*

Heat slid down my spine. On the one hand, it would be fun to get punished for ignoring him. I knew Chase wouldn't be truly annoyed if I felt I had to focus in this meeting. On the other hand... it gave me a bit of a thrill to risk getting in trouble by texting under the table. *Sexting,* no less.

I glanced around occasionally as I replied to

Chase or read a new message from him, but everyone else was either so bored or so desperately trying not to seem bored that no one paid me any attention. I saw Brandon glance at me once or twice, a frown on his face. But he was sitting right across from me, so it didn't surprise me that he noticed I might be up to something.

It was worth the risk. No, more than that. The risk is what made it worth it. I had to keep smothering my grin as Chase and I messaged back and forth.

There are still so many things you need to try, Chase texted me. *So many things I'm going to do to you.*

Promises, promises, I fired back, knowing full well I was begging for punishment later. But Chase liked me bratty—loved it, actually—and the truth was, I enjoyed every second of the consequences.

"Thank you, everyone," Jones said, and I jolted, realizing the meeting was over.

I stood with everyone else, turning my phone face down on the table so nobody could see if a text came in and leaving it with some of my papers while I grabbed my notebook and pen.

I started after my boss, trying to catch up to him. "Mr. Jones, sir, could I have a moment? I wanted to update you on…"

"Yes, of course, that little project of yours and Brandon's for the Monarch," Jones said before I could finish. "How is it coming along?"

I hurried to keep up with Jones, a much taller man with a quick stride, as he walked back to his office and I updated him on the campaign and gave him a rundown on the highlights. He shared his thoughts on changes we ought to make, and I jotted down those suggestions in my notebook along the way.

Jones was the kind of boss who didn't usually have unique ideas but always wanted to feel like he contributed to a project so he could claim he was 'hands on.' I'd learned pretty quickly that I had to take notes on what he said, then find ways to change his ideas and incorporate better versions of them into our projects so that he felt included without ruining the client's overall vision.

Once that was dealt with, I hurried back to the conference room to gather the rest of my things. Brandon wasn't there. I figured he was probably already at his desk, and I'd have to catch him there and talk about how we were going to deal with Jones' latest—

Wait.

An unsettling feeling coursed through me as I reached my seat and I saw my phone on the table, face up. I'd put it face down, hadn't I, because I didn't want anyone to see my screen if Chase texted me again? I'd been careful...I didn't want anybody knowing my personal business.

But now, it was face up.

The only other person in the room was Sharon, one of the administrative assistants, wrestling with the presentation equipment. "Sharon? Did anyone touch my phone?"

"What?" Sharon glanced at me with a frustrated look on her face. "Sorry, I've been dealing with this stupid thing. I haven't seen anybody in here since the meeting ended."

My phone lay there innocently, like it was taunting me to believe my own memory.

I must have been mistaken. I was being paranoid, and even if I was remembering right, who was to say my phone didn't get knocked over onto the floor and someone put it back on the table for me?

This was possibly the worst part of having a stalker, I concluded irritably as I went back to my desk. Knowing someone was lurking about made me second-guess everything, made me jump at every shadow and start to doubt my own perceptions.

I forced myself not to think about it further. I

was under Chase's protection, and he was nothing if not zealous. I was even staying at his place. My project was going well, and our company had a banquet to attend that night, an annual thing thrown by one of the casinos that were our oldest and biggest clients. I had so many more pleasant things to focus on than whoever was trying to spook me.

Especially since Chase was going as my date.

As soon as I'd told him about the event, he'd insisted on attending with me. He'd gone on about there being a ton of people I didn't know at the banquet, that all the exits and entrances provided too many opportunities for someone to strike, and it was better to be safe with him than sorry.

"Are you allowed a plus one?" he'd asked after I'd shared the information with him.

"Yes, we all are, although we do need to RSVP if we're bringing someone."

"Great. Put me down," he'd said succinctly. "I'll be coming with you."

"Wow, assumptions much?" I'd replied with a bit of sass. "What if I wanted to take Violet?"

He'd rolled his eyes at me. "As much as I trust your sister's ability to smash a chair over someone's head if they try to cop a feel, I'm less optimistic about her ability to handle security at a large event like that. Our firm works these kinds of events all the time."

He wasn't wrong, and at the end of the day I wasn't mad that I was going to a fancy dinner on Chase's arm.

I wrapped up work a bit early like everyone else so that we could all hurry home and get ready. Chase picked me up, as agreed, and we separately showered and dressed. I'd stopped using the guest bedroom a few nights ago, but having a second bathroom was definitely useful for times like this when we had a time crunch.

I'd bought my outfit a while ago, a dark purple dress with a slightly plunging neckline and a fuller skirt, and black satin strappy heels. It was a nice, formal event, so I didn't want to go too sparkly or body-hugging, and aimed for tasteful elegance, including arranging my hair into a sophisticated updo and going with a smokey eye.

Judging by the stunned look on Chase's face when I emerged from the guest bedroom, I had succeeded.

He looked gorgeous in a tux with a subtle sheen to the tie and pocket handkerchief, adding a little flair while still being black tie. The suit was clearly tailored, fitting him like a glove, and I was hit all over again by just how insanely handsome he was.

It made me want to skip the party altogether and just beg him to take me to bed and fuck me with the suit still on.

Chase's gaze dragged over my body appreciatively, his eyes dark and hungry. More than that, though, there was something else on his face. It almost looked like—like awe.

Clearly I was imagining things, seeing only what I wanted to see. Nobody was going to look at me and feel *awe* for crying out loud.

"You look stunning," he said, but there it was again, in his voice.

"Thanks." I slid my hand down his white dress shirt, feeling the heat of his chest beneath, and smiled up at him. "You're not so bad yourself."

Chase grinned and offered me his arm. "Let's go."

"Eager to get there?" I asked, slipping my hand into the crook of his arm as he escorted me down to the car. "You won't know anybody and it'll be pretty boring."

"I'm eager to get there on time so we can leave early. And maybe I'm a little excited to show you off." He followed that up with a sexy wink.

My breath felt as though it left my lungs in a whoosh at that compliment. "Leave early, huh?" I gave him a playful look. "Sounds like somebody's making some real assumptions here."

Chase cocked an eyebrow at me. "Should I not be?"

"Just don't think you can take me for granted," I teased.

"Trust me. I don't." Chase's gaze was dark and serious.

My entire body warmed. Honestly, I dared any woman not to feel something for a man when he talked about them like that.

I was grateful for Chase's steadying arm when we arrived at the venue. My gown was floor-length and I wasn't used to wearing one, so I needed to hold my skirt up a bit and be careful walking in my heels.

Las Vegas never did anything halfway. Opulence was the name of the game. This ballroom was in our client's casino at their resort, and everything was glittering and golden. Everyone else was dressed nicely as well. I received a lot of compliments on my dress, and Chase wasn't shy about securing his arm around my waist like I belonged to him. And tonight, for a while, I felt like I did.

I was always quick to introduce him, although I never used the word 'boyfriend' since that wasn't something the two of us had discussed—even if my stupid heart didn't seem to be able to get the memo.

My coworkers all seemed delighted to meet Chase, and then I introduced him to my boss, who asked where Chase worked and they conversed for a few minutes.

"Glad to see Andrea's dating up," Jones said, because God forbid my boss, who clearly had no filter, not embarrass me.

"I'm the lucky one," Chase replied easily, tugging me close to his side. "Andrea's quite the catch."

"She's a real asset to the company," Jones agreed, downing the last of what looked like bourbon in his glass. "The last guy she brought to one of our events was quite…disappointing. We all thought she could do better. Glad to see she's figured that out."

I inwardly winced as Jones finally moved on to someone else. "I am *so* sorry," I muttered, and grabbed a glass of champagne from a passing tray. "My boss needs to brush up on his social cues."

Chase chuckled. "He clearly cares, in his own way."

I sipped my drink, the bubbles tickling the back of my throat. "He's so used to being in charge that he thinks he can just say whatever he wants without repercussions."

"Did everyone really not like Heath?" Chase asked, and I knew he was trying to gather more intel on my ex.

I groaned as we continued to mingle. "I did get the sense that they weren't impressed with him, but nobody said anything to me while we were dating. I think Heath felt a little threatened that I was more successful in my job than he was in his. And this was when we were having problems in the bedroom so it just kind of compounded the issues between us, and his attitude toward me."

"Everyone here seems to respect you," Chase said of the co-workers he'd met. "And," he added with a low chuckle that shivered right down my spine. "Quite a few of the men in this room are attracted to you. You chose a rather daring neckline, you know, and it's hard not to notice what great breasts you have." Chase's gaze dropped down and I could feel myself flush.

I wanted to look good for you, I wanted to say, but I worried that would sound stupid, too intimate and personal. I didn't want Chase to realize that I'd made the mistake of catching feelings for him and make anything awkward between us.

"Oh, wow."

At the sound of the male voice, I turned and saw Brandon standing there. He smiled at me. He looked very nice, all cleaned up, but taking in his attire I could see the difference between a rented tux and a suit that had actually been made and measured just for the man who wore it. He looked like a cheap knockoff compared to Chase.

"You look beautiful," Brandon said, issuing the compliment with a smile that didn't quite reach his eyes. Like he was saying the words, but really didn't approve of how sexy the dress actually was. "The color goes really well with your hair, very dramatic."

"Thank you," I said, feeling oddly uncomfortable with him.

"I'm Chase," Chase said, introducing himself and offering his hand to Brandon, shaking it with confidence, a charming smile on his lips—though I was very aware of him assessing my co-worker. "Sorry, I feel like I've been introduced to a hundred people at this point. You are…?"

"I'm Brandon Smith. I work with Andrea." Brandon smiled tightly. "Sorry, I'm a bit lost. I thought Andrea just had a sister?"

My face burned with embarrassment at Brandon's clumsy attempt to undermine Chase and insinuate I'd brought my brother to the event.

Chase didn't even blink. "No, nothing platonic here," he said with a self-deprecating chuckle. "I'm Andrea's partner. We wanted to keep things to ourselves, since we're both very private people."

The word *partner* instead of *boyfriend* made the relationship seem long term, serious. Mature. I hated that I found it so hot, even if it was just all for show.

"Ahh," Brandon said, and nodded before grilling Chase further, eyeing him with an arrogance that made me internally cringe. "So what do you do? Are you in business? Obviously I work with Andrea, but while at Yale I took some business classes in addition to the graphic design, and no offense but you don't look like the corporate type."

I wanted to melt into the floor. Could Brandon be any more judgmental? Or insecure, really, that he had to try and insult Chase to make himself feel superior? I'd never seen Brandon posture in this manner, and quite frankly, his behavior was mortifying.

"No, not corporate." Chase chuckled easily, seemingly unfazed by the slight. "I don't do anything that fancy or as fun and creative as you and Andrea. I work security."

That was definitely underselling his career.

Chase looked after billionaire clients and high-ranking CEOs and put his life on the line for others. His security firm was arguably the best in the city, and he was making it sound like he just sat at a desk in a museum all night.

Part of me wanted to speak up and point out just how successful Chase was, but the rest of me forced myself to keep my mouth shut. I didn't want Brandon to know he was getting to me with his rude comments, and there was honestly something incredibly attractive about the fact that Chase was downplaying himself. He wasn't playing Brandon's game, and he was confident enough that he didn't care if there was a misconception made. He had no reason to brag.

"Yale, though, that's impressive," Chase continued, inclining his head. "Although the student loans must be insane."

"They were, but I was able to pay them off," Brandon said with a wave of his hand. "Hell, I was even able to get my dream car last year, a Porsche Carrera."

I couldn't recall if Brandon actually drove a Porsche or not but I had to bite my tongue hard. Not only was his salary probably equivalent to mine, just under six figures, everyone knew the people who drove Porsches in Vegas were the douchebags. What the hell was he trying to prove?

"Wow, beautiful car," Chase said, nothing but admiration in his voice.

"Brandon!" someone yelled from another cluster of people, calling him over.

Brandon excused himself and moved on, allowing me to finally breathe.

Chase stared after him, a small little frown creased between his brows.

"I'm so sorry," I said, still shocked by Brandon's superior attitude with Chase. "That was the most embarrassing five minutes of my life, right on the heels of my boss."

Chase glanced back at me, a smirk tugging at the corners of his lips. "He knows only douchebags drive Porsches, right?"

"That's exactly what I was thinking!" I laughed and brought a hand to my face, feeling just how on fire my cheeks were. "God, that was painful. I've never seen him like that, ever. He's usually a nice, decent guy."

Needing some fresh air after that, I guided Chase to the double doors leading out to a terrace and found us a nice, secluded spot, away from the loud party and other people.

"You two work together a lot?" Chase asked

curiously as we stood at the railing, side by side, and looked out over the back end property of the resort.

"Yeah, we're partners on a pretty big project right now," I said, finishing my champagne before placing the flute on a nearby table. "He asked me out a bit ago and I turned him down. I don't date coworkers and he seemed too...well...I had just wasted my time dating a guy who was too passive in bed for me and I didn't want to make the same mistake again."

"You didn't," Chase said, a possessive growl lurking around the edges of his voice.

That dominate tone of his made my nipples tighten. "Regardless, he shouldn't have treated you like that."

"Trust me, I can handle it, and him," Chase assured me confidently, clearly unconcerned. "If I couldn't deal with insecure men posturing at me, I wouldn't be able to do my job."

"I really do feel bad," I said, and sighed. "He just wasn't my type."

"Mmm. You've alluded to that a few times now." He gently rubbed circles against the small of my back and I shivered, longing to feel his fingers tracing across my bare skin. "You want to tell me what your type actually is?" he asked in a sexy, flirty tone.

"Well." I turned toward him, stepping close so that Chase's arm came around my waist completely. I settled my hand on his chest to toy with his lapel, giving him a sultry, seductive look. "Lately I've been drawn to tough bodyguards who drive me crazy in bed." I paused before adding, "even if they're also stubborn, annoying, and always have to have the final say."

He arched a brow at me. "I only have to have the final say with sassy, bratty, stubborn art designers," Chase replied, his voice low and warm and his gaze entirely on me.

"Good thing that's exactly the type I am," I said, keeping my voice light and teasing, but there was no mistaking the way my heart thudded in my chest.

Chase didn't smile. Not right away. He just looked at me, like he was memorizing the moment. Like maybe this thing between us meant more to him than just another temporary fling.

Then quietly, as if it cost him something to admit, he said, "You make me forget how to hold back."

My breath felt as though it left my lungs at that vulnerable confession. My fingers curled into his shirt without thinking, anchoring myself there against him. "Then don't," I whispered.

When he lowered his mouth to mine and kissed me—slow, deep, and full of everything we weren't saying—I knew I was already in way over my head. And I didn't care, even knowing this thing between us would most likely end in heartbreak.

Mine.

CHAPTER 19

Chase

I wasn't lying when I said that Brandon's posturing didn't bother me in the least. It was much more fun to just not react to his annoying behavior and let him think that he'd actually impressed me. Men like him weren't worth the time or energy.

There was, however, something that did concern me.

I was probably being overly sensitive, but we still hadn't turned up anything incriminating on Andrea's ex-boyfriend, Heath. But Brandon, well, there was something about him and his interaction with Andrea that pinged my protective radar and unsettled me. My gut instinct had always served me well, so while Andrea was talking to some work friends after dinner, I slipped away—supposedly to the bathroom—and gave Tate a call.

He picked up fairly quickly. "Do you know where I am?" Tate demanded, sounding piqued at the interruption.

"The club?" I guessed, not that I gave a fuck.

"Yes," he grumbled. "I'm trying to relax and unwind and get laid. Go away."

"Well, the fact that you said you're *trying* means you're not in the middle of fucking someone, so I need you to do me a favor and look up someone for me when you get into the office in the morning and dig up whatever you can on him," I said, rubbing a hand along the back of my neck to ease the tension settling there. "It's for Andrea."

"Oh?" I could hear the sly grin in Tate's voice. "Well, if it's for Andrea…"

"Oh, fuck off," I snapped, not in the mood to be provoked. "Just look the guy up. It's someone she works with. I'm at an event with her and I don't like the vibes he's giving off."

"Text me whatever you've got and I'll go from there," Tate said, taking things more seriously now.

As soon as we hung up I sent over Brandon's

name and the very little information I had on the guy. It wasn't a lot. Mainly, just his place of employment, possibly where he'd attended college and the type of car he drove. Unfortunately, his last name, Smith, was pretty fucking common, but if anyone could find out any dirt on the guy, it would be Tate. Just knowing his name and that he worked with Andrea was all that Tate needed to start making the connections through social media and other digital footprints.

I returned to the party. Brandon was hovering near Andrea now that I was gone, not talking to her, but the way he was watching her, with a disapproving frown on his face, rubbed me the wrong way.

The guy made my spine itch. I just couldn't tell if it was because he was insecure and arrogant, or if it was because he was an actual threat to Andrea. Clearly he wasn't as nice of a guy as he'd led Andrea to believe, that was for sure, but was it because he was the kind of entitled jerk who was angry that a woman wouldn't go out with him? Or was it something more?

Hopefully Tate's inquest would be able to answer that question for me.

I walked over to Andrea where she was chatting with her friends. Fuck, she was gorgeous. She was hot, yes, but she was also *beautiful*, and this dress reminded me of just how stunning she was. The dark purple with her light skin and dark hair was striking, and she'd done some fun dramatic eye makeup that I couldn't wait to see messed up with her tears of pain and pleasure.

"How you doing?" I asked, leaning in close, my lips brushing her ear.

Andrea flushed. She'd been flushing all night, eyes sparkling, as I flirted with her.

"I'm good," Andrea whispered back to me.

"You ready to go?" Now that we'd made our appearance and stayed for dinner and the awards ceremony, I was anxious to leave this fancy event behind and have her all to myself.

Curiosity flickered in her eyes. "Go?"

"To the club," I murmured.

Andrea flushed harder. I could feel everyone in the group staring at us and I didn't give a damn. I'd made it clear tonight that everyone knew Andrea was mine and that I wanted her, and I was just enough of a possessive bastard to be a bit smug about it now.

"Yes," she agreed. "I'm more than ready."

She made her excuses gracefully, and I was sure that everyone knew we were leaving so I could fuck her, even if they didn't know exactly where we were going or what the rest of the night would entail for us.

Lately I've been drawn to tough bodyguards who drive me crazy in bed. Oh, I was more than ready to show her just how crazy I could make her.

I kept my hand on the small of her back as we left and went to the valet to get the car. I headed right for the club. I knew we were both dressed a little fancy for a sex club, but hey, people fucked there out in public. Rules were out the window. People wore gimp suits and played at being puppies or wore bondage corsets and chastity belts. Nobody at the club gave a shit or judged anyone else, which was the beauty of a place like that.

I escorted her inside and I could feel a few people staring—mostly at Andrea. She blushed a little, but I made a point to parade her around the club. She looked amazing and I wanted everyone to see that, wanted her to realize how special she was and, okay, selfishly I wanted every man in the place to know she was *mine*, too.

"Starting to feel a bit like a prize," she muttered crankily.

I laughed and patted the hand tucked into the crook of my arm. "That's because you *are* a prize.

You deserve to know your worth and be the center of attention."

We had made a full circuit at that point and reached the bar again. "Want anything to drink?"

"No, I'm good. I had that champagne earlier."

"Great." I grabbed her hand, anxious to get her alone, strip her naked, and have my way with her. "Let's—"

"Oh my God, Chase?"

I turned at the mention of my name, shocked to see Naomi Starr, the A-list actress I'd spent the week guarding, standing there. She hadn't been an awful client, just a bit self-centered without realizing that's how she behaved. A lot of celebrities were like that. Very accustomed to everything orbiting around them.

Clearly, she'd somehow managed to get herself an invitation into The Players Club.

Naomi was dressed up like she was going to do a burlesque show in the lounge, with lots of rhinestones on her lingerie and sparkling pasties with tassels over her nipples. Not really my thing, personally, but I was sure she'd have no shortage of offers tonight.

"Hey, enjoying yourself?" I asked, stopping for a moment to be polite.

"Oh, so much," she purred, putting her hand on

my forearm and leaning close. "I was hoping to see you here."

My brows flew up in shock, because as her security detail she'd given me no indication that she was attracted to me. Or maybe it was because I wasn't attracted to her and had missed the signs?

"Oh?" I said, not sure how else to respond.

Naomi laughed and stroked my arm. "You can't be all that surprised. It's been so hot watching you do your thing, protecting me and looking so...alpha."

At my side, Andrea had a coughing fit.

Naomi didn't even look in Andrea's direction. It was like Andrea didn't exist.

"I'm flattered." I gently removed Naomi's hand from my arm, trying to figure out a way to let her down easy so I didn't offend her. "But as one of my clients, I'm afraid mixing business and pleasure isn't something I do. I wouldn't want to compromise my professional role."

"Aww, c'mon, don't tell me you don't want to get a little of your Kevin Costner on," she said, referencing the iconic movie, The Bodyguard.

Naomi pouted up at me, her brown eyes peeking up through her lashes. She was beautiful, no denying it, but I suspected she wouldn't be able to handle what I really enjoyed. I already had a woman who did and would and had. And no one, no matter how beautiful, could hold a candle to Andrea.

"I'm afraid not," I insisted. "But I hope you have fun tonight."

I looked over at Andrea. "Shall we get a room?"

Andrea was bristling like a wet cat, claws out. It was adorable. "Let's," she snapped.

I almost laughed out loud at her little tantrum, but I didn't want to provoke her in front of Naomi and potentially extend our conversation. I took Andrea's hand and tugged her along up the stairs, and once we were in one of the private rooms, Andrea whirled on me.

Her eyes flashed with heat and accusation. "Care to explain what *that* was?"

"*That*," I said, stripping out of my tuxedo jacket and setting it on the back of the couch in the room, "was a client who wants to play out her silly little bodyguard fantasies at the club."

Andrea rolled her eyes and crossed her arms over her chest, pure defiance rippling off her. "Like you weren't checking out those perky sparkly boobs of hers?"

I couldn't help it—I grinned, which seemed to only make her more irritated. "Are you jealous?" I asked, casually rolling up the sleeves of my dress shirt.

Andrea huffed. "Why would I be jealous of an over the top diva who wants everyone to worship her?"

"Oh, you are. You're jealous." This *delighted* me.

"I don't appreciate being ignored while she's fawning all over you," Andrea gritted out. "I came here with you, as your guest, and that should be clear. She had the audacity to just come up to you and act like she had a claim to you."

I stepped up to Andrea, and using my index finger beneath her chin, I tipped her head back, forcing her to look into my eyes. "Sounds to me like someone needs to be reminded that one of the most important parts of a dom-sub relationship is *trust.*"

Andrea cocked an eyebrow, clearly not impressed.

"You need to trust," I purred, slowly dragging that same finger down her chest and along the deep plunging neckline of her dress, watching as her nipples tightened against the fabric, "that you're the only woman I want, that you're more than enough for me, and not even a woman in flashy tassels is going to change that fact. What if I'd gone off the handle about Brandon earlier?"

Her lips pursed, her spine still stiff. "That's not the same thing."

"Isn't it? Some guy you work with comes along, posturing, trying to make me feel inferior so you'll dump me and be with him. Sounds similar enough to me." I let my hand fall away, but didn't step back, asserting my dominance. "And I wasn't jealous. I'm still not. Because I know there isn't a chance in hell you'll drop me for that guy. You should have the same trust and confidence in me, and in yourself."

Her shoulders slumped ever so slightly, and I caught a quick glimpse of insecurity in her eyes, telling me what I needed to know. It wasn't that she didn't trust me, it was more that she didn't think she could compete with someone like Naomi.

That was insane. When Andrea was in the room, nobody else existed for me. Not that I could go so far as to tell her that. It would reveal too much of what I felt and just convolute our temporary arrangement.

I figured there were two ways I could take this situation. Go for the painful punishment, or teach her a lesson that would completely unravel her in a different way entirely. Tonight, I opted for the latter, just to show her that discipline didn't always have to be harsh, or hurt. That sometimes, pleasure could be just as effective.

Without another word, I retrieved a silk tie from the cupboard, then returned. Standing behind her, I pulled her hands behind her back, wrapping the material around her wrists as I bound them together. I felt her body going still, just breathing, waiting…maybe even a little confused that I hadn't strapped her down to the nearest surface and grabbed a flogger or crop to spank her.

"I know what you need better than you do," I said, circling around to stand in front of her again. "You don't want to compete with Naomi. You want to be claimed so thoroughly you forget that there was ever another woman in the room." I tipped her head back again, making her look into my eyes. "You want to be the only name I remember. The only taste I crave. And you are."

Andrea made a soft sound, but I could see that she was still holding on to her fire.

"But I'm not letting you off easy," I warned. "You're going to pay for that little tantrum downstairs."

Her chin jutted out stubbornly. "I'm not sorry."

"No, you're not," I said, trying to remain stern

when I wanted to chuckle at her defiance. "And I love that about you."

I guided her back toward the couch in the room, then gently but firmly pushed her down to sit. She looked up at me with parted lips, her wrists still bound at her back, and for a second, everything else dropped away. The club, the bratty comments, Naomi, the whole goddamn world.

Just her. Andrea, looking at me like she wanted me to ruin her.

But underneath that, I saw something else. A flicker of need not just for control or release—but for reassurance. From me. And for tonight, at least, I could give her that much.

"You know what this is, don't you?" I asked quietly, dropping to my knees in front of her and pushing the skirt of her dress all the way up to her hips. "It's not just a punishment. It's a reminder."

"A reminder of what?" Her voice was low, shaky. Uncertain.

I eased her panties down her thighs, then removed them completely, my gaze holding hers. "That you're mine."

Andrea's breath caught—most likely from how much she wanted to believe it. From how deeply she already did.

"I want to touch you," I murmured, my voice

low, the raw vulnerability and desire on her face making me want to worship her like the queen she was. "But I want you to feel every caress. Every intention behind it. This isn't just about control and punishment tonight, Andrea. It's about claiming what's mine in a way you don't forget."

She swallowed, then nodded once. "Then do it. Touch me."

I pressed my hands to her knees and pushed them apart, exposing her damp pussy to my gaze. I lowered my head to kiss the inside of her thigh first—softly and reverently, things she deserved despite how foreign that tenderness was to me when I'd always opted for fast, hard, mindless sex. But I couldn't deny that there was something about being soft with Andrea in a moment like this that felt so damn right.

My hands slid up, thumbs teasing circles against her bare skin. Her breathing hitched as I placed another wet, suctioning kiss higher this time, and dragged my tongue a bit closer to where I knew she wanted me the most.

"I love watching you fall apart," I murmured, looking up at her, my senses drugged with the scent of her arousal. "But I love putting you back together even more."

Her head tilted back slightly, her bound arms

tightening as if she wanted to reach out and touch me, but couldn't.

"Chase...please," she begged, her hips bucking forward.

"See? Punishment doesn't always have to be painful," I said, dragging my thumb down along her slit, then back up to her clit, making her moan deep in her throat. "There are different forms of torment that work just as effectively."

I dropped my mouth back to her pussy, licking, sucking, teasing her for what seemed liked forever, until she was gasping and squirming and pleading with me to let her come. I edged her just like this, again and again, keeping her on the precipice while lapping up the taste of her until it was imprinted in my memory.

I fucked her with my tongue, and she moaned, her thighs trembling against my face as I finally let her fall apart and come. Her entire body shuddered, and she cried out my name as if it meant something. Because it did.

She might have wanted a fight when we'd first entered this room, but she was leaving it knowing exactly who she belonged to.

And right now, tonight, that was all that mattered to me.

CHAPTER 20

Andrea

That night, I woke up from a dead sleep to Chase thrashing in the bed beside me. For a second, I felt completely disoriented, being wrenched from a pleasant dream of walking through an enchanted forest, to lying in bed staring into the dark wondering what the hell was going on.

There was a soft groan next to me, and I rolled over to face Chase's side of the bed, bits and pieces of consciousness returning to me as I realized he was in the throes of a night terror.

I had heard about people having nightmares

like this before, the kind where you tried to call out but were completely lost in the void. What I hadn't realized was how it sounded. The screams and moans didn't sound normal. The person was still asleep, so they couldn't push the words past their lips. It made Chase's moans sound eerie and helpless, his voice completely different from how I'd ever heard it before.

He was covered in sweat, and I could see his eyes moving frantically back and forth underneath his closed eyelids. He gripped the bedsheets so hard his knuckles were white. And those horrified moans, half-formed words, kept slipping out of his mouth. It was heartbreaking, watching as though he couldn't escape whatever was weighing him down. He kept trying to talk but it was like his mouth couldn't work properly—of course it couldn't, he was asleep. But I was sure it only made him feel that much more panicked.

I gently gripped his shoulders. I didn't know what else to do, I just knew that I needed to help him, and I had to make that terror end for him. "Chase. Chase, it's me," I said, giving him a small shake to wake him up. "Chase...you're okay. You're safe, you're with me."

Chase let out a startled, horrified noise, one that honestly chilled me to my core, and then his arm flew up, his fist just barely missing my face, sending me flying off him. I nearly fell off the bed but managed to regain my balance in time, yelping in surprise. I knew Chase was strong, and fast, but I'd never had any of it used *against* me before, like I was an opponent.

Chase rolled over and made a noise like a dying animal. My heart was pounding frantically while I tried to figure out what to do to help him without touching him again, which seemed to set him off. "Chase, please, wake up, please wake up, it's me, it's Andrea, you're safe! You're okay!"

I could feel my voice rising in panic, could feel my own fear try to choke me. I needed to soothe him, but how could I do that when *I* sounded so scared? I watched, helpless, as he kept twitching and moaning. He wasn't ever able to form full words but sometimes it sounded like he was begging.

My throat closed up and hot tears filled my eyes. I had never felt so completely helpless. I wanted to wake him up but he didn't seem able to hear me, and I was honestly worried if I tried touching him again he'd hit me.

He thrashed again, and this time his arm shot out to his side of the bed like he was trying to fight off some threat, hitting the lamp on the nightstand

and knocking it over with a loud crash. Chase's entire body jolted at the sound, and his eyes flew open. He gasped, abruptly sitting upright, his lower body tangled in the sheets, his chest absolutely coated in sweat. For a second I wasn't sure if he could see me, or the room, or anything else.

Slowly, Chase's hands unclenched, but he was still breathing hard, still seemingly trying to acclimate himself to where he was.

"Chase," I said gently. "You okay?"

His gaze snapped over to me, and I was taken aback by the rush of emotions passing across his face—shame, embarrassment, humiliation. It cracked something inside of me just to witness it. He looked haunted. Wrecked by whatever nightmare he'd just had. Like he wasn't fully here.

"Andrea...*fuck*." His voice was hoarse like he'd been yelling—or trying to, anyway. "Are you all right?"

"No, not at all." I gave a shaky laugh that died in my throat. What a ridiculous question. I wasn't the one who'd just had a horrible nightmare, but that entire episode had shaken me badly.

Still, I crawled across the bed towards him to offer him comfort, to make sure *he* was okay, but Chase scrambled up and out of bed before I could touch him, like the idea of being close to me was unbearable to him.

He nearly tripped in the tangled sheets in his haste to put distance between us. "I'm going to go sleep in the guest bedroom."

I gaped at him, shocked at how cold and withdrawn he seemed. "What?"

Chase's jaw visibly clenched as he reached down and grabbed the lamp and set it back on the nightstand. "I'll see you in the morning. Sorry for disturbing your sleep. It won't happen again."

I shook my head in confusion. "What—what are you talking about? Chase, talk to me. Are you okay? Let me be here for you."

Chase's expression was completely blank. Shuttered. Detached, even. "I'm fine. Go back to sleep, Andrea."

He walked out, and the silence he left behind was deafening. The sheets still held the warmth of his body, the scent of his skin. I sat frozen there, arms wrapped around my middle, trying to hold myself together.

I wasn't naïve. I knew Chase had seen and done things in the military that he didn't talk about. I knew he carried ghosts. But seeing him in despair, hearing the way his voice cracked with panic, and then watching him build a wall between us so fast I couldn't keep up...it gutted me.

I wasn't trying to fix him. I just wanted to hold him. To be there in a way he'd already been for me so many times. But he clearly didn't want that from me. Not even for a second.

I curled up into a ball on my side, my heart aching, wondering how I could miss someone who was still just down the hall.

* * *

I STRUGGLED to go back to sleep. I was shaken up, I couldn't deny it, but my mind also couldn't stop racing, thinking about Chase. Several times I almost got up and went into the guest bedroom to crawl in with him and hold him, his stubborn distance be damned, but I always stopped myself.

The middle of the night wasn't the right time for an argument, and that's what this could very well turn into. I'd leave it for morning.

I slept fitfully when sleep finally came, and was in desperate need of coffee when I dragged myself out of bed. Chase was already up and dressed for work when I entered the kitchen and living area.

"Hey," I said softly. "How're you feeling?"

"Fine." Chase's tone was clipped, inviting no

further conversation. He finished his coffee and washed his cup. "I'm ready to go when you are."

I exhaled a deep, shaky breath, feeling extremely off-kilter.

Since I'd moved in, Chase had started making breakfast in the mornings when he woke up before me, although we often swapped back and forth depending on who got to the kitchen first, and he always made me coffee. I poured myself a cup, but didn't make myself anything to eat. I wasn't hungry. My stomach was in knots.

This man felt like a stranger to me, someone I didn't recognize. The Chase I knew had inspired fire in me, and while he'd always driven me insane when we'd met the first few times over the years, before we started... whatever this was... he had never been *cold*. If he'd been like this with me, I never would've wanted him.

I felt so confused and unsure, having no clue how to navigate this emotional landmine with him.

I finished getting ready for work and Chase was silent as he drove me to the office. He didn't talk to me or touch me. Not holding my hand, not a reassuring brush of his fingers along the back of my neck, not even the absent-minded, possessive way he used to rest his palm on my thigh like I was his to protect—his to keep.

It was only then, sitting in that awkward quiet, that I realized just how often he'd touched me before. How casual and natural it had become, like he needed that contact because it grounded him somehow. And I hadn't realized how much I'd started to rely on it, too.

Where had that man gone? Now, his hands were locked on the steering wheel like he was holding on for dear life. And when we arrived at my office, he dropped me off without kissing me goodbye as had become our routine.

Stupidly, I felt like crying.

I was distracted all day. I knew that people could tell something was up. A lot of my coworkers were a bit hungover after last night's party but it was pretty clear that wasn't the issue with me. I felt like a bug under a microscope and could only hope I wasn't becoming the center of office gossip.

Still, I tried texting Chase a few times, but I never got a reply. I tried to keep things casual. Just the usual *what's for lunch? How are things at work?* I even tried to get him riled up by asking if he was looking after Naomi today.

Nothing. So, I texted Austin, who told me that

Chase had gone home early today. Definitely not normal for him.

"Everything all right?"

I jolted in surprise and nearly dropped my phone at the unexpected sound of Brandon's voice. I looked up, wondering how he'd walked into my office without me hearing or noticing. "Sorry. Yeah. Just stressed."

Brandon gave me a concerned look. "I've seen you stressed. This is different."

I sighed and glanced at the clock, knowing I was useless today at work. Especially now knowing that Chase was at home, alone.

I glanced back at Brandon. "Look, if I—if I left early, would you cover for me?"

"Of course." Brandon sounded surprised that I even had to ask. "I'd do anything for you."

I was already standing up and gathering my things. "Thanks so much. I owe you one."

I was going to figure out what was going on with Chase and make him talk about it, one way or another. I'd never backed down from a fight when it came to this man. Why the hell was I letting him rattle me now?

Although, I was going to make him pay me back for the rideshare I had to order. He could just punish me for the bratty attitude later.

When I arrived at his building, I squared my shoulders and went up to his place. The door was locked, typical Chase, but he'd given me a key so I just let myself in.

I walked inside and came to an abrupt stop. My luggage and all my other personal things were packed up and by the front door, his message clear.

He was kicking me out.

CHAPTER 21

Chase

*D*amn it. I'd hoped to be finished before she left work for the day.

I stared at Andrea, who stared back at me like she was seriously considering hitting me over the head with her purse. I'd planned to ask Ford or Tate to pick Andrea up from work and take her back to the townhouse she shared with Violet, avoiding her altogether.

I should've known she'd find a way to fuck with my plans.

"What do you think you're doing?" Andrea demanded. She dropped her purse on the floor and strode over to where I was standing next to her luggage, glaring at me.

I saw the anger blazing in her expression but it was the hurt that sliced me deeper than a knife, when that's what I was trying to avoid. Hurting her. "I've packed your things so they can go back to your house with you."

"Excuse me?" Her eyes flashed with fire. "And you were just going to, what, let me figure it out when you changed the damn locks?"

Everything inside me was twisting with emotions I wasn't used to, but I managed to remain calm. "I was going to have one of my coworkers pick you up and take you home and explain."

"Wow." Andrea folded her arms across her chest. "I know you're a lot of things, Chase, but I never thought you would be a fucking coward."

Inwardly, I flinched at the accusation. The awful part was, I couldn't even deny her claim. The truth was, I couldn't handle facing her after what happened last night.

It wasn't just the humiliation and embarrassment at what she'd witnessed. It wasn't even the night terror itself, though that had been mortifying enough. It had been the fact that I'd been so entrenched in the nightmare, my entire body forced to relive that horrific night I'd lost men, and it wasn't the first time this had happened.

I'd been so rooted in those terrifying memories, unable to escape, thrashing at unknown forces, a prisoner in my own body. I'd knocked a lamp to the floor, and I easily could have hurt Andrea. Not just in the throes of the nightmare itself, but there had been times when I'd woken up from one of these episodes, fists flying, or my hands wrapping tight around a pillow when in my dream it had been the enemy's neck I'd been strangling. There was no goddamn way I was ever going to take that risk with Andrea.

I thought it would be fine as long as I didn't let her get too close—but she had. I'd let her into my life bit by bit without even realizing what was happening until it was too late. And now, she'd seen the ugly, terrifying parts that had forced me to keep her at arm's length in the first place.

Stupid, stupid, stupid.

I should've known better. I never should have let her share the bed with me. I should have kept her in the guest bedroom. I shouldn't have let my guard down with her. Now, she knew—she had seen how fucking broken I was, and it couldn't be undone. All that I could do was make sure I put distance between us before I did something worse, like hurt her the next time the night terrors came.

I'd seen how scared she'd been last night, even if she'd tried to hide it for my sake. Andrea was stubborn and defiant, and I knew she wouldn't ever admit she feared me or what had happened. That fierce pride was what made her my darling brat when we played. But I'd seen the truth in her eyes…she'd been fucking terrified of me.

She had a right to be. She had no idea how bad it could really get. The thought of harming her in any way made me want to throw up, paralyzed me in a way almost nothing else did.

When I was awake, I was in control, for the most part. Even when I had a panic attack, I knew that it was just the trauma, even if knowing that didn't get my body to cooperate or calm down. But when I was asleep, it was all real to me. Blood in my mouth. Sand in my nose. In my lungs. Fighting the enemy with the intent to kill.

"Chase." Andrea dropped her arms, softening. "Talk to me. Please. Let me be there for you."

As if there was anything she could do. Any way that she could mend what was shattered when she deserved a man who was whole and untouched by those lurking demons. This wasn't like a piece of broken furniture she could repair. Human beings didn't work like that. Scar tissue and horrific memories didn't just go away.

"There's nothing to talk about," I said, hating my cold tone of voice, but knew it was necessary. "Please pack up the last of your things in the bathroom. I'll arrange for Ford to pick you up and take you back to your place."

"Are you kidding me?" she said heatedly. "Chase, I'm *worried* about you. What, you're allowed to freak out over me when something happens, but I can't do the same? You can't even let me in a little bit when you've taken over my entire life? You made me move in with you. You won't let me drive myself to and from work. But I see you have a nightmare—"

"I said we're not talking about this," I cut her off, bristling. "And a nightmare is not the same thing as someone fucking stalking you."

No, it was just my bullshit, my trauma, and I had to deal with it. My life wasn't in active danger like hers was. In fact, part of the problem was that my threat wasn't tangible, but I couldn't seem to convince my brain of that once it shut down for the night. A part of me was stuck, forever, in that world of death and loss.

But Andrea's life was in real time jeopardy. Not the same thing at all.

"If my life is in danger, then you kicking me out because you're having some kind of crisis isn't a way to keep me safe, now is it?" Andrea's tone clearly indicated she thought she'd put me into checkmate.

"I have an entire security firm full of men at my disposal, who owe me big-time for favors I've done for them," I reminded her. "I've arranged a security detail for you. 24-hour surveillance and an escort to and from work."

"I don't give a crap about a security detail! I don't want your random buddies, I want you!" Her voice cracked under the weight of anger and something worse. Desperation. "I care about you—"

"Well, you shouldn't." The words came out too fast. Too sharp.

She blinked at me, stunned. "Oh, so you're allowed to care about me but—"

"I don't," I snapped coldly. It was a lie. A vicious, necessary one.

Her expression splintered, like I'd just taken a hammer to the fragile trust we'd built. Her mouth parted slightly, but no sound came out. Just disbelief shimmering in her eyes. Grief.

Inside, I was crumbling. My lungs were tight, like I couldn't get enough air. My heart thudded so violently I could hear it echo in my ears. I wanted to take it all back, to gather her into my arms and hold her until the pain I'd just inflicted went away, for both of us.

But I didn't move because I knew I couldn't give her what she needed. I wasn't the man she deserved. Not with the shit I carried. She wasn't going to be safe as long as she was with me, not emotionally and perhaps not even physically.

"Don't say that," Andrea whispered in an aching tone. "I know it's not true."

It *wasn't* true. Not even close. I cared so goddamn much that it scared the shit out of me. Loving her...it had started to feel inevitable. And that was exactly why I had to cut this off now. Before I failed her in a way I couldn't undo. Before she saw the darkest corners of me that I couldn't even look at in the mirror.

"I'm sorry you've fallen for the belief that you're more to me than you are, but what you are, is my sub," I said, forcing myself to sever the relationship, for her own good. "Which you shouldn't be anymore. You know enough by now to go have fun on your own. I was giving you an education, remember? That was it."

God, it felt like I was driving knives under my

fingernails to say such cruel things to her, things that couldn't be farther from the truth.

Andrea stared at me, bottom lip trembling, and the look on her face...it wasn't just pain. It was betrayal, vulnerable and raw.

I'd never hated myself more.

I wanted to reach for her, fall to my knees, beg her to see the truth, that I was doing this to protect her, not because I didn't care about her. But I clenched my jaw, locking myself down, because the hardest thing I would ever do was let her go. For her. For both of us. Because if I didn't, I was afraid she'd be the one I broke next.

Without another word, Andrea went to the bathroom and packed up her remaining toiletries. She shoved them into the luggage and zipped it up. Then, she glanced up at me, her chin high, defiance blazing in her eyes as if she refused to let me see her fall apart.

"Fuck you, Chase," she snapped. "Seriously, fuck you."

She stormed out, leaving me alone with the wreckage I'd caused and the silence that felt a hell of a lot like guilt and self-loathing.

CHAPTER 22

Andrea

"That's it. I'm beating the shit out of him for you."

I groaned where I lay on the couch with a cool washcloth over my eyes, trying to do something to ease the pounding in my head. "Violet, please don't get arrested for murder."

"Murder's too good for him," she muttered. "Too quick. Too clean. He needs to *suffer*."

I peeled the washcloth off enough to see Violet stomping back and forth across the living room. A living room I'd filled with empty wine bottles and ice cream cartons to drown my sorrows. I'd spent the last week being the most pathetic person in the city. And that was saying something in Las Vegas.

"He's twice your size and ex-military," I pointed out. "I don't think you'll be kicking his ass anytime soon."

"I'll bring my brass knuckles," Violet said, lips pursed. "And trust me, size isn't much against pure rage. You ever tried to wrestle an angry cat?"

The mental image of Violet acting like a pissed-off feline and yowling and scratching and climbing all over Chase was pretty hysterical, and I snorted with laughter. "Look, he wasn't kind about how he ended things, I admit that. But come on. He was right. I saw more into the situation than was there. Chase is... he's clearly haunted by what happened in the military," I said, trying to talk myself down from the heartbreak. "He's hypervigilant, so he took me into his home and I read that as romantic, and that's on me. He never made me any promises and he was straight-forward about our situation. I'm the one who muddied it."

Violet stopped pacing and stared at me like I'd grown a second head. "Are you hearing yourself right now? He pulled you into his life, into his *bed*, practically branded you with that look he gets when someone so much as breathes in your direction. But oh, sure, *you're* the one who misread things?"

I tried to laugh, but it cracked halfway through and came out sounding brittle. "It doesn't matter now, does it? He made it pretty clear I was just a lesson for him. A…phase."

Violet sat down beside me and gently pried the washcloth from my hand. "He's a liar."

I blinked up at her. "Excuse me?"

"He's lying. To you. To himself. That man looked at you like you were sunlight and he'd been buried in the dark for years. And then he threw it away because he's scared of hurting you?" Her voice lowered, gentle but firm. "He pushed you away because he thinks he's broken. That he's protecting you by letting you go. Which, FYI, is the worst kind of romantic bullshit."

"Then why does it feel like it's my fault? Like I'm the idiot who fell too fast, wanted too much, and saw forever with a man who can't give me the same?"

Violet's fingers laced through mine. "Because you're human. And you loved him. And maybe he's too messed up right now to love you the way you deserve, but that doesn't mean what you felt was wrong. Or that you're wrong for still loving him."

I didn't answer. I couldn't. My throat was too

tight and the ache in my chest pulsed too hard to form words. But I squeezed her hand, clinging to the only piece of comfort I had left because deep down, buried beneath all the heartbreak and humiliation, I still wanted Chase Noble. And that terrified me more than anything.

And now here I was, wallowing in a mess that I made myself. It was pathetic, but I couldn't seem to get myself out of this funk. I felt like a zombie the last week. I went to and from work, transported by Ford or Tate—never Austin, I noticed, salt in the wound—and I laid about at home. Like a lump.

In spite of all Violet's attempts to cheer me up, I still felt like shit the next morning, but certainly more defiant. I ignored the security firm's vehicle that was parked across the street for me. I was tired of being chauffeured, and especially by men who all knew that Chase broke up with me. Instead, I got into my own car, flipped off the guy waiting in the vehicle across the street as I pulled out, and I drove myself to work like a goddamn adult.

The car followed me. Of course it did. Ugh. I wished I could be annoyed and tell him to fuck off completely, but I couldn't afford that. My stalker was still out there and even though there hadn't been anything since the flowers, I couldn't quite let my guard down. If Chase still thought I needed protection even with everything that happened between us, I trusted his opinion. I trusted his professional instincts, even though he broke my damn heart.

It had to be Heath, right? Nobody else knew me so well. Nobody else could think of the things this stalker had. And I couldn't get that grocery store run-in out of my mind...

At work, I was doing the bare minimum to get by. It wasn't like me, I knew that, but my mind was so bogged down by other things I'd found it hard to concentrate.

"Skipping lunch again?" Brandon asked, stopping by my office after he'd returned from getting himself something to eat.

I should've known he'd notice I hadn't left, or brought my own lunch. "I'm not hungry."

I knew my eating habits had been terrible. Since the breakup, I didn't eat lunch or sometimes even breakfast, then got home and ate nothing but junk food. A diet of wine and ice cream was not sustainable. It was terrible. I was pretty sure Violet would be staging an intervention soon.

"Sure you are." Brandon pulled something out from behind his back and I saw it was a fresh sandwich from the deli across the street. I often grabbed lunch there, and they catered to us pretty often for meetings. "C'mon, you need to at least try and eat something."

I accepted the sandwich. It was very sweet of him and he got my order right. "Thank you."

He sat down in the chair in front of my desk. "What's got you so down? This really isn't like you."

I didn't like discussing my personal life, especially not with the guy who I knew was jealous of Chase, but I couldn't help it. I needed to tell someone who wasn't my sister. "Chase and I broke up."

Actually, there was nothing to *break up* since we weren't together, but I wasn't about to explain all of that to Brandon.

"Oh."

I shrugged, unwrapping the sandwich, sinking a little more into my pity party. "I should've known it wasn't meant to be. I guess sometimes you just delude yourself, you know?"

Brandon nodded. "Well… now you can find the right guy for you. One who'll treat you the way you deserve. One that doesn't take you for granted."

I sighed. "Yeah. I suppose you're right."

Brandon smiled, like he thought he'd said

something profound. Maybe he had. But the truth was, the only guy I wanted was Chase.

Even now, with everything fractured between us, I still caught myself checking my phone for a message that wasn't there. Listening for the sound of his voice. Waking up expecting the heat of his body next to mine, only to be greeted by an empty bed and even emptier ache in my chest.

I took a bite of my sandwich to keep from saying any of that out loud.

"Anyway," Brandon said after a moment, stretching back in his chair like he planned to settle in. "Maybe we could hang out sometime. You know, get your mind off things."

I paused mid-chew, forcing a neutral smile, because that was the very last thing I wanted. "I think I need a little time on my own."

"Oh. Of course," he said quickly, but the flicker of disappointment in his eyes didn't go unnoticed.

"Thanks for the sandwich, though," I said quietly, wanting to be polite.

"Anytime." Brandon stood, giving me one last smile before heading for the door.

Once he was gone, I leaned back in my chair, staring at the ceiling like the answers might be written there. Clearly, I'd made a mistake with Chase. Gotten too close. Let myself believe in something I should have kept locked up tight. But I couldn't stop hoping, *aching*, for the man who'd made me feel more alive than anyone else ever had.

Even if he'd broken me to do it.

CHAPTER 23

Chase

I tapped my fingers against my desk, my jaw clenched so hard I knew my dentist was going to have a comment about it at my next visit.

Tate wasn't able to find anything substantial on Brandon, and nobody else in the tech department did either. The guy was clean. I supposed it was just a dead end, then. Not a threat, just a mediocre, insecure guy who was jealous that he wasn't with my woman and that I'd won her over him instead.

Well. Not *my* woman. Not my anything. I'd made fucking sure of that.

In the week since Andrea had left my place, I had come to realize how damn sterile the place was. I had the latest technology. Everything was top-of-the-line. But there was no warmth or sense of personality. Andrea had brought all that when she'd moved in, and it wasn't until she was gone that I realized how empty and lackluster my place was.

Truth was, I hated being without her. I felt hollow inside. My bed felt too empty. I hated waking up to an empty place with no bacon sizzling or coffee brewing, no off-key humming from Andrea in the shower. I hated coming home to a place that was now cold and dark. I'd been eating nothing but takeout again. There was no point in making dinner for just myself. But to be honest, everything tasted like shit.

As pathetic as it was, I missed Andrea like someone had taken a spoon and scooped out my organs, and I was lost over it. I had never felt this way about anyone before and I was completely unprepared to deal with the fall out.

The look on her face as she walked out of my place was going to haunt me forever. God. I was a real fucking tool, huh? It wasn't just that Andrea was gone. I had made her leave. I had done this to myself, and I had hurt her in the process. The one thing I wanted to avoid doing, I had done it. And spectacularly.

Christ.

I checked the time, frowning. Tate was supposed to have let me know when Andrea was home from work, that she was safe, but that was twenty minutes ago.

"Knock, knock."

I looked up to see Austin in the doorway. "You need something?" I asked, a little shortly.

Austin put his hands up in a gesture of surrender. "Hey, I come in peace."

I sighed and rubbed my fingers across my forehead. "Sorry."

None of this was Austin's fault, of all people. I had done this to myself. And now I was a mess, nothing but sharp edges and I was inevitably going to cut anyone who got close.

"We had a meeting today," Austin said, settling into the chair in front of my desk. "And we unanimously decided that you look like shit."

"Thanks," I said in a droll tone. "It's always good to know you care."

"Ford told me that you kicked Andrea out. Apparently her sister threatened just about every body part you have, including organs, and your dick," he said, humor lacing his voice. "Ford said

Violet was very creative about what she'd do to those body parts, as well. I think he was impressed."

"Great," I said, annoyed at…well, every fucking thing. "May they have a long and happy life together."

"Don't deflect, jackass." Only Austin could make a word like 'jackass' sound affectionate. "You broke up with Andrea? Seriously?"

"You can't break up with someone that you're not dating. We were never a couple."

Austin's brows rose. "Okay, wow, if you're that bad of a liar it's a good thing the military didn't make you an undercover spy when you enlisted."

"Like you'd know anything about being in the military," I snapped.

Austin gave me a hard look, completely unfazed by my outburst. He didn't flinch. Didn't back down. "You don't get to pull that '*I'm so broken crap*' with me," he said, his voice low and firm, cutting through my defenses like a scalpel. "Yeah, you were different when you came home. You used to be laid back and lighthearted. The Navy changed that. I barely recognized you when I saw you again."

My jaw clenched tight. "Yeah, it did, because I saw shit you can't possibly imagine—"

"No, I can't," Austin said, cutting me off. "But this isn't the goddamn Trauma Olympics, Chase. You know who else has scars? Everyone. Homeless vets, assault victims, kids in war zones—hell, even some of our clients are walking trauma cases, and you never once told them they don't get to be happy."

I didn't answer, and he pushed harder.

"You think Andrea deserves better? Fine. But don't you dare pretend you're doing her some noble favor by pushing her away. She made you happy. We *all* saw it. That woman walked into your life and flipped every switch you'd turned off, and you let her. You were a better man *for* it."

"I'm better with her," I agreed, the words catching in my throat. "But she's better without *me*."

Austin barked out a humorless laugh. "Bullshit. You're not protecting Andrea. You're punishing her for caring about you."

I didn't have a comeback. Not one that didn't make me feel like a hypocrite.

Austin sat forward in the chair, his expression shrewd. "Tell me the truth, Chase. You really gonna sit back and watch her fall for someone else? Watch some other guy touch her, kiss her, give her everything you're too goddamn afraid to?"

That possibility hit me like a sledgehammer, because that wasn't something I'd allowed myself to think about until Austin had forced those images into my brain. The thought of her in someone else's arms made my chest feel like it was caving in. Made me a little insane, too. Not because I didn't think she deserved love...but because she was *mine*.

Austin saw it, and smirked, just a little. "Yeah. That's what I thought. You've got enough ghosts, man. Don't make her another one."

With that, Austin walked out of my office and I sat there, trying to remember how the hell to breathe. Leaving me to wonder, too, when the fuck my baby brother had learned to get the upper hand on me like that.

My phone chimed with a text from Tate: *She's home. Stubborn as fuck, just like you. Hurry up and take her off our hands so she can stop driving us insane.*

I stared at the text until the phone screen went black, then stared a little longer, wondering if I still had the balls to fight for the only person who'd ever made the demons inside of me go quiet.

CHAPTER 24

Andrea

iolet went out of town for the weekend with some coworkers who were also her friends—some kind of *we need to go camping in Joshua Tree before we kill all our clients and burn the casino down* type thing—and to be honest, I was kind of grateful.

I loved my sister, but she was hovering, and between Violet and the nonstop bodyguards, I needed space. A weekend to myself at home would do me good.

Saturday was fine, except for the part where Ford awkwardly knocked on my door and asked me if I knew I could still go out somewhere if I wanted. I wasn't on house arrest.

"I'm fine," I told him. "Go away." Then I slammed the door in his face.

That had felt really good to do. Ha.

The bodyguard who introduced himself to me on Sunday as Garrett was some newer guy I didn't know, but he'd clearly been informed by Chase that his ass was grass if anything happened to me, because he did a whole perimeter sweep and checked my house before he went back to his car.

Once, I would've found it funny that a guy was so scared of Chase. Now, I just wanted to call Chase and tell him that if he was still so fucking paranoid, he could damn well just watch over me himself.

I went to bed on Sunday night, dreading the next day. Going into work could be a good distraction, and probably one I needed, but I just wanted to keep hiding away from the world.

Then, as if my subconscious wanted to punish me, I had a nightmare.

Chase was drowning in a pit of sand, and I couldn't tug him up, no matter how hard I tried. I kept pulling and pulling, but he was still sinking under. I begged him to help me help him, but he wouldn't even look at me. The sand swallowed him up, and I screamed, and screamed, and—

I jolted awake.

My breath was coming hard and fast. I stared up at the ceiling, trying to calm myself down. I couldn't remember the last time I'd had a bad nightmare like that. All of this with Chase was seriously getting to me.

Maybe that was the real issue, at the end of the day. Chase was hurting over something and I wanted to help him, but he wouldn't let me. He'd literally rather be swallowed up, and hurt me as well, than address whatever the issue was. I wasn't just brokenhearted over him. I was worried about him.

But if he wouldn't talk about it, I couldn't make him.

I got up out of bed to get myself a glass of water to calm my nerves. Luckily our place was small. I couldn't imagine how I'd handle a big house right now, everything dark and empty and echoing. I grabbed a glass and filled it with water without even turning on the light, standing in the dark kitchen, enjoying the peace.

An odd scraping sound reached my ears.

I froze.

It was quiet—maybe I had imagined it?

There it was again. It was a sound that was familiar, but it took me a second to place it, because, I realized as my blood went cold, I'd only ever seen/heard it in movies.

Like horror movies.

Someone was picking the lock on the back door.

The glass of water nearly slipped out of my hand, but I clamped down and managed to set it in the sink. I couldn't let this person know I was awake.

Trembling all over, I tiptoed in my pajamas to the front door. My heart hammered in my throat. I winced as I slowly undid the lock and turned the handle. Once the door was open, I slipped out, running across the street to the car that was parked, faithfully, on the opposite curb.

I banged on the rolled up window, and the bodyguard jolted, dropping the book he was reading. "There's someone trying to get in to my place!"

To his credit, Garrett moved damn fast. He rushed out of the car and ran towards the house. I followed at a distance, burning with curiosity over who it could be even while simultaneously terrified that someone had tried to break in while I was alone and vulnerable.

There were crashing noises from inside the house and then the sound of the back door slamming. I hurried through to see a dark hooded figure hopping the back fence, the bodyguard just exiting the house to tear after him.

I waited in my doorway, trembling in the aftermath because I was fairly certain that whoever it had been was my stalker.

After a few minutes, the bodyguard came back, already on the phone to someone. He shook his head at me as he approached. "Whoever the guy is, he was fast. And I didn't get a good look at him because of the hoodie he was wearing."

Shortly thereafter, I could hear sirens in the distance and sighed. Yeah, the police would have to be told about this. They arrived just a few minutes later, but they weren't the only ones. A familiar car screeched to a halt in front of my house and Chase sprinted out, eyes wild. I figured Garrett must have called him, along with the police.

"Andrea!?"

I was sitting on my front stoop at that point, in my bathrobe, feeling horribly embarrassed as police officers swarmed my place. "Hey."

He reached me and immediately pulled me up so I was standing, checking me over for injuries. "You're okay?" he asked frantically. "You're not hurt?"

"I'm fine, Chase—"

Before I could say anything more, Chase was rounding on the bodyguard, his expression livid. "What the hell is wrong with you? The guy gets into her house and you were doing, what, a fucking crossword puzzle?"

"Chase!" I snapped in shock. "Garrett was in the car out front. How was he supposed to know that there was something going on at the back door? He chased the guy. He was right there the moment I called for help, leave him alone!"

Chase jammed his fingers through his hair and scowled. "Ford never should have let some wet-behind-the-ears guy take over surveillance tonight—"

"And this wouldn't even be a problem if you didn't kick me out, you idiotic jackass!" I finished heatedly.

Several officers stared at me for a moment, and then went back to what they were doing. My face burned with embarrassment, but I squared my shoulders and faced Chase down.

"I was safe when I was with you, but you made it clear that you didn't want me around anymore," I said, my anger rising. "That's your choice, okay, fine. But I'm on my own now, and that means I'm going to do things my way. That also means that I might get hurt. You don't get a say anymore."

"You're not alone," Chase said, his voice low and rough with emotion, contradicting the closed off man I'd left behind that day I'd walked out of his place. "You'll always have me to protect you."

I jabbed him in the chest with my finger. "You protected me best when you had me in your bed."

Garrett made a strangled noise and quickly found somewhere else to be. I didn't blame him.

"Doesn't matter," Chase insisted, lips pressed into a firm line. "You'll always have me there to protect you."

He wasn't making sense. None of this did. "No, I don't. You can't have it both ways, Chase," I said, confused by his words, and his behavior. "What is wrong with you? You can't be there for me and also push me away! And I'm not going to stand around for weeks or months or years while you figure your shit out, because if there's one thing I can thank you for, it's teaching me that I deserve to stand up for myself, because the right person will appreciate it. I know my worth now, so thank you, and that means I'm not going to—"

Chase grabbed me and yanked me to him, crushing his mouth to mine. I gasped in surprise as he kissed me senseless. My train of thought came to an end as my brain shut down. Goddamn him for being a such good kisser. I melted against him, my fingers curling into his t-shirt as I clung to him, kissing him back.

The police radio went off and I jolted, shoving Chase back as I came to my senses. I stared at him in shock. My lips tingled and my heart pounded. I couldn't even begin to process what had just happened.

I shook my head and went inside my house while the police wrapped up outside, my body shaking. I didn't understand what was going on. Why would Chase say those things to me and kiss me like I meant something to him?

"Andrea..." Chase followed me inside.

I whirled on him, feeling raw and confused after that kiss. "No, you don't get to do that. You don't get to go back and forth with me like this, playing with my emotions!"

"Andrea. Do you have any idea how lucky you were?" Chase's gaze held mine, and he looked genuinely distraught. "If you hadn't woken up for that water, you could be dead right now."

He sounded shaken. Like he'd seen a ghost, and maybe he had. Maybe it had been mine. "And do you want to know why I woke up in the first place?" I asked, swallowing past the sudden lump in my throat. "I had a nightmare. About you. I dreamed you were sinking," I whispered, feeling the hot sting of tears in my eyes as I remembered the vision. "I couldn't pull you out, because you wouldn't let me. I couldn't save you. You chose to just... get swallowed up."

He flinched, and for a second I saw it—his soul stripped bare. He appeared to struggle internally with something, his jaw clenched and his eyes clouded over with memories. When his gaze finally came back into focus, his expression was somber.

"The police are going to go," he said quietly. "Why don't we make some coffee. I want to tell you something."

I hesitated, but the vulnerability on his face wasn't something I'd ever seen from him before and it softened my anger toward him. I wasn't ready to forgive him for pushing me out of his life, but I could sense that this was important to him, and I needed to hear what he had to say.

With statements given and evidence taken, the police finally cleared out, and the poor guy assigned to watch me went home for the night. I brewed coffee, and Chase and I settled down on the couch.

He was silent for a long moment, leaning forward, hands clasped between his widespread legs, his gaze on the floor. He seemed to be trying to figure out what to say and I waited patiently for him to speak.

"I have these nightmares," he finally said quietly. "It's always the same and they always feel real to me. I have a lot of shit that I carry from my time in the military. An assignment that went sideways, losing people I cared about because I couldn't control the fact that we'd been given bad intel. These soldiers were my responsibility, and they died."

My throat tightened, and I reached out and grabbed one of his hands. Much to my relief he didn't pull away, just laced our fingers together tighter.

"I've gone to therapy for my PTSD but… I don't know, I still feel pretty fucked up." He exhaled a long breath and met my gaze. "And these nightmares I have…there have been times when I've woken up with my hands around a pillow, because in my dream I was choking out an enemy, and the possibility of me doing something like that to you scares the shit out of me."

It was hard to hear what he was saying, but I sat beside him, silent, letting him finish while I listened.

"All I wanted to do was protect you from me," he continued. "I thought I was doing the right thing, that if I pushed you away now, it would hurt less than if I let you all the way in and failed you later. The thought of ever hurting you, Andrea..." He shook his head and shuddered.

I'd never heard him sound like this, like the emotion was choking him. It made my heart, my lungs, my very bones ache.

I gently disentangled our hands so that I could move over, climbing right into Chase's lap and looping my arms around his shoulders, holding him tightly. He stiffened at first, startled, then slowly, achingly, he relaxed against me. His arms locked around my waist, his face pressing into my throat like he needed the contact just to breathe.

"I thought I could do this alone," he whispered against my neck. "I thought I *had* to...until you."

"You're not alone, Chase." I took his face in my hands, needing to look into his eyes. "You have me and I'm not going anywhere. But you need to stop pushing me away, because I'm going to keep coming back, until you finally see what I already know. You're not broken. You're just a man who's been through hell. And I'll walk through it with you, in any way you need, if you let me."

"It's effort, Andrea," he said gruffly. "I'm not going to pretend it isn't going to take work."

"And you're worth that effort, Chase." I said,

meaning it. "You are worth it, to *me*. I promise. Yes, you are my dom, you are in charge when we're playing, but that's not what I want our relationship to be all the time. I want us to be equal. You take good care of me, so let me take good care of you. Let me be there for you."

Chase tightened his grip on me, then kissed me again, but this time it wasn't desperate, it was reverent and sweet. Like he was finally coming up for air and choosing to believe that he could truly have it all.

"Take me back to your place, Chase," I murmured against his lips.

"I won't let you leave again, if I do," Chase warned me, but he was grinning now. "I don't plan on letting you go ever again."

"That sounds good to me," I whispered. I kissed his cheek, and pressed our foreheads together.

We stayed like that, holding each other for a long, long time.

CHAPTER 25

Chase

*A*fter we finished just embracing and slowly breathing together, I took Andrea back to my condo, where she belonged. By that time it was pre-dawn, so I made her call in sick to work so she could sleep in.

Having Andrea back in my place made it seem that much more like home. And, knowing she was safe with me was an added bonus. Her stalker was still out there, clearly getting bolder, and my only priority was finding the person responsible for all these threats.

We were both too exhausted to talk when we

arrived. We just passed out in bed together. I slept deeply, no dreams, but feeling the weight of her in my arms even when unconscious, I was secure in the knowledge that she was exactly where she belonged.

The next day we moved some of her things back over to my place. I didn't officially tell her that she was going to move in with me on a more permanent basis than just the stalker situation, but I was pretty sure there wasn't going to be an argument when it happened.

I figured I'd wait a couple weeks before I started asking her what paint colors she'd like for the walls or when she'd like to move her art prints over. Actually, I was excited to buy her proper original art pieces of her own. Vegas always had some kind of art show going on, and I was in the mood to spoil her. Especially knowing that Andrea had endured such financial insecurity. I wanted her to know that I could get her not just anything she needed, but anything she wanted.

Even though this stalker was getting braver, Andrea insisted on going back to work on Tuesday. "I only skipped a day because I would've been falling asleep at my desk," she said.

I leaned against the bathroom doorway, watching

as she finished doing her hair for the day, just enjoying her presence and this lighter feeling inside me after our conversation at her place earlier. I felt happier...and hopeful about our future together.

"Breaking into your townhome is a major escalation," I said, not happy that she was leaving the house at all.

"I know that." Her gaze met mine in the bathroom mirror, and I didn't miss the stubborn set to her jaw. "But I can't let this guy stop me from living my life. If I stay home under house arrest all day, every day, hasn't he won in a different way? Doesn't that give him the control over me that he wants?"

I couldn't argue her point, as much as I wanted to. "I hope you know how brave you've been about all of this. Most people would have stayed cooped up inside and demanded we send an entire army to protect them."

"I don't know if I'd call myself brave," she said, giving me a sassy smile. "I think obstinate and headstrong are better terms."

I snorted in amusement, then grew serious again. "This isn't a scene. You aren't being a brat to enjoy a punishment or get a rise out of me. You're choosing to keep living your life even though you're scared and you know it's a risk. That's bravery."

Andrea turned around, her face beautifully flushed. "Well. Thank you."

I dropped her off at the office before heading to work myself. I gave her a kiss before she slid out of the car, and I grinned as she waved goodbye to me before heading into the building.

I still had to do the security detail that I was paid to do, but I found time late in the afternoon to head back into the office and go over the files on Heath that Tate had sent me. I was sure he was the stalker. He didn't have any priors, but that didn't mean he was innocent, either.

Heath knew about the tattoo, and about Andrea's personal life. He'd shown up in her neighborhood at a grocery store, exactly when Andrea had been there, and he'd made it clear he wanted her back.

Unfortunately, and worryingly, we couldn't find him.

Heath had moved out of his last place about a month ago, leaving no forwarding address. I tried calling his workplace but was told that he'd taken some time off using his accumulated vacation days and they hadn't heard from him in a few weeks.

That definitely didn't allay my suspicions at all. In fact, it heightened them.

I just had to figure out where the fuck this guy had gone.

I was just getting ready to leave to go and pick up Andrea from work when my phone buzzed with a text from her. I grabbed it and looked it over.

Hey, handsome, going to be a little later than planned. Brandon and I are staying after hours, just the two of us, to push through on this project. Which is your fault for making me skip work yesterday by the way.

I grinned and texted her back. *Excuse you, but I don't recall twisting your arm to make you do anything. You were exhausted. But sure, next time I'll make you get up and go to work with only four hours of sleep.*

Now that's sadistic, Andrea texted me back. *And not in a fun way.*

And here I thought you enjoyed pain and punishment, I teased her.

"Yo, Chase?"

I looked up to see Tate standing there in my office, a folder in his hand. He looked a little worried.

"Hey." I put the phone down. "What's up?"

"You remember that guy you asked me to look into?"

I sat up a little straighter, thinking *this must be it*. Finally. Heath's location, or some proof that he'd done this sort of thing before. "Yeah?"

Tate tapped the folder against his hand. "Well, I kept digging, and it took me a bit of time, but I was able to unearth a juvenile file."

I leaned back in my chair and frowned. "Juvenile records are generally sealed."

"I know." Tate grinned at me and winked.

I was impressed, knowing Tate had most likely hacked into the system to retrieve the information. "Damn, you're a master of your craft."

Tate passed me the file and I opened it.

"He was arrested twice for stalking and assaulting former girlfriends," Tate said, giving me a quick rundown. "He was fifteen one time, seventeen the next. Because he was under the age of eighteen all records were sealed, and as far as I can tell he basically got a slap on the wrist for it. You know how it is, the guy's young, so they want to give him a chance to grow up and do better."

"Yeah, and after that, he clearly got smarter. Knew how to do it so he wouldn't get caught," I murmured. I stared down at the file, expecting to see Heath's name there at the top—and froze.

It wasn't Heath.

The file said *Brandon Smith*.

I looked up at Tate, my blood going cold. "This is—this is the coworker I asked you to look into."

"Yeah." Tate sounded a little confused. "I'm still tracking down the ex-boyfriend. But this is pretty concerning, right?"

More than that. My heart slammed against my chest and I threw the file aside and got to my feet, grabbing my phone. "I have to go."

I was pretty sure this man had tried to break into her home just two days ago and now he had her alone at the office. I had to get to Andrea. *Now.*

CHAPTER 26

Andrea

I checked the time on the computer again as I finished tweaking another video. 5:30 pm. Ugh. At this rate, it was going to take us at least another hour to finish the presentation we needed to turn in by tomorrow morning, first thing.

Unless Brandon started doing something other than stare at me, which I was beginning to find disconcerting. We were in the conference room, sitting across from one another at the table, and I could feel him looking at me. It was taking everything in me not to snap at him.

I exhaled a deep breath and told myself it was just the stress from the last couple of days. On top of the stress from the last week. On top of the stress from the last couple months.

Wow, I needed a vacation.

Brandon was probably just worried about me, but I suspected that wasn't the case. I had appreciated his sympathy and listening ear the other day, but I had the feeling that he was going to try to ask me out again and I really did not have the patience to get it through his stubborn skull that I wasn't going to date him. Ever.

Brandon was a good guy. But no matter how many good qualities a guy had, they could piss you off if they wouldn't take 'no' for an answer.

You're just being paranoid, I told myself, sighing and sitting back in my chair. I had been an absolute wreck for the last week. Of course I was going to start getting pissed off for no reason at people who didn't deserve it.

I couldn't wait to get back to Chase's place. I was sure he'd find a way to get rid of the stress for me...

Brandon cleared his throat. "Andrea?"

I glanced over at him. He was still staring at me. "You okay?" I asked.

"I'm—I'm fine." Brandon smiled at me. It was a

341

cute smile, he was a cute guy, but I suddenly felt the hairs at the back of my neck stand up. "I'm actually doing really great, because you and your boyfriend broke up. I know that sounds harsh, but it's the truth."

I wasn't sure what to say to that, so I didn't say anything at all. But that uneasy feeling inside of me increased.

"I'm sorry you were hurt, I really am. I never want you to be hurt," Brandon continued, sounding robotically sincere. "But that's why you need a different kind of man. A kind, nice person who will show you just how special you are. I hope that you're ready to see that now. You just had to go through that breakup with that *jerk*, to appreciate what you really need, what you really want."

I opened my mouth to tell him *actually, the last thing any woman enjoys is being told what she wants,* and then forced it shut again because I didn't want to do or say anything to antagonize him. I had to remind myself that most people weren't like Chase, they didn't like it when I was defiant and prickly.

Still, Brandon was delusional, and I couldn't ignore that horrible sick feeling swirling in my stomach. Some instinct in me screaming that something was wrong, and I didn't know *why*, but I knew that I needed to listen to that voice.

"Brandon," I started slowly. "You've been incredibly kind to me…"

My phone buzzed and I glanced at it. It was from Chase.

"Sorry, one sec…" I opened the text.

IT'S BRANDON, Chase's text read. *GET OUT OF THERE NOW. I'M COMING FOR YOU.*

Panic jolted through me, and I felt my expression change to reflect that apprehension the second I read the message. *You have no poker face,* Violet would always tell me, laughing. She wasn't wrong.

Brandon. It's Brandon. Brandon was my stalker.

I slowly looked up, trying desperately to stay calm and keep my expression neutral, and I found myself staring at a complete stranger. The man sitting across from me was Brandon, of course he was, but he was not at all the man I knew. Something completely shifted, and now I could see a dangerous, gleaming light in his eyes, a tightness to his face.

He knew that I knew.

I swallowed hard. I wanted to flee, terror gripping me, but I ignored it. I'd never backed down before and I wasn't going to back down now.

Whatever happened, I was going to go down fighting.

I stood up, and he did the same. A standoff, it felt like, judging by the way his gaze narrowed in on me. I calculated the distance to the door, but knew he could easily intercept me, so I remained where I was for now.

"You're my stalker," I said, calling him out on his shit. "It's you."

"Of course it was me, Andrea." Brandon sounded completely unashamed. Pleased, even. Relieved, like he was happy that I knew. "Who else would love you enough to do what I've done?"

"Love?" I gaped at him in shock. Yep, definitely delusional, but weren't most stalkers? "That's what you call it?"

"That's what it is." Brandon shrugged and gave me a smile that was no longer cute, but creepy. "I'm so glad that it's all out in the open now. It's been exhausting waiting for you to figure it out. To open your eyes and see what's right in front of you. I've been patient, *love* must always be patient, but even I have my limits."

"You don't even know me."

"Of course I know you," he said, tapping his fingers on the conference table. "I know everything about you, even the parts that you don't want people to see."

"You have no *idea* who I am," I snapped. "Following a person around doesn't mean you know them! So you saw my shoulder tattoo, and you figured out where I live. That doesn't mean you know jack shit about *me*."

Antagonizing Brandon probably went against everything you should do when facing a potentially violent psychopath, but I figured I just had to keep him talking until Chase arrived. I only had to hold out until then. And I wasn't very good at being diplomatic.

"I know jack shit, huh?" Anger vibrated through Brandon's voice and flared to life in his eyes. "I know exactly what you get up to, you little slut. Visiting an exclusive sex club and letting that asshole put his dirty, filthy hands all over you. You can do so much better than him, Andrea."

I was sure my horror showed all over my face. Brandon had been doing far more stalking, and for far longer, than I'd realized. I wanted to throw up.

He started around the table. "I tried to be nice. I really wanted to be a gentleman, but clearly you like it rough, and dirty, and I'm more than happy to accommodate those desires, too."

I backed up instinctively, my heart pounding so

hard I thought it might rip straight through my chest, but I forced myself to stay upright. Alert. In control.

"You don't want to do this," I said, forcing my voice to stay level, despite the terror coiling through me. "If you touch me, there's no coming back from that. My boyfriend is former military and works at a private security firm. He'll make sure you never see daylight again."

"You mean *ex*-boyfriend," Brandon sneered, moving closer. "He threw you away like trash. I'm the one who's been here for you. Watching out for you. Loving you. I *see* you. He doesn't deserve to breathe the same air as you."

He was unhinged. Fully gone. There was no kindness left in his eyes, and I knew I had no choice but to try and make a run for the door. I started in that direction, but Brandon was faster. He lunged in front of me, grabbing my arm and yanking me back. I cried out in pain.

"What's the matter, baby?" Brandon asked, his voice eerily soft. "Isn't this how you like it?"

I glared at him. "Let go of me, *now*."

"I know you don't mean that," he said, shoving me back against the conference table. "Now I know exactly what you want."

He grabbed my throat and I gasped as my

airway closed off. I clawed at his arm, but couldn't dislodge his hold. Brandon leaned in close, eyes bright with what my terror-addled brain could only describe as madness. "You. Are. Mine. Got it?"

"Fuck *you*," I gasped out, and I brought my knee up as hard as I could between his legs.

Brandon doubled over, crying out in pain, his hands grabbing his crotch. I sprinted for the door, kicking my heels off as I ran. I didn't bother with the elevator but lunged for the emergency stairwell, running down them. I could hear movement above me and I knew that Brandon, even with the injury, was hot on my heels. And now, even madder than before.

I hurtled down to the lobby. Of course, of *course* the security guard wasn't there. Probably doing his rounds now that most people had left for the day. I screamed with frustration, tears pricking my eyes.

Behind me, I heard the door to the stairwell slam open. Fuck, I didn't have much time. I sprinted for the front doors, rushing out into the parking lot—and right into the path of a car. The car screeched to a halt and I felt my entire body sag in relief as Chase emerged.

"Andrea—"

I saw his face change to unconcealed rage as he

looked behind me, and the next moment I was shoved aside, put behind him, as Brandon emerged from the lobby the same moment Chase charged toward him. Chase moved faster than I thought possible. He grabbed Brandon by the wrist and used Brandon's forward movement against him, twisting his arm and flipping Brandon over on himself.

Brandon hit the ground hard on his stomach, arm bent behind him, Chase's knee planted firmly in the middle of his back, keeping him pinned.

"If you ever come near her again," Chase snarled at him, "I'll make damn sure you regret it. I will fucking *destroy* you for even looking in her direction then bury your fucking body somewhere in the desert where nobody will find you."

Brandon thrashed, trying to buck him off, but Chase didn't budge. His entire body radiated fury —controlled, focused, deadly.

Chase dug his phone out of his pocket with his free hand and dialed. "Hello? Yes, I need police immediately..."

My entire body shook with delayed shock. Tears burned the back of my eyes, but I refused to let them fall. I was still standing. Still breathing. Because of Chase.

Chase kept Brandon subdued until the police

arrived, and once they took him into custody, Chase walked toward me like I was the only thing left that mattered in the world. When he reached me, he gently cupped my face in his hands, his intense eyes searching my expression.

"Are you hurt?" His voice was rough with emotion, like he was scared the answer might undo him.

I shook my head. "You got here just in time."

The words felt inadequate. Nothing could capture the pure relief flooding through me. Nothing could express the way my knees nearly buckled from the weight of what *could* have happened, had Chase not arrived.

"You're okay," Chase promised, his voice calming me as he enveloped me in his strong arms, anchoring me. "You're okay."

"I know," I whispered, burrowing my face against his chest. "You're here."

As long as Chase was here, I was safe.

CHAPTER 27

Chase

The police arrived and I was able to hand Brandon off and finally, *finally* take Andrea into my arms. She trembled like a leaf, but didn't cry. My girl was strong and resilient, holding herself together like the badass she was.

I held her all through the interview process with the police, glaring when some of the cops tried to get me to step back. Andrea wanted me there, and I wasn't all that inclined to let go of my girlfriend after she'd nearly been assaulted and God knew what else by that man.

Finally, things wrapped up, and I was allowed

to take Andrea home. Brandon was being charged with a whole list of offenses, starting with aggravated assault, and even if the district attorney's office only found a couple of infractions, I'd find a lot more. Our company had fantastic lawyers.

"C'mon," I murmured, kissing the top of Andrea's head. "Let's get you home."

She gave me a tremulous smile. "I like the sound of that. Home."

Once we arrived back at my place, I insisted that Andrea sit on a stool at the kitchen island while I started making dinner—baked chicken, seasoned potatoes, and broccoli.

She watched me prep the fresh ingredients, decompressing after everything that had happened. "No take out?"

I glanced over my shoulder at her and grinned. "You deserve better than take out."

"Look at you, being all domestic," she teased.

"Speaking of domestic," I said, retrieving the pots and pans I needed. "You deserve a home that's not just white walls and boring furniture I bought from a catalogue. What do you say we take this weekend and go shopping? Pick out some paint colors, stop by some furniture stores?"

Andrea looked at me with wide, searching eyes.

"Are you asking me to... *properly* move in with you?"

"Yes," I said, meeting her questioning gaze. "If you'll have me."

Her lips parted, like the words stunned her. Then she softened, the shock melting into relief. "Of course I'll have you, *always*."

She stood up and walked around the island to kiss me, slow and sweet, like she wasn't just saying yes to the idea of moving in. She was saying yes to me. *All* of me.

I wrapped my arms around her and held her tight, as if I could somehow absorb the fear and trauma she'd just been through. "I'm sorry it took me so long to figure out it was him."

She leaned back just enough to look up at me, fingertips brushing my jaw. "You have nothing to be sorry for. How did you figure it out?"

I explained about his juvenile record. "I should've figured it out sooner. You were almost hurt. That's on me."

Andrea shook her head, fiercely. "No. You saved me. You've been saving me from the beginning, whether you realize it or not." Her hand slid down to my chest, resting over my heart. "You've been there every time I've needed you, even when *you* were hurting. You've gone above and beyond."

"You did a little saving yourself." I thought about the way she'd stood her ground in the conference room, refusing to cower, even when he'd cornered her. I'd heard the statement to the police. I'd heard the tremble in her voice when she recounted how she'd defended herself.

"That guy never stood a chance," I said, gently tucking a stray strand of hair behind her ear. "That's my girl. Brave as hell."

"Well," she said, eyes glinting as a smile curled her lips. "After dealing with *you*, he was a piece of cake," she teased.

That made me laugh, a sound that felt damn near foreign after the day we'd had. But then the amusement faded and the serious moment returned. I cupped her face in my hands again, gentle, loving. "I mean it, Andrea. I will always keep you safe. I promise. You are my everything."

She nodded, eyes shining. "I know. I always feel safe when I'm with you."

God, I loved her. And the moment I thought it, I realized I should say it out loud, for the first time ever to a woman. "I love you, Andrea Corbin."

Andrea stared at me for a moment, a bit in shock, then a smile spread over her face, one I'd never seen before. I realized it was because I had never seen her *this* happy. So elated and content.

"I love you, too," she said.

I kissed her, soft, lingering, like a vow I didn't need words to make.

We ate dinner quietly. Andrea didn't say much, so I didn't either. I just sat with her, letting the weight of the evening settle. When we finished, I stood and gathered the dishes.

"I'll clean up." I told her. "Why don't you go take a shower? Get warmed up and relax."

Andrea nodded gratefully, her expression soft, eyes distant, but not vacant. Just...tired. She'd been through a lot and all I wanted to do was take care of her.

While I rinsed the plates and loaded the dishwasher, I kept an ear out for her. The sound of the water turning on was oddly reassuring. A reminder she was just down the hall. A reminder that she'd survived.

When I finished, I wandered toward the bathroom, the need to be close to her pulling me like a tether. The whole room was filled with steam, and I could just make out the shape of Andrea through the frosted glass door.

My mouth watered and my dick stirred. My hands flexed at my sides. I wanted to worship every inch of her skin. Not just because I craved her, but because I needed her to feel everything I couldn't say in words. I needed her to feel cherished. Chosen. *Safe.*

Andrea was mine to love, and protect, and honor. She'd let me lead her in the bedroom, at The Players Club, in our dynamic. But this...what we were building now...this had to be different. This needed to be the beginning of everything real. It was time I finally let someone in all the way.

I raised my hand and tapped gently on the glass door. "Mind if I join you?"

There was a pause, then the glass door creaked open slightly. Steam swirled around her. She was bare, glistening, flushed pink from the heat of the water, but it was her expression that undid me. Open. Vulnerable. Trusting.

"You don't even have to ask," she said, smiling, almost shyly, like this was our first time.

Maybe, in a way it was. All the emotional barriers between us were finally gone, and what was left was raw and honest. Something more intimate than anything we'd done before. This wasn't about sex. It wasn't about dominance or submission. It was about trust. About choosing each other in the aftermath of fear, in the quiet space where love was louder than lust.

I stripped off my clothes and stepped inside, pulling her gently into my arms, letting the water rush over us both as I held her close, skin to skin. I could hardly believe I got to have this, *her*, for the rest of my life.

Andrea lifted a hand and placed it flat on my chest. I covered it with mine.

"I was scared today," she admitted, looking up at me. "I haven't let myself say that yet. Not to the cops, not even to myself. But I was scared, Chase."

"I know," I said, my voice hoarse. "I was, too."

My cock was already hard, and her breath caught when she felt my shaft pressed against her. I wanted her, that was a given, but whatever happened tonight was up to her.

"What do you want?" I murmured, seeing the lust in her eyes, but also something deeper. Something aching and raw. A need to reclaim something that had been taken from her.

"You," Andrea whispered. Her voice trembled, but never wavered. "I want...I want to stop feeling him. He put his hands on me. I want you to wash it away. Make me forget."

I exhaled slowly, gently brushing a hand over the bruises on her arm, then over the faint red marks lining her lower back. She was lucky she wasn't bruised on her throat, too, but he hadn't grabbed her tightly enough for that, thank God. He hadn't really been trying to choke her, just scare her.

Each mark made something dark stir inside me, something protective and violent, but I didn't let it show. Tonight wasn't about him. It was about her. That bastard wasn't ever going to touch her again.

I turned off the water and we dried off together, her skin warm and damp and smelling like my shampoo and soap, smelling like *me*. "I want to do something different tonight," I said.

"Oh?" she murmured, looking up at me curiously, her lips parted slightly in invitation.

I just smiled, lowering my head and brushing my mouth across hers. I tugged her along, walking backwards and continuing to kiss her until we got to the bedroom. When we hit the mattress, I turned and pulled her down with me, over me, her body sliding over mine like warm silk. My shaft prodded her stomach, but I didn't rush things. I wanted to savor this, and her.

We'd never fucked like this before. Taking our time and enjoying the moment and each other. There was always some fun goal involved. I loved doing our scenes, but I also wanted us to have this...just sex, for the pleasure of being together. No other reason.

Her hand reached down to my cock and wrapped around me, her touch featherlight but purposeful, her fingers gliding over my piercings like she was remembering exactly how to unravel me.

"Stop teasing me," Andrea murmured against my lips. "I want you inside me."

"If you want me," I said, my voice low and rough. "Then take me."

I guided her to straddle my lap, and when she hesitated, I looked into her eyes, seeing the surprise and confusion there because I was clearly giving her all the control and power, and I didn't do that often.

"Tonight, you lead," I told her, my hands sliding down to her hips. "I want you to take exactly what you need."

Desire sparked in her eyes as she slid her hands over my chest, bracing her palms flat, then raised herself up and slowly sank down on my cock. I groaned as I filled her, that tight, warm heat pulling me under. She gasped softly, and once she was completely seated on my shaft, she began to move. She kept her eyes locked on mine as if she didn't want to miss a second. Her rhythm was deliberate, like she was reclaiming her body, her pleasure, her power. Every slow grind of her hips, every hot clench of her pussy taking me in again and again, threatened to send me over the edge. Holding back, waiting for her, took every ounce of restraint I possessed.

It was basic sex compared to the other things we'd done together, but it felt like the most connected we'd ever been. She moved with growing confidence, her breath catching as she rotated her hips, and I bit back a curse. She was stunning like this, flushed, glowing, alive.

Her fingers slid into my hair and tugged me into a kiss that was deep and messy and perfect. Then she pulled back and whispered against my lips, "Take what you need, too."

"I need *you*," I rasped. "Just like this. Don't stop."

My girl rode me like she was claiming every inch of me, body and soul. She didn't ask for control, she took it, and I gave it willingly. Her moans turned breathless as she neared the edge, her movements losing that rhythm.

She clutched at me, panting. "I love you, Chase," she whispered. "I love you, Chase, love you love you," she chanted.

I felt her coming around me and I gave myself over to the pleasure, climaxing right along with her. She collapsed on top of me, gasping, trembling, holding on.

When the shaking stopped and the world came back into focus, I whispered into her ear, "He doesn't get to leave a mark on you. But I will. Every kiss, every touch, every mark, will be mine."

Andrea lifted her head to look down at me, tears shimmering in her eyes, but her smile was the most powerful thing I'd ever seen. "Good," she said. "Because I'm yours."

And I knew, deep in my bones, that I was hers, too. Forever.

EPILOGUE

Andrea

I couldn't believe six months had already passed.

Chase and I had fun tackling his place as a couple. We painted the walls, and redid the kitchen, giving both color. My art prints hung on the walls as well as some new art that Chase had bought me. New furniture filled the living room, and I was putting some sexy touches on our bedroom décor, opting for a black and deep purple palette. We'd even had his mother and father over for dinner when they'd been out visiting—his father checking on things at the Las Vegas division of Noble and Associates, and his mother doing some interior decorating for The Players Club.

Jillian and Dean Noble had raised a fine man. An honorable man. And I made sure they both knew it during their visit.

I wasn't the kind of person who wanted to be constantly spoiled, but I understood what Chase was doing by letting me transform his place. It was his way of taking care of me. Letting me know that we had enough money for things like art, and redecorating, and really, anything my heart desired. I wasn't ever going to worry about going hungry or being evicted. Chase would always be there.

Work had been busy, but we'd still found time for each other. I had gotten a promotion after Brandon's arrest, my bosses telling me that my campaigns had been successful and they wanted me in a position to provide more oversight to the others in my department. Especially since it was clear that I had always done more work than Brandon did on our joint projects.

Brandon... thank God that was all over. When news of his arrest got out, a few other women had come forward, testifying as his victims. He'd never done anything that the police could pin on him and so any reports made had just... sat there.

Nobody had ever followed up, nobody had bothered to do anything. These women had been forced to change their names and move to new cities, to live in fear that one day he would come back.

Now, they would finally get justice and see him behind bars for a good long time.

It felt so good to be able to walk around freely and go anywhere I wanted, all on my own, and not worry that someone was following me. Even six months later I still felt incredibly grateful for that freedom every time it happened.

I entered the casino and made my way over to Violet's table, watching her from the side as she dealt a hand to the players sitting in front of her. I didn't want to distract her while she focused on her job.

Casinos never made me very comfortable. Between my lack of poker face if I played and the memories of my father's behavior and gambling addiction, it put me on edge. But Violet was in her element here, in full command of her table, and I loved watching her work.

When she wrapped up her shift, another dealer came up behind her as the players left and tapped her on the shoulder. Violet stepped back, the other dealer stepped forward, and the next round began.

Violet saw me and grinned, walking over. "Hey! You made it!"

"Why do you say it like that?" I teased, hugging her hello.

"Because you're always so busy with that hot man of yours," Violet teased me right back. "C'mon, I get to eat at the buffet for free."

We made our way over to the casino's buffet, one of the many insanely delicious restaurants that Vegas was famous for. We filled up our plates, and I waited for Violet to notice the new accessory on my left hand.

By the time we'd sat down, she still hadn't.

I was right-handed but I did my best to eat with my left hand so she could see the two carat diamond ring catching the light, but Violet was too busy talking about her day. I kept trying to hold back my laughter.

Finally, I couldn't stand it anymore. "Notice anything different about me?"

Violet frowned, examining my face. "If he knocked you up and I'm supposed to notice because your boobs are getting bigger or you're glowing or something…"

"Oh my God." I rolled my eyes and thrust out my left hand. "*Look.*"

Violet's eyes went wide. She dropped her fork

and grabbed my hand. "Oh my God!" she squealed in excitement.

I grinned so hard it hurt my cheeks. My heart felt like it might float out of my chest. "He proposed last night."

"That's amazing!" She pressed a hand to her heart, smiling. "I'm so happy for you. What did he do?"

"He made dinner and set it on top of my dessert," I said, laughing.

Violet's brows rose. "He's really getting into cooking, huh?"

I shrugged, but my heart did a little flutter when I thought of him in the kitchen, sleeves rolled up, brow furrowed in concentration. "He likes to cook, and it's one of the ways he enjoys taking care of me. And I think it's therapeutic for him."

"Putting the ring on top of a dessert?" she asked, shaking her head. "Kind of cheesy. But of course you loved it."

"Of course I did. And it's not cheesy if it's the right person. Then it's just… earnest and sweet."

Violet feigned a gag, but she was grinning. "God save me."

"Someday, you're going to eat those words. Just you watch."

"I don't need a boyfriend."

"But you could use some fun, right?" I asked, reaching into my purse. My fingers brushed the invitation I'd brought for her, and pulled it out with a flourish. "Ta da."

Violet took the invitation, her face lighting up like I'd handed her the keys to her own private fantasy, and I guess in a way, I had. "Thank you thank you thank you, did I mention you're the best sister ever?"

"So, is this sufficient bribery for being my maid of honor?" I teased.

"Oh, well... I suppose..." Violet leaned over and hugged me tight. "I'm so happy for you. You deserve this."

And for once, I didn't argue. I didn't deflect or downplay it. I just...accepted it. Because the truth was, I did deserve this. I'd fought hard for my happiness, for my life. And Chase was the best part of it.

When Violet went back to her shift, I floated out of the casino on a cloud of joy, eager to get home. My body still ached in the best possible way from last night's celebration—hot, desperate, passionate sex—and I couldn't wait to spend the night in Chase's arms again.

But when I walked through the door, Chase

was fully dressed, shoes on, jacket in hand, tension written across every line of his body.

"What's up?" I asked curiously.

"You didn't answer my texts," he said, glaring at me. "I didn't know where you were."

I blinked. "Oh, please. Just because you put a ring on my finger doesn't mean you get to use it as a leash. You should've just put a tracking device in the damn thing if that's the case."

He didn't laugh.

Okay, I'd gone too far.

I softened. "We talked about this. You can ask where I am. You can even tell me you're worried. But don't go dark and broody and possessive on me. Not without context."

He arched a brow at me, looking very...dom like. "I don't think you're taking this very seriously."

"Of course I'm not," I replied, my tone light and playful. "But I can say I'm sorry and pretend I care if it'll make you feel better."

His lips twitched. There it was. The slight crack in the armor. "I had a feeling you'd say something like that. You might want to go and get ready. And dress nicely."

"Why?"

"Because we're going to the club tonight," he

said, dropping the act and letting his grin finally break through. A sly, wicked grin that made my pulse quicken.

I laughed, stepping into his arms and rising on my toes to kiss him. "I can't wait to see how you punish me, *sir*. I've been very bad, haven't I? And not very apologetic at all."

His hand smacked my ass, just hard enough to sting. "I guess you'll just have to wait to find out what kind of punishment you've earned."

God, I loved this man. I loved the way he balanced darkness and light, pain and tenderness, control and chaos.

Tonight, I'd walk into The Players Club wearing his ring. Letting everyone see it. Letting everyone know who I belonged to, in every sense of the word.

My dom. My partner. My future.

This wasn't just the start of our new life together. It was the start of our forever.

Up next in The Players Club Sinners series is Violet and Ford in PLAYING WITH TROUBLE.

To stay up to date on Erika Wilde's latest releases, please sign-up for her newsletter here: erikawilde. com/subscribe

To learn more about Erika Wilde and her upcoming releases, you can visit her at the following places on the web:

Shop all things Erika Wilde:
www.irresistibleromancereads.com

Website:
erikawilde.com

Facebook:
facebook.com/groups/erikawildesfanclub

Instagram:
instagram.com/erikawilde1

Printed in Dunstable, United Kingdom